Goodbye Dear, I'll Be Back in a Year

Goodbye Dear, I'll Be Back in a Year

Patricia Abbott

Five Star • Waterville, Maine

First Edition, Second Printing.

Published in 2002 in conjunction with Patricia Snyder.

Photo of man on cover courtesy of the author.

Set in 11 pt. Plantin by Elena Picard.

Printed in the United States on permanent paper.

Library of Congress Cataloging-in-Publication Data

Abbott, Patricia.
    Goodbye dear, I'll be back in a year / Patricia Abbott.
      p.   cm.—(Five Star first edition women's fiction
    series)
    ISBN 0-7862-4077-6 (hc : alk. paper)
    1. World War, 1939–1945—Ohio—Fiction. 2. Ohio—
    Fiction. I. Title. II. Series.
  PS3601.B39 G66 2002
    813′.6—dc21   2002023085

I dedicate this to Lee, whose tales I borrowed
or fictionalized, to Larry Names who started it all;
and to the DFW Writers' Workshop whose support
and good cheer helped me finish it.

One

April 1941

"Oh, look, it's Jack! What's he doing here this time of day?" Ginny Fairfax watched him climb out of his Model A Ford. He stepped back, whipped out his handkerchief and gave the shiny black hood a fast swipe. First car or not, Ginny couldn't understand why he spent so much time washing and polishing the thing. It looked so high and funny compared to all the others. But he was proud of it, something Ginny found kind of sweet and cute.

He paused at the sidewalk, brushed back the blond wavy hair that hung over his forehead, and patted his shirt pocket. He seemed to frown a little before leaping up the steps onto the porch.

The fleeting expression sent a warning vibration through Ginny but the sensation turned to laughter as her teenaged sister rushed to the window. Carey grinned as she peeked through the lace curtains, holding them carefully so Jack wouldn't see her. "Yeah, it's the hubba, hubba man himself."

Ginny gave her a light shove and darted for the door. "Hands off, kid. This one's mine."

"Owww. That hurt."

"Go tell Momma, baby!" Ginny couldn't help laughing. Carey was the one who climbed trees and swatted baseballs.

7

Ginny reached the door just as the bell rang, threw it open and found herself in the arms of Jack Andrews. He bent to kiss her but she drew back. "Carey's—"

Giving him a mischievous grin, Carey sauntered toward the kitchen. "Hi, Jack. I guess I need a glass of milk."

He released his hold on Ginny to make a playful lunge for Carey. "How's my second-best girl?"

She sniffed. "Hmpf. It's first or nothing. I'm not waiting in line for anyone, thank you."

Jack raised his eyebrows and shrugged as though offended. "Okay—but remember, you had your chance."

Ginny took him firmly by the hand and led him to the living room. He sat on the mohair sofa and put his feet on the pie-crust coffee table.

Ginny glared.

"Oops. Sorry." He put his feet down and leaned over and kissed her.

She fought the rush of blood to her head and looked around. "Carey . . ."

He tried again. She kissed him back for a moment, but she was too curious. "How come you're here so early?"

"I'm sorry, guess I should have called only I got something in the mail." His hand lingered over his pocket for a moment, then drew out a white envelope.

Not too happy with the look on his face, Ginny hesitated. Something was up. He had that embarrassed-to-be-pleased-with-himself look.

She snatched the envelope, almost afraid to look at it but she'd never let him get away with whatever it was. Her heart sank when she saw the return address. *Selective Service Board No. 17 of Lucas County, Ohio, 423 Broadway, Toledo, Ohio.* Postmarked April 21, 1941.

"Oh, Jack! When?" She handed it back without opening it,

unwilling to face the "Greetings" she knew was inside. *Damn!* She didn't say it aloud. She didn't suppose Jack would faint or anything, but her mother probably would have if she heard it.

Why did it have to happen now when things were going so well? Worst of all, why did he look almost happy about it? He ought to be upset.

"Not until July eleventh. Fort Belvoir, Virginia."

Two and a half months away. Well, she supposed it could have been next week or something. Virginia wasn't too far, was it? She asked. "How many miles away is that?"

"About five hundred, I think."

He put his arms around her, kissed her gently, then again more firmly.

This time she didn't look around but it was hard to concentrate on kisses. "I'm too upset right now." She wanted to cry. No she didn't. She wanted to punch out whatever Ohio senator voted for the darn draft.

"It's only for a year."

There it was again. That look. He could be so exasperating. "Just a year," like he'd say, "It's just a penny." Sure. He could go away and forget all about her. Or maybe find a new girl. Anything could happen. Jack was too good looking. She didn't want him out of her sight that long.

She looked sideways at him. When he smiled, he reminded her of Robert Taylor, the movie star, except that Taylor's hair was black and smooth. Jack's lay in deep blond waves. And Taylor was maybe a little too slick. Jack had an open boy-next-door face. Only this boy-next-door was a lot handsomer than any other boy she knew.

Her mom had once peeled an apple with the skin all in one piece and told her if she threw it over her left shoulder she'd dream of the man she was to marry. But Ginny didn't need an apple skin to dream that. She'd decided to marry Jack the first time she saw him. Now her plans were ruined. Unless she could get him to propose before he left.

"It's only for a year," he whispered again, nuzzling her neck as he said it. He was flattered by the gleam of tears he saw in her eyes. They'd met only a month ago in the Purple Cow restaurant. Even though they were going steady and he liked Ginny a lot, he wasn't ready to settle down. He was new at his job with the advertising company. Right now he only got the boring assignments. He knew he was good and that would change, but until it did . . .

Then, too, there were things he wanted to do while he was still a bachelor. "Or heat things up," the cautious Jack whispered in his ear. He paused in his nibbling long enough to sneak a look at her. She was pretty. Good sense of humor.

He would miss her. Except for that, being away for a year might not be bad. Pratt, Whitney had to hold his job for him. Part of the draft act. He might even like being in the army for a while. He'd been in the Civilian Conservation Corps in Yellowstone and enjoyed that. Besides, if the U.S. did enter in the war, well . . . Roosevelt kept saying we wouldn't, but it didn't look so sure. Jack knew he'd volunteer, so what was the difference?

He tried to see how upset she really was. Did she look more angry or tearful? Her brown eyes had that glint of red that made him want to get out his paints and scrabble around in the burnt sienna to try to capture the color. One day, he'd do a portrait of those delicate bones. And that copper colored hair! He'd always remember that first sight of her. He'd almost tripped over his own feet.

His lips sought hers. A loud thump from the kitchen stopped him.

Ginny sat up straight. "Are you okay, Carey?"

Carey's head appeared in the doorway. She was laughing. "It's okay. I dropped the milk. It didn't break. I don't suppose either of you want some? Some of what's left, that is." She held out the half-empty bottle.

Ginny scowled at her.

Jack grinned. "That's all right. You keep it. Growing girls need their milk."

Carey wrinkled her nose and waved the bottle at him. Drops splattered on the rug.

He threw her a clean handkerchief from his pocket and laughed. Glancing at his watch, he turned back to Ginny. "Look, I've got to go now. I promised Mom I'd pick her up downtown. I'll see you later. *The Great Lie* with Bette Davis is on at the Paramount, and *Ziegfeld Girl*'s at the Valentine. Six-thirty, okay? I don't want to miss the newsreel." His eyes laughed at her. "And, of course, Tom and Jerry."

He winked at Carey. "Did you know your sister cries over a stupid cartoon?" Ginny punched him on the arm. Jack grabbed her wrist, drew her to him and gave her a quick goodbye kiss. He went out laughing.

The two sisters watched from the window again as he drove away. Ginny drawled, "Thanks a heap, kid."

"Sorry. I didn't mean to break up anything. If he couldn't stay, what'd he come over for?"

Ginny snorted. "He's been drafted."

Carey's eyes grew round and tears welled in the corners. "Oh, Ginny. That's awful. When?"

With an annoyed little laugh, Ginny said, "He has to be at Fort Belvoir on July eleventh. Apparently, he doesn't think it's so bad."

Carey searched Ginny's face. "Gosh, if I were you, I'd

11

be bawling my head off."

"What do you know about anything, anyway? You're just a kid." Here the guy was, running off for a whole year! The worst part was, she had to face the risk he'd find someone else. She didn't feel like crying, she wanted to howl.

Carey wrinkled her nose. "I'm practically seventeen. Two and a half weeks. If that were my guy going off to war, I think I'd be scared to death."

"In the first place, we're not in a war. In the second, it's only for a year." *I keep telling myself!* "And don't stare at me like that!"

"I'm not staring. I just think it's awful. I know the draft's supposed to be for a year, but I can't believe it."

Ginny frowned at her. "Congress promised we wouldn't get into it. We're just being prepared, that's all." She got a craving for chocolate when things went wrong. She marched toward the kitchen, Carey at her heels. She dug out a pan, measured cocoa, then eyed the bottle of milk. *Just about enough!* "You spilled it all. Better get some more or Mom'll be upset." She mixed the cocoa, set it on the burner, then rinsed the bottle and put it in the rack by the back door.

Carey took down a cup for herself and continued the argument. "That's only what they say. Roosevelt's dying to get us into it."

"Look, you don't know what you're talking about. England isn't going to last. They don't stand a chance. When they give up like France did, the war's over."

Carey insisted. "That bombing of London's going to make people change their minds. A lot of my friends already have. Some of them are even into bundles for Britain, knitting scarves and socks and all that stuff. Been thinking of doing it myself."

She pushed back her shoulders, stuck out her jaw, and

lowered her voice, speaking slowly and distinctly, imitating Churchill's ponderous manner. "I have nothing to offer you but blood, toil, tears, and sweat. We will fight on the land, on the sea, and on the beaches. We shall never surrender." She wiped away a big tear from the corner of her eye. "Churchill's great. People like that don't lose wars."

Ginny shrugged. "It's not our war. They dragged us into that other one. We ought to just stay out."

"Roosevelt can't afford to let England lose. None of us want to face this war. The news is worse every day and the longer we delay, the bigger the hole we'll have to dig out of." She put her arm around Ginny. "I don't want us to go to war, either. Jack! Ted! It's awful." Tears glistened in her eyes.

Even if Carey was three years and one month younger than Ginny, Carey always made her look like the little sister when they stood together. Now, Carey hugged her. "I've got homework to do."

"Yeah," Ginny was thoroughly depressed. There was still tonight, though. "I guess I'd better iron something." She wondered how many more nights there might be for her and Jack.

Two

Tom and Jerry scampered across the screen of the Rivoli. Jack stuffed a folded handkerchief into Ginny's hand and whispered "Here, you'll need this."

She wanted to laugh at his "ain't I clever" grin, but didn't intend for him to see it. The real tear jerker, *Wuthering Heights* hadn't started yet. She'd need it then. She was sure she didn't have enough tissues.

He said, "You're not disappointed about the other movies?"

"The lines were too long. Anyway, I wanted to see this one again."

"It's the third time, you know."

"I know, but Olivier is gorgeous. It's so romantic. We don't need to stay for the second feature. That's only a 'B.' "

"Heck. I like The Saint."

She turned up her nose and snuggled against him, letting the mood of the film absorb her. When her tissues ran out, she tried not to sniff, but by the end, she gave up and tried to steal the handkerchief back. Jack put his hand over the pocket, then, with a look like Tom's when he caught Jerry, handed it to her with a flourish. She swallowed a quiet sob and dabbed at the tears as Lawrence Olivier carried the dying

14

Merle Oberon to the window to have one last look at the windswept moors that echoed her own spirit, that were part of her soul.

Ginny was still sniffling as they left the theater. How could Jack's eyes be so dry? It was all so sad.

He pulled his Model A to a stop at the far end of her block. She snuggled against him, still haunted by the desperate love of Heathcliff for Cathy, hearing in her mind Olivier's agonized cry of "Cathy, Cathy," over the haunted moors. She hugged the bittersweet moment to herself and looked into Jack's eyes, those eyes that always turned her to butter. "I wish you didn't have to go."

He kissed her forehead and opened his mouth, but she beat him to what she knew he was about to say. "Yes, I know . . ." They both said in unison, "It's only for a year."

From where they sat in the car, she could see the pool of light cast by the street lamp in front of her house. She put her head on his shoulder, trying to soften him up.

On the way home from the movie she tried to convince him to get old Doc Milton to pronounce him 4-F, even now. "He can say you've got flat feet. It'll be easy. He has to be at least sixty. Probably can't tell a good foot from a flat one anyway. You could just turn your arch in."

Of course, she knew Jack wouldn't go for it, but it was worth a shot. Here she was, on the threshold of her greatest romance, and he had to go away. She pictured herself at the door of their cottage, the mist hanging heavy in the morning air. He would turn to her and wave. She would smile bravely at him and . . .

The tender farewell was interrupted as Jack moved and accidentally hit the horn on the steering wheel. They jumped and laughed.

Wistfully, Ginny asked one more time, "Sure you don't

want to be Four-F?"

He stroked her hair, following its curve down her cheek, fingering the curl at the end. "You know better than that."

At least he wasn't mad that she'd said it. Maybe he understood, but men never let on about things like that. She automatically brushed at her hair. Page boys were supposed to look smooth.

"You are so pretty. Do you know that?"

"Oh, Jack." She lay her head on his chest. "I want to cry."

He put his hand under her chin and raised her head. "It's okay, Ginny." He kissed her, softly at first, then harder. His hand wandered to her thigh but still lay on top of her skirt. When she didn't resist, he moved his hand up slowly, kneading with his thumb. He paused at the top of her stocking and the garter hook, then moved to slide his hand under the skirt.

She grabbed his arm and pushed it away. "Don't!"

He kept his hand on her knee and kissed her again, slowly moving along her stocking until he found the hook.

The moment he touched it, she jerked upright, pushed at his hand and said again, "Don't."

"Why not?" He tried to burrow into her neck. "No one's looking."

"No one except probably every house on the whole street."

"It's dark."

"No. You're going away."

"What if I stay?"

She sat up straight and looked him in the eye. *Stay?* Was he actually going to talk to old Doc Milton? Maybe he really did have flat feet. Could guys with flat feet dance? But his eyes sparkled. She huffed. He had no intention . . .

His mouth turned up at the corners, finishing what his

eyes had hinted at, then he put his hands on her shoulders, drew her close, and kissed her gently three times. Between kisses he murmured, "Not far."

"You might not come back."

He pulled back, his eyes crinkling at the corners again. "I'm only going to Virginia. Besides, that's supposed to be *my* line, you know." He lowered his voice and tried to sound sexy and continental like Charles Boyer. "We must live now, chère, for we may not have tomorrow."

She sniffed and scooted away from him toward the car door.

The look on his face had to be the one the wolf used on Red Riding Hood. "I'll still respect you."

"No, you won't." She was beginning to feel silly. They sounded like five-year-olds, little kids taunting each other with, "Yes, I will," and "No, you won't."

"You let me kiss you on our first date and I still respect you."

She moved her head to catch any glint of humor in his eyes. How could eyes laugh? His certainly did. Those eyes. They were the bluest she'd ever seen, like Ohio's October skies. She was feeling that melting sensation again. She took a deep breath. No. She wasn't going to give in to him.

She reached for the door handle then remembered the argument his eyes had distracted her from. "That's right. Tell the whole world I kissed you on a first date! Brag about it like all you men do!" She almost never kissed a guy on the first date. There were too many braggarts and she didn't intend to give them anything to talk about. Jack was so dreamy she'd decided he was worth the risk. But only that risk. Her mother kept telling her, "If a man gets free milk, he won't buy the cow."

She knew he understood, even if he didn't want to. Once

she'd complained about some guy who hadn't wanted to take *no* for an answer. The guy had been a real jerk and she'd told him to get lost. Jack had said, "A real man won't try to talk a nice girl into things. He'll respect her." Then he'd laughed. "Dad says a decent man wants a good girl."

She wanted to reach out and touch the lock of hair hanging down on his forehead, gaze into those eyes until her butter sizzled under his touch. She didn't dare. She liked him too much. Not quite sure whether she believed that business about the free milk or not, she still had to watch her reputation. Her mom said more than once, "Where men are concerned, there are two kinds of girls—the ones they bring home to meet their mother, and the ones that say *yes.*"

She figured he expected her to refuse, something like a kid who wanted a piece of chocolate but didn't want to take it out of the pretty gold wrapper.

Jack kissed her ear. "Yeah, you're right. I go down the street and tell everyone I meet, Ginny Fairfax kisses on a first date." The line around his mouth deepened. "Let's go." He started the car.

He parked it in front of her house.

The house was just what she dreamed of for herself someday, white frame, green shutters, with a nice deep porch across the front, and lots of lawn. Unlike Jack, her family had been lucky. Her dad hadn't lost his job during the depression. He was a pharmacist. Like doctors, people couldn't do without them.

She said, "Come on. I'll get you a beer." Lights glowed in two of the upstairs bedrooms but the rest of the house was dark, except for one light on the porch that spotlighted the wooden swing. Her dad's intention, she was sure of that.

Jack looked at her with a raised eyebrow and then at the swing in its spotlight.

She laughed. "I don't think Dad trusts you guys." She didn't wait for him to open the car door but stepped out and walked to the porch.

She turned out the light, then curled up close to him on the swing. He put his arm around her shoulders and she lay her head on his chest. This was agonizing. She wanted him to kiss her until she fainted, but it wouldn't be "nice." And what if he did go away and never came back? She'd be ruined. Frustrated, she took a deep breath and let it out slowly.

He touched her lips with his fingertips, then put his hand under her chin and drew her to him, brushing her lips softly. He leaned back and looked at her wistfully.

She sighed again. Happily this time. His kisses were ambrosia. If only he'd stay. "What about your job?" she whispered.

"The law says Pratt, Whitney has to hold it for me, but we don't have time to talk about that." His lips searched for hers but she held back.

"Eleven weeks." She'd counted. She pecked him on the nose. He had a great nose, thin but not sharp, and not too long. "Shall we go in and turn on some music? We'd have to keep it low."

"Your mom and dad in bed?"

"Their lights are still on."

"Well, we don't want to keep them up. Can you fix it so we can listen out here?"

"I guess I could. Want that beer?"

"I don't think so."

She opened the window and put the white bakelite radio near it, dialing to find a local version of "Make-Believe Ballroom." She turned the volume down. Soft strains of Miller's "Moon Love" floated out to them. She stood and held out her hand. "Want to dance?"

"Out here?"

"Well, you said no one was looking."

He took her in his arms, pressed his cheek against hers and swayed gently from side to side with the music. "Your cheeks are so soft . . ."

He held her as the song ended and the announcer's voice crooned, "And now, we have Ray Eberle with a tune for you boys who'll be taking some time out from your regular jobs, 'Goodbye Dear, I'll Be Back in a Year'."

Jack shook his head.

Ginny tilted her head toward the music, listening. "And when I come back, I'll be all tanned and brown. We'll buy that cottage right outside of town." He *would* come back all tanned and brown, and maybe with enough money for the cottage, too. In Perrysburg, a nice little place with wide streets, lots of big old trees and pretty houses set way back from the road. "Damn." She put her hand to her mouth. She'd said it out loud without even realizing it.

He raised an eyebrow and clucked at her, then smiled as he smoothed her hair. "I'll be back."

Sure, she thought, she'd be here and he'd be there, and with all those girls chasing him, too. They always did, like the two neighbor girls who used to try to coax him to go on picnics. According to his friend Tom Gordon, however, the picnics of those two girls included more than food. Jack never went, but he always blushed when Tom teased him about the invitations.

Just as he leaned over to reassure her with kisses instead of words, the sound of a siren, the red flash of a fire engine screamed past the corner of her street. He stopped in mid-kiss and jumped back. He had that guilty look again.

To her annoyance, he kissed her quickly on the cheek and backed off. "Gotta go. G'night—I'll call you." He fled down the steps.

She put her hands on her hips. "What are you? Some stupid Dalmatian?"

He paused in his escape only long enough to send her that silly grin. "Yeah. Gotta go." He jumped into his Model A and waved.

She glared after him and muttered, "Damned Dalmatian." She wanted to yell it. This wasn't the first time he'd taken off after a fire engine. The other times she'd been in the car with him, a captive audience. She clucked her tongue. Just like a little kid, afraid to miss something.

She sighed and addressed the spot where he'd been, "And you're as romantic as a dead rat!"

She marched to her door and let herself in, letting it bang. She didn't have to worry about waking anyone. They'd all be waiting for her.

Her mom's voice floated downstairs to her. "Ginny? Everything okay?"

Her dad coughed.

Nuts. She was a grown woman, practically. When would they stop waiting up?

"Just ducky! I'll be up in a minute."

Cocoa! That's what she needed. She went to the kitchen and checked the refrigerator. *Hope Carey got some milk.* Good! She had. Ginny put the kettle on, stepping out of one shoe, giving the other a kick that sent it flying.

"Ouch," Carey complained from the doorway. "Don't take it out on me!"

"Take what out?"

"I know why you're mad. I had the window open."

"So you're spying on me?"

"It's April, remember? Springtime?" Carey opened the cupboard and got herself a cup.

Ginny shrugged and muttered, "Don't ever get involved

with a man. They never grow up. Chasing fires, yet!"

Carey's face lit up. "Yeah, that's what makes him so cute. He's different."

Ginny nodded in disgust, but she admitted it was funny, too. "He definitely is different."

"Yeah, and he's kinda shy for a guy who's so good looking."

"He and his family got hit hard by the depression and I think it gave him some kind of complex. His dad got laid off right away and Jack was really poor in high school." She stirred her cocoa thoughtfully. "His mom's kind of snooty. Thinks no one's good enough for her Jack. But it must have been awful for them. He worked his way through art school."

"Well, any time you get tired of him, I get first dibs. He's a real dreamboat."

Ginny nodded vaguely. He certainly was and a real catch. She looked at Carey. "Yeah, he's sort of sweet. Did I ever tell you about the time he ran away from a girl?"

Carey scooted her chair forward. "This I have to hear."

"One day we ran into this girl. She practically stood on her head to get his attention. When she left, I asked him, 'Who was that?' He had a dumb grin on his face and said, 'Oh, just Mary'."

Ginny took a sip of her chocolate. "I wanted in on the joke. He finally admitted, 'She was my first real girl'."

"I figured that wasn't enough to account for that grin. He got all red. Then he said, 'Well, we were on her porch. I kissed her and she opened up the side zipper in her dress. I got scared and ran home'."

They both giggled and Carey beamed. "Only Jack."

"Yeah, only Jack. He is sweet."

Ginny looked at her kid sister. Carey hadn't quite grown out of her baby fat, but when it wore off in another year, she'd be really pretty.

The two of them were like Rose Red and Snow White in the old fairy tale. Carey, rounded but tall, with long straight blond hair and green eyes, contrasted sharply with small-boned Ginny with her sienna eyes, auburn hair, and angular features. But the resemblance was there sometimes: maybe in the dimples in their chins, or perhaps the residue of life in the same house, the same atmosphere, like old married couples who looked alike.

"What are you doing up?"

"Baseball game. Ted played tonight. We went to watch."

"Well, you'd better stick to Ted, because in the first place, I intend to marry Jack. He *is* a real dish and he's my dream-boat, not yours. In the second place," she reached out and tousled her sister's hair, "you're still a baby."

"Spare me the big sister act. You've been twenty for a whole two weeks. Besides, I don't have a crush on Ted anymore. That was kid stuff." She'd had a crush on her girlfriend Toni's big brother for years. Until she saw Jack. With Jack, though, it wasn't a crush. It was complete heart failure. But Ginny didn't need to know that.

Carey glanced at the third finger on Ginny's left hand, wondering if she'd be wearing a ring pretty soon. Carey was a bit relieved one wasn't there now, but she was also resigned that Jack was Ginny's, and that was that. She pushed away her feeling of envy and asked, "Are you going to get engaged before he leaves?"

Ginny looked at the spoonful of chocolate left in her cup. She drained it and took it to the sink. "He hasn't mentioned it." She turned to Carey and smiled, "I still have eleven weeks."

Three

August 1941

Jack sat in his underwear on his bunk with its olive drab
blanket at Fort Belvoir, croaking, "Goodbye dear, I'll be back
in a year." Well, less than a year now, he thought, ten months
and a couple of weeks and he'd be home.

A shoe sailed past his head, missing him by an inch. "You
sound like a damn frog, Andrews."

He raised an eyebrow and asked innocently, "Who, me? I
think I'm pretty good." Of course he knew better. He'd heard
that complaint all his life. No one in his family, except his
little sister, Littlebit, could carry a tune. Still, if he felt like
singing, he damn well would. He started over. Three voices
from the back of the barracks joined the groan of the redhead
who had lobbed the shoe at him.

Jack ignored them, took out his shoe polish and began rubbing the toes of his shoes. His eyes scanned the sea of drab
around him: bunks, lockers, clothes, even some of the guys.
As an artist, the color offended every instinct in his soul.

"You know the worst thing about this army?" he asked no
one in particular. "It's this green. I think it's another endur-
ance test. If you fail, you get to be a lieutenant. If you pass,
you get shipped off to one of the hot spots in China to be an
advisor of some sort." *Thank goodness, I get to wear my own*

24

underwear. At least that's white.

He laughed, thinking of the time when he was little and couldn't find any clean shorts. He was in a hurry. His friends were waiting. In desperation, he picked up yesterday's from the foot of his bed just as his mom came up with the clean laundry. She'd clucked and said, "What if you got in an accident and got sent to the hospital? I'd never be able to face the nurses if you had on those things!"

The chuckle, though, wasn't enough to lighten his mood. He hated living like a caged animal on public display even more than he hated the drabs. A monkey in a zoo had more privacy. It could disappear into its little cubbyhole in the corner of its cage and hide from the goons who came to stare at it.

Remembering the big chimp at the Toledo Zoo, Jack laughed aloud then coughed to cover the sound.

The redhead didn't let it go. "What'cha laughing at?"

Jack didn't bother to share his thoughts on the lack of privacy. Red was the lion in the outfit. He raised his head, roared, and pranced through life, the king of the jungle. Being on display twenty-four hours a day didn't bother him in the least.

Jack hesitated, then grinned as he explained, "I was just thinking of this chimp in the zoo back home. It used to spit at all the gawkers, then he'd hold his head in his hands like he had a headache. Sometimes, if you took his picture, he'd ham it up and actually pose for you."

Red stared blankly and Jack shrugged. Obviously the guy hoped for more, some explanation that said, "that was funny!" Well, the redhead wasn't one who would make the connection between an ape in the zoo and a man in the army. Jack took a stab at explaining. "I don't know about you, but being a private in this man's army makes me feel related to

25

that chimp. No privacy around here at all."

Red launched into a story about his most recent date.

Jack tuned him out and concentrated on polishing his boots. Maybe deep down he was a little envious, but mostly, he didn't like men to brag about sexual conquests. Some things were meant to be private even though the word didn't exist in the barracks. In this olive drab zoo, everything was up for inspection, including a guy's most private parts. The variety of remarks on that passing parade astonished him. The guys never quit. Jack, on the other hand, zealously guarded his mental and emotional privacy, fencing off areas where only a select few would be permitted.

He stretched out on his bunk and pondered the ceiling, imagining the waters of the Maumee River. He longed for the old swimming hole and the rowboats at Walbridge Park. He and his next door neighbor, Tom, tried to rent the same boat every time, although at least four others had their initials scratched under the seats. They stuck a matchbox under No. 43 and left a dime to buy ice cream cones. They never lost their dime.

Tom had picked up the polio germ somewhere, maybe from the river. He was lucky. He survived with only a paralyzed leg. It barely daunted him and he still swam like a fish.

Careful not to laugh aloud this time, Jack replayed the memory of the time the pair had tried to sneak home more than a little late and more than a little drunk. The still night air magnified the squeak of Tom's crutches on the sidewalk until each step sounded like the squeal of bad brakes on an old car. They started to snicker, then laugh so hard they could barely walk. They might have stood there laughing until dawn if not for the porch lights that flicked on from four different houses.

Red's words jolted Jack back from his daydreams.

"Y'know, the worst thing in this outfit's the damn food." Red was the nearest the army had to an aircraft carrier, with his flat-top hair cut, broad shoulders, solid chest, and long, slim legs. His bright red hair flew like an admiral's flag at full mast in a stiff breeze.

"The worst thing's people who don't shut up and let you get some sleep," complained a voice from the back. A second guy barked loudly, "Yeah, it's Sunday, and as long as we gotta be in this stinking barracks, we wanna sleep."

Jack pulled a box from his locker. It held two squares of chocolate fudge. His last. He gave one to Red who now sat at the foot of Jack's bunk. They lowered their voices.

"From Ginny?"

Jack shook his head. "Her kid sister." He let out an exaggerated sigh. "I sure wish I could see Ginny, though."

"Look, this is the last week we're confined to base. We have passes next weekend. Why don't you ask her to come out? I'm asking Barb. They could come together. Barb's easy to get along with. They should like each other."

Red was from Columbus, only about one hundred twenty miles from Toledo. Most of the fellows in the company were from Ohio.

"Yeah! Good idea." Jack threw the empty box into the air. He closed his eyes and breathed in deeply, trying to capture the scent of Ginny's perfume, the warmth of her skin. When he opened his eyes, chocolate crumbs lay all over his blanket and the floor. "Damn." He scrambled to pick them up and spent the next five minutes policing his area. He sure as hell didn't want to end up restricted.

Red joined the hunt for crumbs but instead of sweeping them together for the trash, he licked his fingers and ate the bits that stuck.

"I swear you'd eat worms, Red."

"Naw. But I ate a rattlesnake once."

"Shut up!" The three voices from the back roared.

Red held up his hand in submission and nodded toward the door.

Jack finished dressing and joined him outside. "Want a Lucky?" he asked, offering a cigarette from a white pack with a green circle.

Red shook his head and pulled out one of his own. "I think the only good thing about the army is the cheap smokes."

Jack blew a smoke ring and watched it drift away. "I sure want to see Ginny. But I wonder if her folks will let her come to an army base."

"You engaged?"

"Thought about it a bit, but I don't know." The end of his cigarette dimmed and then glowed brightly again as he inhaled. He wasn't sure. "I like Ginny a lot, but we haven't known each other very long. If a war starts, marriage might not be smart. Too much can happen. Why rush into something? No sense being stuck for life because of the pressures of a war."

"Well, she could tell her mom you're engaged. She'd probably let her come then."

"Yeah, but I don't think she'd lie to her mom—especially a big fib like that. She's a nice girl."

"Mmm. One of those. Well, you won't know if you don't ask."

Jack thought for a moment. He didn't like talking Ginny into lying. His own mom used to call the easy girls, party girls. "You don't want to marry one of those," she'd said. Ginny sure wasn't a party girl. Besides, even if she did say they were engaged, he'd be surprised if her mom would allow Ginny to visit. Of course, she was twenty, but something like this . . . Well, he could hear her now. "Huh, I have to live with her, don't I?" But maybe with Barb along, she might.

He sighed and gave in. "Okay, I'll call her." There was a phone at the end of the barracks, but the thought of the whole unit listening made him feel like his chimp pal. No dice. "Come on, let's go to the stand."

The three phone booths at the tiny store where they could buy cigarettes all had long lines. Red eyed the rows of men critically, then nodded. "This one."

Jack followed and got behind him. "Are you crazy? This is the longest line."

Red smirked. "Yeah, but its got the smallest guys. If they take too long, I'll start massaging my muscles. They'll get done real fast."

The line did move quickly. Jack figured Red had nothing to do with it, but in ten minutes he found himself listening to Ginny's kid sister's voice. "Hi, Carey. How's my second favorite girl?"

He was surprised how pleased he was when she squealed, "Jack?" She was cute. Give her about six years and she'd be almost as pretty as Ginny. What was she, fourteen? He heard her calling, "Ginny. Quick! It's Jack. Long distance!"

She started to ask, "How do you like th—"

He heard a hushed squabble, then Ginny. "Jack! Are you in Virginia?"

"Yeah. I'm still on base. But they're going to turn us loose next weekend." Red nodded at him from the open door of the booth. "Do you remember me telling you about this guy, Red McCann?"

"Yeah, I guess." She didn't sound interested.

"He's from Columbus. His girlfriend Barb is coming for the weekend. Do you think you could come down, too? Maybe you could take a train and meet her, then come down together."

"But I don't know her."

"I've seen her picture, and from her letters, you'd probably get along. She sounds kind of sweet." With Red he figured sweet also meant dumb, but he couldn't say that. He crossed his fingers and waited.

"Mom'd never go for it."

"Barb could be your chaperone. You are twenty, you know."

"Ha. I have to live here."

Bingo! He didn't say anything, hoping she'd weaken. When she was silent he coaxed, "Tell your mom you would stay in Alexandria, at the YWCA, and Y's never let guys past the lobby. That might help."

She was still quiet. Finally, she said, "A girl has to watch her reputation, you know!"

"What if you told her we're engaged? She'd let you then, wouldn't she? And then no one could talk." He badly wanted her to come, yet part of him would be relieved if she didn't give in and agree to lie.

He cleared his throat. Why didn't she answer? Or say something. "Ginny?"

"I don't think I can do that, Jack. Lie about being engaged, I mean."

Her tone was coldly disapproving. His guilt warred with his disappointment. He'd better say the right thing now to stay in her good graces. He traced the outline of a heart with someone's initials scratched in it on the wall of the phone booth. He really wanted her to come. Finally he said, "Okay. Will you, then?"

"I just told you. I can't."

He shook his head. Was she playing dense? "I mean, *marry me.*"

He heard something that sounded like a croak then a voice

with a soft southern drawl broke in. "Your three minutes are up. Please stay on the line for additional charges when you're finished."

He almost shouted, "Yeah, operator." There was no sound on the line as the operator cut out. Frantic that she'd be gone, he almost shouted. "Ginny?"

"I'm still here."

He swallowed and summoned his courage. "Well, will you marry me?"

"I heard you."

He thought she laughed and then he heard a loud sigh. "This has to go down in history as the least romantic proposal I've ever heard!"

He blushed, glad she couldn't see him. "How many have you had?"

"Well. Ever heard of, then. But yes, I will marry you." She added wryly, "And thanks for asking."

He breathed like a man coming up for air, an uncertain mixture of relief, pleasure, and panic. Ginny's laughter added to his confusion. In the background, Carey squealed.

The guy in line behind him tapped on the glass of the booth. Jack nodded and mouthed, "One minute."

"Listen, I gotta go. Barb's got your number. She'll call you." He held his breath. "You'll come?"

"Yes, I'll try. 'Bye. I love you."

He opened his mouth to say "I love you, too," but stopped. He'd never said "I love you" to any girl. Before he could speak, she was gone. He reached out and touched the receiver hook twice. Funny, he hadn't realized until now that he loved her.

Jack got the operator back on the line and listened to his pile of coins clang in the box. Sort of like wedding bells, only flat. Oh, hell. He hadn't meant to propose. He wasn't at all

31

sure getting married was what he wanted right now. But he had to admit, she'd be nice to come home to.

He stepped out of the booth and shouted, "Whoopee!"

The soldiers standing in line grinned and gave him a round of applause. They knew exactly what it meant. There had been a number of *whoopees* in the lines today.

Four

"Good dinner. Actually, it's a nice place," Ginny said, noticing for the first time, the dimly lit surroundings in the Cabin Club. She'd been too busy looking at Jack to worry about food or atmosphere until now.

He put his arm around her waist and hugged her to him. The Club was a small place on the outskirts of Alexandria where a lot of GI's from Belvoir took their dates. The walls were rustic wood and it had a primitive look, but the white tablecloths were clean and starched. The steaks had lived up to the recommendations from the other guys.

Ginny beamed at Jack. She didn't care about anything except that she was with him. Her eyes devoured him. Jeepers, he was handsome in that uniform, and just like the song said, "all tanned and brown." She had a moment of panic. Did he know any girls down here? What if he liked the army and stayed in?

She held her breath before she dared to ask, "Do you guys like the army?"

Jack and Red looked at each other and roared. Jack finally managed, "Well, it is better than prison."

"Yeah, this place is nice." Barb echoed belatedly.

Ginny groaned to herself. *Nice. I don't think I'll ever use that word again.* She fiddled with her fork, not daring to look at Barb. The girl had been so darn *nice* on the way down, she'd almost driven Ginny out of her mind.

Ginny raised her head and looked at Barb with narrowed eyes. She really was a patsy. If only she'd say something disagreeable, anything, even just *no.* It seemed Barb's and Red's entire relationship depended on the girl being agreeable, *nice.* Ginny decided Red was a creep.

She turned to study him. As much as she wanted to despise him, she found herself fascinated with his roguish, almost animal, sex appeal.

As though he'd read her mind, Red looked at her and turned his charm on high. "Gosh, you gals have no idea how good it is to see someone in a skirt who still has hair." He rubbed his hand over the field of red corn stubble the army had left him when they took clippers to his hair.

Ginny squirmed. If Gable had wanted to play a no-good wolf, he could have used Red for a model. She'd pictured Red small, more like Danny Kaye, not big and muscled. He wasn't as handsome as Jack, his features not as refined but some kind of strange appeal was there.

Embarrassed by her response to his magnetism, she turned abruptly back to Jack. At least he didn't look shaved on top. The way his hair curled, it was hard to tell just how long it was. Then maybe the barber hadn't had the heart to really cut that beautiful stuff any shorter.

Jack's face displayed his pleased-with-himself grin as he echoed Red's remark on girls. "Yeah, if it hadn't been for Red's picture of Rita, I'd have forgotten what a girl looked like." Then he added, "Except the colonel's wife, and she doesn't count."

Red snorted. "She doesn't count because she looks like the Wicked Witch of the West. A couple of weeks ago, the

Looey had to go to dinner at her house." He sputtered the rest of the story. "He hasn't been the same since."

They both roared and Ginny wondered if it always took so little to make servicemen laugh. Maybe the two of them were just feeling like monkeys out of their cage.

A waitress with a full bosom that spilled over the top of her uniform brought dessert menus and cleared the dinner plates. "You boys don't sound like you need it, but do you want something else to drink?"

Jack watched her, taking care to cover his surprise. Poufy colonial dresses were far from sexy, but on this girl, they took on unexpected dimensions. "We do want a refill. Another round of Seven and Sevens?" He looked at the others for approval.

Red nodded absently, his eyes on the waitress's chest, his expression one of unconcealed lust.

Hurt flickered in Barb's eyes. Ginny bristled. How could anyone be so stuck on a guy that she'd put up with such disregard for her feelings? Where was her backbone?

Barb was tall, only a little shorter than Red, and had a sweet, round face with a pretty pink glow. Almost meek, Ginny thought with scorn. Barb's blond hair had a faint strawberry tinge and just a hint of darkness at the roots. The cut was short and old-fashioned.

"Dessert?" the waitress asked.

Jack groaned and Ginnie said, "No, thanks."

Red stopped leering at the waitress long enough to think about it, then shook his head without asking Barb.

The leader of the small orchestra stepped up to the microphone. "Ladies and gentlemen, if you'll please clear the floor, we have a surprise, a dance contest." The audience clapped. "Contestants will be judged on three dances, the fox trot, jitterbug, and tango. Couples who are tapped will return to their seats. The winner gets his party's dinner check paid."

Red didn't ask. He stood up, reached for Barb and led her to the floor.

Ginny and Jack looked at each other and by instant, mutual agreement, stayed. She loved to dance, but Jack's bobs and bounces, his two b's, she had teased him, wouldn't pass in a contest. He'd made some improvement since their first dance together. She hoped he hadn't forgotten even that little bit.

Ginny's foot tapped time under the table as she watched the couples. Red and Barb glided and dipped in their fox trot as though they were skaters on ice. Barb responded easily to Red's faultless control. His grace, in contrast to his size and Tarzanish manner, came as a surprise to Ginny and she felt her blood stir again. She stopped tapping her foot and took a drink, then to relieve her tension, commented, "He moves like Astaire. Did you ever notice how Astaire leans when he dances?" As if in response, the couples swung into the tango. Red and Barb managed to look like poster dancers listing at a forty-five degree angle.

The two judges continued to eliminate couples until only five pairs remained for the jitterbug. All five couples jumped and twirled and threw the girls like rag dolls, but again, Red and Barb led the pack. This time, Barb was the star. She did a boogie that stopped the other dancers, and the whole audience rose and clapped with the beat. When it was over, Barb received a standing ovation.

They returned to the table breathless and triumphant.

Ginny brushed away her envy and hugged Barb. "You were wonderful. Where did you ever learn to dance like that?"

Flushed with pleasure, Barb turned the praise away. "We do a lot of dancing. Red's real good at it."

A waiter presented them with champagne. As he poured,

Red bragged, "Taught her everything she knows."

Ginny frowned. She couldn't help thinking, *It's okay to let the guy think he's a big shot, but at least, Barb, take credit for your own ability.* She turned back to watch Red preen. Reluctantly, she admitted again that along with that sex appeal, he was a great dancer. She felt sorry for Barb. It would be easy to play Jane to his Tarzan, but not smart.

Red's eyes met hers and held her with a knowing look. She shivered and turned abruptly away, but not before her hands went to the tips of her ears to see if they were as hot as she felt. She spoke too loudly as she addressed Jack. "The band's good."

He rose and held out his hand. "Well, we can't match them," he smiled, "but we don't have to. Dance?"

He drew her to him as the saxophonist practically cried "Stardust." She melted into his arms. Next to kissing, nothing was quite as romantic as the warm feeling of her cheek against Jack's broad, muscled chest. He wasn't a big man, but he sure had a nice chest. She rubbed her cheek against him like a contented cat.

For a change, Jack seemed to have caught the tail end of Red's magic. He forgot to bob, and slid into long, gliding steps. Ginny slipped her hand from his and moved it to his shoulders, feeling a warm flush at his strength. He moved his left hand between her shoulder blades and held her close. They danced in silence for a while.

Jack bent his head and nuzzled his cheek against her hair. "Sorry I don't have a ring for you to wear. Can you wait?"

"Mmmmm." In his arms like this, he could have said, "I'm sorry, I just turned blue," and she wouldn't have cared.

"They don't allow new recruits off the base. This is the first time we've had a pass. But if I get a real leave, I'll get you one."

Ginny's head popped up so suddenly she almost cracked his jaw. "Why do you say *if?* You've been in almost three months. Aren't you due?"

Jack drew her back to him, but the song had ended. "Sorry, I should have said something. I forgot you didn't know. Scuttlebutt has it we aren't getting out in a year like congress promised." He squeezed her hand. "We might be shipped out pretty soon."

"Oh, Jack. No! Where?"

He didn't answer at first, just stood looking guilty. Ginny's eyes grew watery, and Jack tried to soften the blow. He said, "I'll be surprised if we get any leave at all."

Before she could say anything, the orchestra leader approached the mike. "I know you guys are here in uniform because you all wanted an army career." Sarcastic barks and mocking laughter echoed around the room. He nodded to acknowledge that the joke was on them. "Well, this next number's not for you. It's for your girls. And here's April to sing it."

"Goodbye dear, I'll be back in a year—" April didn't get to finish. The place erupted in a giant roar. The orchestra played on but she stood there smiling and moving in rhythm.

Jack shrugged. "See what I mean? Even the orchestra is teasing us."

Red and Barb were at the table when Ginny took Jack's hand and led him back. This was not what she had in mind. She wanted that cottage outside of Toledo, her white house with green shutters in Perrysburg. She didn't want to be an army wife, even for a while.

Jack pressed her hand to his mouth, held it for a moment, then kissed her fingers. He pulled out her chair for her. "Rumor is we're headed for the Pacific. And this time, I think the rumor is probably true. Japan's been making bigger headlines than Hitler lately."

He turned to Red, who was nuzzling Barb's ear. "That right, Red?"

He looked up at Jack and laughed. "Nope. We can't go to no island."

Ginny jumped at the words. "You mean you won't have to?"

"I mean, we aren't allowed." He punched Barb on the arm lightly. "See, there were these two little old maids, and one of them decided they should go to St. Thomas for a vacation. The other one started to cry. 'What's the matter, my dear?' the first one asked. Number two blew her nose and said, 'I guess you might as well know. I've never told anybody, but do you remember Tommy Jones?' 'Yes, I guess I do,' the first one said. Number two started to cry again. 'Well, that's why I can't go.' The first old maid couldn't understand so she asked, 'What in the world has that to do with anything?' 'Well, they're virgin islands!' "

Red roared, Barb groaned. He winked at Jack. "And we ain't no virgins!"

Jack commented wryly, "Well, the Virgin Islands aren't in the Pacific, are they? I doubt if the army makes such restrictions!"

Ginny wanted to laugh, but it wasn't really funny, was it?

Even Red didn't smile. He rose and led Barb back to the dance floor.

Ginny made a face and dismissed him. "I just don't believe this." She had concentrated so hard on the idea of just one year, determined to believe nothing would change that. "Roosevelt promised. Only a year." She spoke frantically, raising her voice, sure that if she said it loud enough it would be true. "He'll work out something. He always does. Besides, Japan's so small. All they know how to make are those cheap toys and copies of things. They wouldn't dare go to war."

Jack tipped her chin up and kissed her, then took a long drink and fiddled with his glass. "I think that's why we'll probably go to Hawaii. Try to scare them off."

"Oh." She made lines on the tablecloth with a forgotten spoon and a tear rolled down her cheek. So much for rose vines and cottages. Jack touched the tear as if to catch it and keep it. "Will you marry me?"

She looked up at him and the tear became a stream, a stream that carried surprised laughter in its wake. "Oh, Jack. You're *not* a dead rat, are you?"

He did a double take, looking half amused, half insulted.

"When you ran after that fire truck instead of kissing me goodnight, I called you a Dalmatian. I figured romance came *after* fire trucks, burying bones, and any other distractions. And I actually said you were as romantic as a dead rat! I'm sorry!"

"Oh." The corners of his mouth turned up but his eyes didn't laugh. They sent a message of wonder. He held out his hand, drew her near, and pressed his cheek against hers as they reached the dance floor. The horns cried, "Fools Rush In" and the singer chimed in with the song's warning, her throaty voice lamenting that even angels were afraid of love.

Ginny's cheek was warm and cozy. He could get to like this comfort. Still he wondered, were they fools? Would there be a war? Would she wait for him? Should she? He couldn't imagine being away somewhere, all alone, no one to hold on to. No one to come back to.

He held Ginny close, clinging to her warmth for reassurance. They couldn't go to war. He lay his hand on her head and pressed it against his chest, trying to believe that even if Japan did get up the nerve to declare war, it wouldn't last long. A tiny island like that! But what if he didn't come back?

He closed his eyes and held Ginny tight, basking in the warm moment, but knowing the possibility of war wasn't going away. Roosevelt and Churchill were getting thicker and thicker. Even if they didn't get into conflict with Japan, Hitler was just around the corner. At least if he and Red got sent to Hawaii, there'd be palm trees!

Ginny snuggled against him, her head pressed hard against his chest. They danced slow, tiny steps in a slow, tiny circle. If only time would stand still.

But it didn't. Red and Barb danced over to them. He tapped Jack on the shoulder, "We've gotta get the girls back pretty quick. Let's trade for one dance."

"I don't know. Do you give lessons, Barb?" Jack's eyes sparkled as he took her arm and disappeared into the crowd.

Ginny gave Red a weak smile. The evening was spoiled. She might as well.

The band played a smoothie, and under the spell of Red's effortless moves, her gloom left her for a moment. He held her close and led her across a floor that had lost much of its crowd. He made dancing feel like floating. She tingled under his touch and her pulse raced. His hand on her back reminded her of Gable's enormous hands around Scarlett's head when he threatened to crush her. She missed a step but hoped he hadn't noticed. She drew back a little, afraid of the butterflies that flitted around her insides.

The song finally ended. She touched her hair and smoothed the skirt of her dress.

Jack folded her in his arms for the last dance and she clung to him.

They took a cab back to the small hotel Barb had arranged for instead of the Y. She'd said it was nearer the base, leaving more time with the men and less time in a cab.

Ginny waited while Jack paid the driver. By the time they were inside the lobby, Red and Barb were nowhere in sight. Jack led Ginny into the little bar, whispering, "Come on, let's find a corner." It was quiet and dark.

No one paid attention to their kisses.

Would she ever see him again? If he went, how long would he be gone? She tried to put a lifetime of kisses in each one, but they seemed like bits of fluff in a high wind. She held onto him hungrily until Red appeared.

"Gotta go, chum." Red left to wait outside the bar.

Jack held her close. "Maybe none of this stuff will happen. But tonight may have to last us for a long time." He drew back and looked at her, trying to burn her image into his mind.

They rose and walked to the elevator, Jack's arm around her waist. When Ginny reached her room, she handed him the key. He unlocked the door, pressed the key into her hand and took her in his arms. He kissed her hard. Ginny backed into her room, froze the picture of Jack's longing eyes into her mind, and closed the door with a quiet sob.

Five

Jack stood at the window of his barracks at Schofield Army Base on the far side of Oahu from Pearl Harbor. His gaze skimmed the pineapple fields and wandered beyond to the horizon. He sniffed the morning air. Ohio mornings had been soft and rain-washed, colored in siennas and ochers, earthy. These Hawaiian dawns were vibrant, salty, in blues and greens. Ohio mornings called in the mellow voice of the robin. Hawaii put an orchid in her hair and sang a siren song.

His only real regret was leaving Ginny. He closed his eyes to recapture that last kiss, but imagination was a poor substitute. He'd only had twenty-four hours with her after the Virginia weekend. In the movies the guys all got weeks—well, at least one, for furloughs. He felt cheated, especially since he'd had to divide the time between Ginny and home. Well, no use feeling sorry for himself, he had a lot of company.

They'd arrived in Honolulu on the seventeenth of October. Not counting the drills, and even with the hard work, it had been weeks of enchantment. Hawaii's lavish landscape had given him a better understanding of the lush Gaugin paintings in the Toledo Art Museum. He glanced back at his Spartan barracks and wondered what would happen if he

43

suddenly set up an easel in the middle of the scrubbed floor and started to paint.

He sighed and turned back to the window. Mornings were the worst time of day, even here—bittersweet, with melancholy moments of quiet Ohio dawns, and a freshness, an eagerness for the new day it promised.

"C'mon, let's go." Goat Carter tossed Jack's shoes at him.

Ron Carter, better known as Goat, had been the last man to join the outfit, and as the smallest, he immediately became the butt of their jokes. He accepted it all with his natural good humor and dished out as good as he got. One of the guys had once asked him, "Doesn't anything get your goat?" The nickname stuck.

Jack sat on his bunk and slipped on his shoes. He and Goat were the only ones awake. The rest of the men, including Red, were still round lumps under their blankets.

Goat prodded Jack. "C'mon, I'm so hungry I could eat roof shingles."

"Go get the damn shingles. We don't care," came a voice from the bunk across the aisle.

Goat lowered his voice. "We have to be nuts, you know. Look at those slobs. They plan on spending the whole day in bed." He scratched his head and looked at them half wistfully. "If we had any sense after last week, we'd do the same."

Jack gave his bunk a final pat and headed for the door. "Not me. I'm not wasting my Sunday in bed. I can't wait to wash the dust from those maneuvers off my feet." He strummed an imaginary guitar. "Oh, you golden sands, here I come."

"Yeah. Right. Myself, gimme a girl." Goat followed, swaying his hips and humming "Sweet Lelani". As they passed Red's bunk Goat paused, his eyes dancing. "Shall we wake him?"

As if in answer, Red snorted. Jack grinned. "Sounds like an old pig, doesn't it?" Red was well ahead of the unit in the dirty tricks department. Jack and Goat both owed the guy a few, but caution held them back. Their buddy, Private Johnson, was the most recent GI to wear a purple badge, and not the medal for being wounded in action. Johnson's badge was the purple bruise under his eye, the direct result of a Joe Louis punch from Red. Red had a habit of taking an automatic swing at people who woke him from a deep sleep. He always apologized, but the guys were careful to stay away.

Jack backed off and shook his head. "You do it. My mother didn't raise no fool." Only three hours ago, Red had crawled into bed after a night at the Blue Ocean Cafe.

"How'd he get away with being AWOL?"

"Friends in the right places, especially up there." He pointed at the heavens and flapped his arms like wings. The stubble of carrot-colored hair, the only part visible above the covers, rolled over. Red seemed to know every girl in town and had offered to get him a date, but the thought of Ginny back in Toledo stopped him. That, and his reluctance to catch any number of disgusting diseases.

Goat bobbed and weaved and jabbed at the heap.

Jack shook his head. "Better not, Goat."

Red turned over and groaned. Goat backed up like a man faced with a hot grenade, then shrugged. "Naw, I'm saving myself in case those Japs decide to get brave."

A voice from the lump on the bed next to Red's grumbled, "You ain't gonna live long enough to face no Japs if you don't get the hell outta here."

Goat winked at Jack. He tiptoed up to the sleeping Red, who lay sprawled on his stomach with one bare leg and an arm hanging off the bed. He blew gently on the red hair. Not a muscle twitched.

Reassured by Red's coma, Goat dug into Red's footlocker, and came out with a long tie from a Japanese robe he had bought in Honolulu. He looped one end around the leg of the cot, crisscrossed the other under and around a dangling leg, and tied the ends. Four inches separated the leg from the bunk corner. Red grunted and snored but didn't move. Goat held up his fingers in the "V" sign for Victory.

Jack rolled his eyes and punched him on the shoulder. "Come on. Let's get out of here and get some chow."

Jack and Goat joined the small Sunday morning group of men who wandered toward the mess hall. Schofield's barracks were neat, many-windowed wooden structures fronted with deep verandas. They stood in groups of four, militarily correct and square, around a flawless, immaculate quadrangle. No stray grass dared grow in the cracks of the walks. No long, unruly weeds had the nerve to push up into the lawn. The whole camp seemed to stand at attention.

Jack looked at his watch, then up at the sky. Six 'til eight. The day was passing; he wanted to get going. Waikiki's golden sands beckoned him like California's gold had called to the forty-niners. "I think I ought to learn to play a uke."

Goat snorted. "I hope you play better than you sing."

Jack offered a lopsided, self-conscious grin. "Those ukes and Crosby used to make me dream of the islands, but boy, I never thought I'd really be here." He took a deep breath. The air gave him a cheap drunk. Last week in the field had been hell, but today made up for it. Heaven had waited.

Goat looked at the sky and squinted. "Funny, sounds like thunder." He turned in a circle, looking for the source. "Think maybe a volcano blew? Listen. Hear it? Over toward Pearl. It can't be raining. There ain't a cloud in the sky."

Jack listened. He heard the deep rumble but saw nothing. The sun still smiled and the blue sky stretched out like a great tarp above them. He shrugged. "Must be navy. Gunnery practice."

Goat scratched his head. "Nah. It's Sunday."

Suddenly the tropical horizon vanished in a veil of gray dust. Had the munitions exploded? The pair turned and stared at several black specks in the sky above the dust. The specks grew larger until they could be recognized as on-coming, low-flying planes. Jack, Goat, and the other men heading for the mess hall gawked, bewildered. The planes were firing. One of the forces had gone nuts. They weren't al-lowed to use live ammo.

The men jabbered. "What the hell? Are those Wheeler's?"

"Fixed landers. Must be Marines from Ewa."

"Must be target practice."

"Boy, somebody's ass'll be scorched for this."

"Yeah, wait'll the admiral at Pearl gets a load of it."

They stopped, frozen in disbelief as a deafening boom and explosion hit the far barracks and planes roared down on the quadrangle. Bullets raked the dirt, raising staggered bursts of dust.

Jack's brain told him these planes couldn't be there. He'd once seen a car drive toward him on the wrong side of the road. His mind hadn't believed that then, he didn't believe this now.

One plane roared toward him bearing . . . a solid red circle! Not possible! Red circles meant Japs! His mind may have doubted what his eyes saw, but his body hit the dirt and tried to disappear, to become a mole and burrow back to the main-land. The plane passed. He jumped up and sprinted for the protection of the verandas. Goat had beat him there.

When he caught his breath, he realized his right hand hurt. Was he hit? Would he lose his hand? How could he draw without his right hand? Was he going to die? Slowly, he opened his clenched fist. Deep marks showed where his fingernails had bitten into his skin. His palms were dirty and wet with sweat.

An air raid siren whined and then screamed through the noise of the explosions. Goat poked him and pointed at the barracks door. "Hell, Jack. Red's in there!"

The picture of a tethered Red flashed in Jack's mind. It wasn't funny, but it was hysterical, a hysteria quickly cut off by a stream of bullets that sent showers of dirt into the air. "Gotta get Red." They ran, doubled over, for the door.

"Raid! Air raid!" they yelled as they dashed through the door of the barracks. Some of the men stood at the windows, some were struggling into their clothes, and all were trying to figure out what the hell was happening. A chorus of questions erupted around the room. "Why would we raid this dump?" they asked each other.

"Not us, the Japs. The Japs." Jack snapped as he ran toward Red's bunk.

"It's real. Real stuff. Japs. Damned Japs!" Goat hopped he was so mad.

As he struggled with the knot that held the snoring Red captive, Jack fought against the reality of the attack. Soon he would wake from this chaos. But it wasn't a dream, it was real. Those yellow, copy-cat rats were really doing this. How'd they get the nerve? They must be crazy. Where was Roosevelt? He wasn't supposed to let this happen.

Goat yelled again. "It's no drill!"

Red, awake now, tried to roll over on his cot. He tugged at his leg, yanked at the belt and bellowed like a mad elephant. "What the hell!"

Jack was glad for the chaos. He'd rather face the Japs than that bellow of Red's.

"Get me out of this damned thing," Red roared as he

tried to roll onto the floor.

As Red fought his tether, the sergeant released the rifles from the lockup. Jack grabbed his weapon and helmet, dashed back to Red and sliced the kimono tie with his bayonet. An explosion rocked the barracks. The two of them hit the floor and rolled under the cot.

Red punched the underside of it. "A helluva lot of good this thing'll do. Let's get out of here." They rolled out and dashed for the exit. The men poured out the doors between bursts of bullet spray and darted for any shelter they could find.

Ammo. They needed ammo. Jack, Red, and Goat ran for the next barracks and huddled between the two adjacent buildings. A plane flew over and Jack cursed and glared at his empty rifle. "Come on, damn you. I dare you. Come on down here where I can get you!" He swung the rifle like an axe and cheered when Goat took off his shoe and threw it at the retreating plane.

Their enthusiasm didn't last. They hit the dirt again as more Jap bullets tore up the ground in front of them. The plane turned for another run. Jack, holding onto his helmet as though it were a steel blanket, his eyes tightly closed, pressed himself into the dirt.

Goat, nearest the front of the building, yelled, "Well, one ain't no good," and threw his second shoe as the plane shot past. But the steam had evaporated from his gesture. The trio jumped up, skirted the back of the barracks, hugging the wall as long as they could, then dashed into the pineapple fields.

As they disappeared between the rows of plants, Red cursed and yelled, "Ammo. Gotta get ammo."

Jack began to laugh and couldn't stop. He yelled back waving his puny little rifle. "Gonna shoot 'em down with these pea shooters?" All the same, live ammo would have given them some feeling of security.

He eyed the path to the munitions hut. Scattered barrels, planted as an obstacle course to delay invaders, stood between them and the ammunition. Jack crouched low and dodged between them. Bullets pinged and ricocheted. "Dear God, get me out of this. I promise I'll be a bloomin' saint, won't even say GD anymore. Won't make another pass at a woman." Crazily he added, "Except Ginny. We're engaged, Lord."

He looked up as another Zero skimmed over. The pilot seemed to be looking straight ahead. Jack whispered, "I'll be a priest. No, dammit, I'll be one of those monks that don't even talk. I'll forget Ginny."

Crouching low, he ran forward, hoping the officers knew what the hell they were doing when they had taught him to zigzag. A straight line would be a hell of a lot shorter. At the storage facility, a sergeant stood screaming at the men banging on the lock with their rifle butts. "I ain't got no orders. You can't do that."

"The hell we can't." A couple of burly soldiers shoved him roughly aside and kicked in the door.

Ammo passed quickly down the line but the Zeros were coming back. The men scattered, dashing for the field again, for whatever camouflage lying among pineapple plants could supply. Red got his rifle loaded first and raised it at the oncoming pilot. "I'll get you. You sonofabitch."

Goat punched Jack, pointed at Red and snickered. He shouted, "You'll never hit it, Red. Even something that big."

Jack could see men lying in the dirt, not moving. Were they dead? He'd never seen a man die before. He choked at the possibility. Damn, he wanted to get one of those Japs. One. Just one. He took a deep breath, squinted and took aim as the pilot skimmed low over the barrels. White teeth glistened in a grinning mouth. "Goddamned sonofabitch." The man actually looked happy. Jack fired wildly after the retreating plane. "God—" Then he remembered his pact. "Sorry, God, I promised not to say 'GD' any more. Just get me through this and I'll get those bastards."

For a moment, the skies were quiet and Jack realized the irony of promising God he'd kill someone. He would gladly have killed the damned pilot, but could he do it face to face? His hand went to the bayonet. He remembered the force of it biting into the practice bags and shuddered, praying that his bullets would be long distance ones.

He looked over at the guys he'd thought dead. One of them had moved. Another lay still. Red-hot anger swelled. Yes. Right now, he could use that bayonet and not think twice.

He scanned the sky that was, for the moment, eerily empty. Where'd they go? He'd be willing to bet Goat's picture of Betty Grable that it wasn't over, yet the drone of planes had grown distant.

Maybe they'd finally been shot down. Maybe they'd quit and gone home, wherever that was. But why? And how in the hell had they gotten here without being seen?

Smoke and flames were visible in every direction. The rumble from Pearl seemed to jolt the whole island. He shuddered to think of all those ships tied up in the harbor for the weekend. How many had the Japs gotten? Had the guys been able to shoot any of the planes down?

He lay in the field, waiting and wondering, almost wishing they'd come back, and that somehow, this time we'd be ready. But most of all, he feared he'd get that wish and they *would* come back. With landing ships.

The men waited. Jack didn't know how long, but it seemed forever. He stared at a dark green leaf, bent and broken, an inch from his nose. A clear gob of sap hung from the edge and a tiny rainbow glinted in the fluid. He reached out and touched the drop. Sticky, like the blood that might be seeping from some of those guys lying still in the field.

Jack rolled onto his back, pushed his helmet off and used its upturned shell for a pillow. Even though the planes were gone, that magic blue Hawaiian sky no longer smiled. It hung over him like the belly of a giant bat, waiting to drop and smother him. He felt like a fly waiting for the fly swatter.

His mother and Littlebit's faces came to him. Ginny's voice whispered, "I love you." He tried to bring her face close to him, but the image resisted. He tried again and she seemed further than ever.

He tried to call up the image of her in that nightclub in Alexandria, to feel her in his arms. She came near and he heard again her soft laughter as the bandleader introduced their song, "Goodbye Dear," then the loud, sarcastic roar of the recruits in the audience.

He choked, smothering a bitter impulse to laugh. Yeah. Sure, he'd be back in a year, if he was lucky. But which year?

Red reached out and slapped him hard on the shoulder.

Goat sighed and shook his head. "T'aint funny, McCann."

Jack stopped choking and pushed back the lock of hair that hung down on his forehead. "Fellahs, I think we're in for one helluva long year."

That night after beach patrol, Jack sat staring out over the dark water that could hide anything, wondering if the Japs were there now. Were they waiting for dawn, or would they come back tomorrow with ships and armies, or just more planes? He pulled out a small notebook. Until now, there hadn't been much to say. It read:

Friday, July 11, induction
Friday, October 11, left Frisco 1:10 p.m.
Friday, October 17, arrived in Honolulu 0300 hours

That week on the troop ship to Hawaii had been a hell of a trip. The packed hold had been so hot, they'd slept most nights on deck and ugh, the seasickness! Even now the thought made him want to wretch. It had been so bad he'd looked at the rail and thought about just rolling right over. But the fierce, dark water lapping against the hull had looked even more terrible than the sickness. Six days. Well, he hadn't died then. He hoped he wouldn't die now.

He took out his pen and added:

Sunday, December 7th. Japanese air raid on Pearl.

He looked at the dates, eleven, eleven, seventeen and seven. Seven come eleven, and it was one more big crap shoot whether he'd get out of this alive. But then, when it came to craps, when he was down to his last cent, he usually ended up a winner. Maybe he'd be a winner this time, too.

The words in the book looked insignificant. There ought to be something enduring to say about today, but the disaster was too complete, too numbing. And tomorrow? Oh, hell. He put his book and pen away.

How in the hell could Roosevelt let this happen, anyway? All those no-war promises. The country'd been fooled.

Later, after his duty ended, he sat on the edge of his bunk listening to the tales of disaster, still unable to comprehend it. According to the talk, almost the whole Pacific fleet had been sunk or damaged. Kaneohe, Ford Island, Pearl, Hickam, Wheeler, all of them had been devastated.

God, how could such a thing have happened?

He reached into his locker and took out his stash of letters.

He held them as though he could squeeze the past out of them, bring yesterday back. He stared at his name and began counting. Fifteen from Ginny, fifteen. Just about two a week for the seven weeks he'd been here. Littlebit's pile was almost as big. Four from his mom. He laid them down and ran his fingers over them. They moved at his touch and a pink envelope slipped apart from the others. He smiled. That was from Carey, Ginny's kid sister. Cute kid. Funny letter.

He stacked them up and put them back in a shoe box that had once held the brownies Carey sent. He stared at the lid, then laughed wryly. "You know, Goat. We never got breakfast."

Six

Ginny watched an auburn-haired girl in a parrot-green bathing suit dig bright red toenails into the Waikiki sand, watched her breathe deeply and close her eyes, luxuriating in the warmth and moistness that oozed between her toes. A light breeze thick with the scent of wild orchids playfully ruffled her page boy, then drifted onward to stir the leaves of the tall palms. The girl raised her chin and the light from a tropical full moon caressed her forehead, accentuating her loveliness. Beside her, a bronzed, blond man took her in his arms and kissed her passionately. She felt the ripple of his muscles, the heat from his lips.

Ginny opened her eyes. No, that wasn't right. Strike the moonlight. Instead, let there be a glorious sunset that sets the girl's auburn hair aflame in its crimson glow. Yes. Better. Ginny closed her eyes again and once more the man kissed her, overwhelming her, conquering her with his passion.

Nuts.

She sighed and rose from the bed where she'd lain fully dressed. Imagination was useless. How could she dig her toes in this dumb blue rug? Her only flowers were in the draperies and the only glow, the polish on the new mahogany dresser she'd bought for her dream house.

She took off her Sunday church dress, hung it up, and took the new gray wool slacks from their hanger. The slacks were the dubious prize of another Saturday shopping spree with her girlfriends, although it hardly qualified as a spree. She sat down on her bed and pouted, counting off the months on her fingers. Jack had left for Belvoir on July eleventh, then sailed for Hawaii in October, also the 11th. November, December. December seventh. Four days less than five months. Nuts. Another seven long, boring months until he got back.

Jack, at least, had the sand and sunsets of Hawaii to enjoy. She was stuck here. No dates, no nothing. She raised her hand and glared at her red-tipped fingers. Not even a ring to show for it.

A tear appeared at the corner of her eye and threatened her makeup. She blinked it away. If he'd been home they'd have spent the summer dancing at Luna Pier and swimming in the quarry, maybe even gone up to Cedar Point. She heaved an *I'm so sorry for myself* sigh. Now that it was December, at least there would be Christmas shopping.

She stepped into the slacks, leaving the zipper open, then played the *I don't have a thing to wear* game with her blouses, sliding them back and forth on the closet rod. Nothing seemed right. The red one too old, the blue boring. She tried on a white, frowned in irritation at her image, and discarded it for a new yellow cotton she'd been saving. What she saved it for, she didn't know.

Maybe she shouldn't have accepted Jack's proposal— waited until he got back. At least she'd be able to date. Nothing serious. Just go out. But he had been so cute. How could she say no? And if she had refused, she might not have him at all. She pictured him putting a lei around a dark, exotic girl in a grass skirt, touching her shoulders.

He'd better not!

She picked up the photo he'd sent from Honolulu and made a face at him, flicking him on the nose with her finger. *Take that for making eyes at girls in parrot-green bathing suits.* Well, maybe she'd been smart after all to get engaged. This bird in the hand was better than all of the rest of them in the bush.

He'd said the shirt was custom-made. He looked like an officer. His blond hair was almost white against his tan and she wondered how he got away with the length of the top. Maybe after the guys were in for a while, they stopped buzzing with the clippers. He smiled at her from the photo, showing perfect white teeth. She kissed his mouth, amused by the thought that if it were really him, with that big grin, she'd be kissing his teeth. But she still warned the image, "You'd better not be whistling at those hula dancers. Anyway, I hope they're all short and fat."

She put the photo back on her dresser, mooning over the silly grin of his and how he'd blushed that time he'd whistled when he she came downstairs for their first date. She'd worn her black dress with the rhinestone necklace.

Taking the dress from the closet, she pressed it against her waist, and preened in the mirror. Maybe she should get unengaged. But she knew she wouldn't. She wanted Jack.

Could any guy be as innocent as he looked? He wasn't immune to a pretty face, but if an old girlfriend's name was mentioned in conversation he'd get that shy smile and say, "She kinda liked me," as though it were a surprise. All the same, any guy that good-looking wasn't a sure thing 'til you had that wedding ring around your finger. She frowned at him. *Don't forget, you're mine.*

From the kitchen, pans clanked ominously and her mother's voice held barely restrained impatience, "Ginny!"

Oh, joy. Now I get to peel potatoes.

She ambled dreamily downstairs. Did Jack ever get KP duty? He'd never complained about it. The movies always showed the guys with mounds of potatoes, but mostly for punishment. That wouldn't be him. What would he be doing right now? When she reached the kitchen she asked, "What time is it?"

"It's twenty-five after two. Would you please hurry up with those potatoes? The chicken's almost done."

That was what Hawaii time? Five hours. Nine twenty-five there. Would Jack be in church? Would he go? Maybe he'd be at the beach.

Her mother opened the white oven door to baste the chicken. The scent of roasted meat and sage dressing rose from crisp brown skin. Her mouth watered. That's one thing he didn't get on the islands, Mom's baked chicken. Was he chowing down right now on soggy toast and watery oatmeal? He wouldn't get creamed beef for breakfast, would he? In his letters, he griped about rice, but that sounded better to her than the dried boxed potatoes the army tried to pass off as real.

Would he be finished with breakfast and already on the beach? With some other girl in a green suit? She wished she were there. It irritated her when he bragged about Hawaii. Men had all the fun.

Her mother frowned. "Ginny, stop daydreaming and get on with it. Pay attention."

"Yes, Mom. Where's Dad?"

"One of his friends asked him to help fix his car. He said to go ahead and eat, save him some dinner. He'll be a while."

Ginny nodded. Her dad was a nice guy. It surprised her how many different things he could do. She wondered if Jack would be that handy when he settled down. She knew he could fix cars, too, because he'd worked on the Model A when he bought it.

Wistfully she turned on the radio, ignoring its hum and squawk while she turned the dial until she found some bearable music. Something romantic. At least the church stuff was over.

"Virginia! Please!"

"Sorry, Mom." She picked up a knife, but her mother frowned. Ginny sniffed in exasperation, put it down, and got the peeler, attacking the spuds on the enamel drain board as though they were the stupid congressmen who'd passed the draft act. She held the potatoes under the faucet to rinse them and turned the faucet on too hard. Water splashed over her and her mother, who gave her another annoyed look. Cripes! Was everyone in the world going to be crabby today, or was it just herself? "Where's Carey? You spoil her. She never has to help."

Mrs. Fairfax raised an eyebrow at her childishness, but said patiently, "She's next door at Antonia's for dinner. They're going to an early movie this afternoon."

"Why do you call her Antonia? It's such a long name for a little spoiled brat. Toni's better." Even an argument would relieve her restlessness.

Her mother didn't take the bait. "My, aren't we cheerful today?"

"Everything's so boring. Sometimes I wish I'd waited to get engaged."

Her mom patted her shoulder. "A year's not so long."

Alice Fairfax, at forty-three, was younger than the mothers of most of Ginny's friends. If girls turned out to resemble their mothers when they were older, Jack wouldn't have to worry. Just a wee bit round from years of good cooking, Mrs. Fairfax was still pretty, with light brown hair and translucent green eyes, the color of glass marbles.

Her mom didn't upset easily, but when she did, Ginny

59

said, "Yes, ma'am. No, ma'am." Ginny thought her mom too old-fashioned, too strict about dating and boys. And it seemed half their conversations were about the proper way to act. The right way. Her mom had even given her an Emily Post book of etiquette on her sixteenth birthday. It was the price she paid for being the older sister. She felt it part of her duty to Carey to campaign for a little easing of the rules.

Now her mom said, "You know, Ginny, I have to confess, when I first met Jack, I was worried. He was just too good-looking. I thought he'd be trouble, but I think he's very well behaved. I like him."

Ginny's back was to her mom, who couldn't see the silent laughter. It was as if her mother had read her mind. Yes. Jack and Emily Post would make a great couple.

An excited voice from the radio distracted Ginny from her musing. "We interrupt this program for a special announcement." Then, a dramatic pause. The announcer's tone became as grave and measured as Churchill's had been in his famous blood, sweat and tears speech. "This morning, December 7, 1941, at 7:55 a.m., the Japanese attacked Pearl Harbor—"

Ginny's peeler wavered over her potato. Was this another one of Orson Welles' bad jokes? It wasn't funny if it was. She tried not to listen, but the voice continued. Talking. Talking. Jack was at Pearl, well, Schofield. But then this wasn't real, so she didn't need to worry. Someone was trying to create another sensation like that Mars invasion broadcast. They said people had jumped out of windows when they heard the program.

But the voice didn't stop and her mother was looking at her in a funny way. In a trance, Ginny watched the plate her mother had been holding float lazily downward in slow motion. It hit the kitchen floor and spun for a moment like a played-out, wobbly top, then fell over and cracked into two pieces.

Ginny stared at it for a moment, then picked up the halves and tossed them into the trash. She reached over and snapped off the radio. "They shouldn't be allowed to do that. It isn't funny." It had to be another fake. Japan couldn't.

Her mom put her arms around her and pressed Ginny's cheek against her shoulder. She reached back and turned the sound on again. She said gently, "We have to hear."

The announcer continued to describe the havoc.

Ginny struggled and fought free of her mother. She stared wide-eyed at the radio, then pounded her fists on the little brown plastic box. It crackled, then went right on talking. No. No. It wasn't true! It was a hoax!

Finally, she conceded. What the man was saying had to be true. The Japs had bombed Pearl Harbor. She put her hands to her mouth. "Jack." She closed her eyes. Pictures of bombs falling, Jack falling, flashed through her mind. She shuddered and let out a low moan. Dear God. No. Not Jack.

Her mother spoke sharply, "Ginny."

She gave her mother a frightened look and repeated, "Jack! Jack!"

The agonized voice on the radio recounted the story in awed and disbelieving tones, using words like "total disaster" and "complete surprise." Ginny stood rooted as the details rolled out. "The *Arizona, Oklahoma, Ford Island, Nevada.* Our Pacific fleet—"

This couldn't happen. Jack was supposed to come back in July. Strictly a defensive posture, the president had said. Roosevelt had promised. Japan? Those little yellow rats, all they knew how to do was make cheap celluloid dolls. How did they hope to get away with it? How dare they? We could crush those little pipsqueaks in a month. Who did they think they were?

61

Dear God, let Jack be safe. Don't let anything happen to him. She buried her face in her mother's arms and sobbed.

Her mom brushed at her hair, trying to soothe her. "The worst of it seems to be at the naval base. They're talking about ships. He's on the other side of the island. Maybe he'll be all right. We'll pray, Ginny. We'll pray."

Carey, red-faced, her eyes wide and glistening with tears, rushed into the kitchen, letting the door slam behind her. "Ginny, Mom! Did you hear?" She stopped at the sight of her sister in her mother's arms. Carey's own tears poured down her face, unrestrained.

Her mom looked at her over the top of Ginny's head. Her eyes were filled with tears but she didn't cry. She reached out to Carey in a helpless motion, as if to say, "I'm sorry."

Carey walked over and hugged both of them, then turned and went out onto the back porch. It was cold, but she couldn't stay inside and watch her sister sob. She sat on the step alone, resting her forehead on her crossed arms. *Jack. Dear God. Not Jack.* She wiped at her tears with the back of her hand and sniffled. He wasn't at Pearl. He'd never said "Schofield," but his buddy Red had called home and Red's girl had written. No matter how hard they tried, it was almost impossible for a whole army to be kept secret.

Dear God, let him be safe. Don't let him get hurt.

Damned Japs. She rarely cussed, but she meant it now. Damn. Damn. *Damn!*

War. For years now she'd listened to and watched news reports of wars over there, in Europe, Asia. But not the U.S. World War One. Thank goodness she was too young for that one. Every year on November eleventh she'd had to listen to long, boring speeches about the Great War, as it was called, and Armistice Day. The War to End All Wars. That had never seemed real. It might as well have been the Civil War or the Revolution.

The real truth and horror of those awful stories about the trenches, going over the top and that awful gas, came to her for the first time. It had been more than just a history lesson to those men. It could happen to Jack.

But the wars she read about and watched in the newsreels now—Hitler in Europe, Japan in China—wasn't in trenches. It was everywhere, like the bombs in London. She'd felt safe because the United States was clear across an ocean from it all.

The war movies had mostly been about Hitler and England, and that was the war she'd worried about getting into. China and Japan were different. Even with the pictures of the Chinese, like the one in *Life* magazine of the baby sitting in the middle of a bombed-out road, alone and crying. The East was a fairy tale world, and Japan a place that made little toys for the five and ten cent stores. Little islands like Japan just didn't attack big countries like the United States.

Carey's friend, Toni, came over, sat and put her arm around Carey's shoulders. "Don't worry, Ted'll be okay if he ever has to go."

Carey looked up in surprise and blushed with guilt. She smiled weakly and sniffled. She'd thought only of Jack, not Toni's brother, Ted, but she couldn't say that to Toni. Carey put her arm around her friend.

From where she sat, she could see the neighborhood women gathering over their back fences. They hadn't even put their arms into the sleeves of their coats, just draped them hastily over their backs. They sent anxious glances toward her house. She knew why they looked, what they were saying. "Ginny's Jack is there on Hawaii." He was the only one in the neighborhood who'd been drafted, the only one at Pearl. She suddenly resented them, then felt ashamed. Most of them had sons. If the war lasted, then . . . She left the thought unfinished. Surely . . .

"Oh, Toni. It's awful. How long do you think a war could last?" The Chinese had been fighting the Japanese forever, but China didn't have the war materials they needed and they weren't very modern. But everyone admitted the U.S. wasn't ready either. The country had geared up to help Britain with Lend-lease and for the sake of "preparedness" but was no where near any fighting strength.

The hope now lay in the fact that a country with the resources of the United States could out produce both Japan *and* Germany.

Toni commiserated with her. "I don't know how long a war can last. Look at China, Manchuria and Japan. That seems like it's been going on forever. The Spanish one lasted four years, but that was because of help from Germany and Italy."

Four years! "Oh, Toni. I'll be almost twenty-two. I'll be an old woman and all the boys will be gone." She didn't say, maybe they'd all be killed. She hugged her friend. Even Ted, Toni's brother, just twenty, would have to go. "What does Ted say?"

Toni's face reddened and tears filled her eyes and spilled down her cheeks. "He said he was going down to the recruiting office and sign up for the Army Air Corps right away but Mom was really upset. She talked him into waiting 'til the school year ends." She got up and shivered. "I wish I were a man. I'd go show them a thing or two."

Carey stood and hugged her. "Don't worry. By the time he's in and learns to fly, Japan will be licked."

"Yeah, but Roosevelt's been wanting to get at Germany, too. We're in it now. All the way."

Carey wiped the tears from her face. She looked wistfully at Toni and Ted's back porch where they'd all had so much fun. "Remember how crazy I was about Ted?" She hated to admit that it wasn't really that long ago. Ten months. Since she'd first laid eyes on Jack. After that, Ted and all the other guys had faded out of her life. She sighed and said aloud, "Why?" thinking, why do I have to be seventeen? Why does Jack have to be so old? Twenty-three. I'll never catch up. And why does he have to be engaged to my own sister?

"Yeah," Toni repeated. "Why does there have to be a war?"

Carey huddled against her friend and stared out at the backyard. Her warm, cozy world looked soiled now. Dirty remnants of an early snow lay against the fence, turning the soft brown earth of fall into the bare hard clay of winter. Even her glorious rose bushes were unfriendly, their thorny branches menacing, the grass brown and dead.

She'd been too upset to be bothered much by the cold before, but now she shivered. "You know, Toni, it's never, ever going to be the same again."

Seven

Carey checked her watch. Six forty. Ted would be here any minute. He hadn't wasted any time enlisting. The day his exams at school were over, he'd headed for the recruiting office. Hadn't even waited to be drafted. She closed her eyes, refusing to worry about him yet. He'd have to learn to fly. That would take a while.

She frowned at the blond image in the mirror and flipped back her long hair, wondering if she should cut it.

She swept it up in her hands and piled it on top of her head, then tilted her head in her best Rita Hayworth imitation. She tried a toothy look, then grimaced. *Rita definitely has no competition here. For that matter, neither does Ginny. Jack still thinks I'm a little kid.*

She pinned the top and sides in Gibson Girl rolls and stuck her tongue out at her image. *Oh, for red hair like Rita's!* Maybe if it was short. Maybe she would look older. She swooped it up to her ears.

Her sister's reflection appeared beside hers in the mirror. Ginny reached for a comb. "It looks good long." She gave Carey's hair a few flips, letting the blond hair fall in a cascade of soft curls. She nodded. "There. That's nice."

"It makes me look like a baby."

"You are a baby." Ginny patted her on the head, then laughed at Carey's glare. "I know. You're a big-shot senior now. I'll never forget how grown-up I felt."

"Yeah. Well, just remember, when you're thirty, I'll only be twenty-six."

Ginny wrinkled her nose. "Twenty-seven. Ted's waiting."

"Okay. I'll be right down." Carey scrabbled hastily through a pile of lipsticks looking for the match to her nail polish. When Ginny frowned, Carey raised an eyebrow. "Well, say it. What's the matter?"

Ginny waved her hand and shrugged. "Nothing's the matter. I just wondered."

"What?"

"You aren't going to get engaged to him, are you?"

"Where'd you get that idea? We're friends. This is only a goodbye dinner." *I hope.*

Ginny assumed her big sister look. "You've been pals for a long time and with him going into the air corps . . ." She shrugged. "I'm worried he'll want someone to come home to."

You and me too! That was exactly what worried Carey. Ted had said only, "Let's make an evening of it. My last weekend home." She couldn't refuse yet she was afraid he'd make more of this date than she wanted him to. For herself as much as Ginny, Carey insisted, "It's not that way between us. I outgrew that puppy love a long time ago." *As soon as I laid eyes on Jack!* She eyed Ginny enviously.

"Well, don't be in a hurry. You're just a kid."

Carey gave her a disgusted look. "I was eighteen in May."

"Seventeen, eighteen. What's the difference? You're still too young and it looks like a long war. Don't get stuck like me," Ginny tossed over her shoulder as she left.

Surprised by that remark, Carey watched the image in the

mirror retreat, wondering, *Does she really wish she wasn't engaged to Jack? That would be something. But even if she doesn't want him, Jack will still think I'm a kid.*

She tried to swallow her cheeks like Marlene Dietrich, twisting and turning to see the effect. Hopeless! No matter what she did, it wouldn't make any difference. She had Ted, whom she liked but didn't want, and Jack, whom she wanted but couldn't have.

For years, she'd hung around Toni's big brother, hoping for some crumb of attention. Two and a half years older, Ted had appeared grown-up and glamorous. Now that seemed a long time ago. Lately, though, he'd been different, teasing her less and treating her with more reserve, more courtesy. More than once she'd turned to find him watching her. He tried for her attention like she used to try for his. This business of the shoe on the other foot unnerved her.

"Carey, Ted's waiting!" Ginny sang again from the stairway.

Why did big sisters think they were mothers? One in a house was enough. If only she'd been born first.

She took a last look at her image, added another touch of lipstick, and went downstairs.

Ted's face lit when he saw her. He stared for a moment and raised an eyebrow, "I suppose if I whistle, you'll hit me!" All the time he bounced on the balls of his feet like a boxer before a fight, then grabbed her hand, practically dragging her to the door. "C'mon, we've got to catch the bus."

"Can't we take the Studebaker?"

He didn't stop. "Just about used up my gas ration. I gave the car to Mom so she could have it while I'm in the air corps. I let her register it so she'd get the coupons."

They reached the corner just in time to wave down the oncoming bus. It skidded to a quick stop. The driver smiled.

"Almost missed me." They gave him their tokens and wended their way to the back. Saturday night busses were always crowded.

Ted wiped his brow and flapped his jacket front.

Carey, in her cool, blue linen dress looked at him smugly. She loved the summer bareness of sleeveless dresses. Especially this one with its long waist. No belt to add warmth. She ran her hand over the pleated skirt, smoothing it. "You men are idiots for putting up with those coats in the summer."

"Yeah, I guess, but I need one tonight. I thought we'd stop at the Hillcrest after the show." He glanced at her appreciatively.

She squirmed inwardly but couldn't help being pleased. And worried. The Hillcrest usually signaled *big plans*. She tried to ward him off. "I'm impressed, but we won't have time, will we?" The hotel boasted a first class, expensive restaurant with a small dance floor, but it wasn't really downtown where they could catch the midnight bus.

"*Road to Morocco* ends about ten. If we run all the way from the theater to the hotel, then run to the bus afterward, we can do it."

She looked at her three-inch heels. "I hope you're kidding."

Patting his pocket, he grinned and reassured her. "I think we can take a cab. My last fling."

"Madison," the driver called and pulled to the curb. The bus emptied quickly and everyone seemed to head for the Paramount and Hope and Crosby. Carey waited inside the packed lobby while Ted bought the tickets. They had to settle for the balcony, but managed to get seats near the front railing. She sighed with relief. She never liked the back rows with all the kissing couples. She knew some of the girls back there tonight. They had a reputation for being fast.

The Paramount, with its lush wine velvet, gold trim, and baroque scroll work around the ceiling and walls, was her favorite theater. She settled down contentedly and let it transport her to Vienna or maybe Paris.

The organ pit stayed closed. No monster rose majestically from the depths, the organist playing full throttle to accompany Bela Lugosi rising slowly from his coffin. The sound always thrilled her but she felt a bit silly singing along with the dumb little ball that bounced over the words on the screen. She wished she had a voice like Jo Stafford's or Peggy Lee's.

Ted slipped his arm around her shoulder and she tensed, worrying again that accepting this date had been a mistake.

She sensed rather than saw his smile as he pressed her shoulder but he made no other move. Thankfully, the lights dimmed, and from the screen, the Pathe News Rooster crowed into the dawn. The audience stirred, underscoring their anxiety as the news clips detailed the war highlights. Since the final victory at Midway early in June, the Japanese front had been comparatively quiet. She wondered where Jack was, what he was doing, whether he'd been anywhere near Midway. Was there even one person in the audience who didn't have someone in the service, someone to worry about?

The week's big news was the main German summer offensive that started on the twenty-eighth of June and the Russian evacuation of Sevastopol on the thirtieth. That news now filled the screen.

Ted's hand gripped her shoulder as they watched the reports. "I can't wait to get over there." She reached up and touched his hand. He didn't take his eyes from the screen, but the grip eased. "Sorry."

Carey could feel the tension that virtually crackled in the theater. Then Eisenhower's face came on the screen and the electricity evaporated. His grin and open Midwestern face ra-

70

diated confidence. He'd been appointed Commander of the U.S. Land Forces in Europe on June twenty-fifth.

A collective sigh could be heard as the clips ended and a buzz of conversation filled the void. Even though the shots were at least a few days old, the newsreels were so much more compelling than newspapers or radio. Carey thought maybe she should be a foreign correspondent. She could travel and avoid guys who wanted to be serious. Life was becoming very complicated.

A Tom and Jerry cartoon followed, then, finally, Hope and Crosby filled the screen. She was glad to put her problems behind her while their wise cracks kept her laughing. Yet, beneath the laughter, she was conscious of Ted's arm still around her shoulders and his nearness. It would be tempting to fall in love with love, and kiss the soldier goodbye as he bravely went off to his war.

Like Ginny. The thought rose unbidden. Once, when they were kids, they'd had a fight over Sir Lancelot in the tales of King Arthur. They both wanted to grow up and marry him. Sometimes she wondered if Ginny ever outgrew the dream of a knight in shining armor.

In the dim light, Carey studied the firm line of Ted's jaw, his classic Roman nose, curly dark hair, and rather square face. Ted Giordano. She couldn't see herself as Mrs. Giordano even though she had no chance of ever becoming Mrs. Andrews. Yet wars upset many relationships.

A roar from the audience brought her back to the movie. Ted didn't show any signs of daydreaming. Evidently excited by the prospect of flying off into the wild blue yonder, his laughter was even harder and louder than most.

In the cab to the hotel, he talked nonstop, then overtipped the cabbie. "The last of the big spenders."

Carey managed a few "mmm hmm's" and was relieved

when they were seated at a table. She glanced quickly at the white and gold menu, then laid it down and looked at her watch. Her mom would be worrying. "Order for me, will you? Anything but the fish. I'd better call Mom. She'll be looking for me on the last bus."

"It's okay. I told her I was bringing you here. We can take the cab home, too. I want the evening to last as long as it can."

"Oh, boy. I can just hear that conversation. 'Now you're not to give her any alcohol'." She raised an eyebrow and her head. "I'll even bet she told you not to drink."

"I don't think she was worried." He reached over their table and twirled the end of a strand of hair around his fingers. He gave it a playful tug. "With a face like yours, they'd never serve you."

She slapped at his hand. "Well, you're not exactly a man about town." Her mom was partial to Ted, but like Ginny, she worried they might become engaged or even go steady. Her mom said often enough, "You're too young." She *was* too young—for Jack. Now if Jack were Ted's age . . .

A quiet hum filled the crowded dining room. Carey soberly watched the other diners. Nearly all were service men, both army and navy. Toledo had no camps of its own. Most of these men probably came from the Great Lakes boot camp or Camp Perry, a few miles down the lake.

The presence of so many uniforms seemed to exhilarate Ted. He ate little, talked a lot, and kept looking around. Fidgeting with his fork, he said, "I can't wait to get my wings. I hope I make fighter pilot."

She reached out and put her hand on his. "You've seen *Dawn Patrol* too often. You'll be part of that soon enough." Regret for the loss of her nice growing-up fun world as well as sadness for these men settled on her. She wanted to cry for

Ted and Jack, for all these boys and men, the handsome white-jacketed officers here, the cute little sailor in his bell-bottoms over in the corner, and the one lone marine. He looked like he was fifteen, not old enough to be in the service. And the gray-haired army officer—Carey couldn't be sure from this distance, but it looked like eagles on his coat. He had an air of control, as though he assumed no one would disagree with him.

She felt a sad sisterhood with their women. Like the pretty one at the next table holding hands with the army lieutenant who had a face that looked maybe nineteen after a bad day. Carey met the girl's eyes and read the anguish in them. Perhaps it was the end of his leave.

Ted took her hand. "Let's dance."

The small dance floor allowed little exhibitionism and they settled into a cheek-to-cheek fox trot. Ted held her tighter than she expected and hummed softly in her ear. She wanted to put a little distance between them, but that girl's sadness and the melancholy of the sax was overwhelming. She didn't move away. The singer added to the spell with her complaint, "Don't Get Around Much Anymore."

They danced two sets before Ted said the words she'd been dreading, "I don't suppose you'd want to be engaged?" At least he said them lightly.

She didn't answer right away. His cheek was still against hers, but she could tell he was smiling. Even though she'd expected it, the suggestion brought a tear to her eye. She suddenly felt old and tired. Why was it always the wrong one who wanted you? She was tempted to put more physical as well as emotional distance between them, but didn't want to hurt his feelings. They were friends.

She did put a little daylight between them. "You may be gone for a long time. A lot of things could change." She summoned up a smile for him, "Wait 'til you get your wings. You'll have so many women after you, you won't even remember my name." *I hope.*

He sighed. "I guess I knew you'd say that." Then he got that teasing look he used to get when she was a pesky kid trailing him.

Her heart turned over.

"What happened to that crush you had on me?"

"Who said I had a crush on you?"

"Are you kidding? You were like a little puppy dog hoping for a pat on the head. I always wished you were a little older." His eyes laughed at her. "You were a cute little brat."

She sighed. The brat part was true, anyway. She almost wished it still was. She wasn't sure she liked growing up in this world at war.

He tried to pull her close, but she kept the space between them. She couldn't read the expression on his face when he asked, "So what happened? Did you grow up or did I?" Was that look amusement or wistfulness?

She finally said, "I do still like you a lot. I just don't know about love."

That wasn't the greatest answer in the world, but it was as close as she could come to honesty. She wished she had a definition of love. Was that what she felt for Jack? How could it be? She hardly knew him. It had better not be love. He belonged to her sister.

She had a funny feeling about her sister and Jack, though. She wasn't at all sure Ginny knew what real love was any more than she did.

She realized Ted was looking at her with that same unidentifiable expression. He said, "Well, will you wait for me?"

She held her breath, wanting again to cry, but not daring to in front of him. Not with her mascara and her handkerchief still in her purse. She was tempted to snuggle close, to hold onto those wonderful times when she wasn't quite so grown-up and he was still her hero. She finally said, "Oh, Ted. Who knows what can happen. I don't think you ought to make commitments. Besides, I'm . . ."

"Yeah, I know what you're going to say. You're only eighteen and you want to go to college." His mouth smiled as he said it, but she read hurt in his eyes. He sighed and pulled her close for a moment then let her go. "I think it's going to be a long war, Carey, and I do love you." He shrugged his pain away. The little grin that made him look like Peck's bad boy returned. "I don't know when it happened. There you were, my kid sister's bratty friend, then suddenly here you are, maybe only eighteen but more grown-up than most girls I know, and definitely the prettiest."

In spite of herself, a tear spilled from her eye. She tried to focus on the blue of the dress of the girl dancing near her. Anything to distract herself. She mustn't cry.

He didn't wait for her to speak. "I guess right now, you aren't in love with me. But I'm not in a hurry. I'll wait."

She was glad when the band broke into "Cow-Cow Boogie" and they were too busy dancing to talk. By the time the song finished, she was breathless.

The band left for a break and a young woman sat down at the piano. Ted listened intently as she played her own version of the boogie. "She's good." He played a pretty mean piano himself. Carey was relieved to have him distracted.

He looked at his watch. "We'd better go before one of us turns into a pumpkin. I'd like to close the place, but your mom will get worried if we're too late." He kissed her lightly on the cheek. "At least you'll send me cookies and fudge, won't you?"

She raised her eyebrow at him. "Depends on whether or

not I can find a black market to buy some sugar. Of course, I could go to jail for that, you know."

He pouted.

She laughed and gave in. "Okay. You win." She reached out and touched his hand. "Of course, I'll send you cookies!"

"And write?" He pressed her hand in his.

Her uneasy feeling returned, but what else could she do? She nodded. "And write."

He released her, and brought out a picture from his wallet. "I'll put this on my locker door."

"Oh, not that one! That was last summer. Look how fat I was."

He laughed and sang, "I don't want her, you can have her, she's too fat for me." He waved the photo in front of her. "Either this, or get me a new one."

She held up her hands. "Okay, y'got me. I'll get ya m'mug."

"Okay, sister. Don't forget or it's curtains. Got it?"

"Just wait 'til you get your wings. You'll need two lockers just to pin up all the girls chasing you. You won't need me."

He shook his head. "You're the only one I'll ever want to pin my wings on." He leaned over the table and kissed her softly for just a moment.

She mustn't cry.

Eight

August 1942

Ginny put a final daub of suntan lotion on her legs and tossed the tube on the blanket. She looked up at the cloudless August sky and sighed contentedly. "I'm sure glad we're not on those twelve to nine's anymore. If that telephone company didn't have these split shifts in the summer, I'd go crazy."

Her friend, Sylvia Atkins, agreed. "It wouldn't be so bad if they didn't gripe all the time about us talking. It's okay when you're busy, but really!"

The two of them had planted themselves on their favorite spot at the old LaFrance stone quarry. Sylvia grabbed for the suntan lotion. "Mom would have a fit if she knew I was swimming here."

Ginny nodded. "Yeah, I know. You only have to mention 'quarry' to someone and you get another story about someone drowning." She looked out at the cool, green-blue water sparkling innocently under the glaring sun. The quarry was an abandoned gravel pit that had filled with water. Everyone claimed it was really deep and there were always stories of someone who got trapped under the ledges that jutted out under the water.

"Anyway," Ginny continued, "I think it's a swell place. Never crowded, not too deserted either. I just don't dive into it." She closed her eyes, waiting for the sun to turn her skin golden brown. "It was nice of Matt to drive us out. Where'd he go, anyway?"

"Over there, talking. It'd be nice if he'd stick around for five minutes." Sylvia's slight eastern Kentucky drawl made the words sound like a kitten purring.

Ginny opened an eye but then closed it again and wriggled her back against the blanket. It seemed that a different guy took Sylvia home from work every night. A regular parade. "Where do you find all those fellows of yours, anyway?" Ginny had heard that Sylvia was in Ohio living with an aunt. She was a cute strawberry blond but not spectacular enough to account for the stream of guys. She'd never heard anyone say that Sylvia was fast, either.

"Finding guys isn't that hard with two navy, two army, and a marine for brothers. They all have pals."

Ginny nodded toward Matt. "He seems like a real swell guy."

"Yeah, but he'll be shipping out. I don't want to get tied down."

Ginny said nothing. She wanted to but it sounded so cheap and unpatriotic to say she wished she wasn't tied down. Not that she didn't love Jack, she did. But life got boring. Especially she couldn't say that when Jack might be in the middle of a battle. On the seventh and eighth there'd been landings at Guadalcanal. The news said it was mostly marines. Pray God Jack wasn't there.

Even if he was still in Hawaii, he was far away from mom and apple pie. He ought to be out here with her now. The best years of her life were plodding past.

She decided to change the subject. "The Sausage called me over today."

Sylvia turned on her side and giggled. "The what?"

"Miss Wells. She reminds me of a sausage. That corset she wears sort of squeezes everything upward." Ginny laughed. "Haven't you noticed how she walks around with raised eyebrows all the time?"

"Yeah. Now that you mention it, she does look like a sausage. Maybe a tree trunk. What did she want?"

"Oh, it was about Marjorie again. I can't believe they like the way she sounds. 'Lo-ong diss-taance. Threeya sevon nyon nyon. Th-ank youuu,' " Ginny trilled, imitating Marjorie's exaggerated syllables and sickly sweet voice.

"She's such a mealy-mouthed little fake. It makes me cringe to listen to her. I'm glad she's not my supervisor."

"You're lucky. She plugged in on me today again and started nagging me about the lack of expression in my voice. I was tempted to use a real sexy voice with the next guy, but I just made it sound like her." She grinned at the memory.

"You're going to get yourself canned."

Ginny snorted. "Great. I've been there one whole year and I can't stand the supervisors breathing down my neck all the time. I mean, how hard is it to dial a telephone number?"

"What did Marjorie say? Or didn't she even notice?"

Ginny sniffed. "You'll never believe it. She actually said that was better." She threw up her hands. "I don't know what she really thought. Doesn't she know how awful she sounds? Everyone makes fun of her."

"I suppose she squealed to old Sausage Wells then?"

"Yeah. Wells repeated what Marjorie said to me. I told her I'd been complimented just that morning on my voice by a customer. She just sniffed and complained that I'd been late twice, talked too much, and all that good stuff."

"That's a real bunch of hep cats there."

"I'd quit, only they say I can't. It's a war priority job."

"Looks like a long war, too. Have you heard from Jack?"

"Two letters last week." In an amused tone she added, "He thanked me for the cookies, but I never sent him any."

"Sounds to me like there's something going on."

"Oh, no. It was just my green-eyed kid sister, Carey, worrying about his morale." She closed her eyes and let the heat seep into her flesh. "I think men stationed in Hawaii should have to send cookies home to keep up *our* morale."

They lay quietly for a few moments, then Ginny turned on her side and poked Sylvia. "Hey! I just had a great idea. Do you know what we ought to do?"

Sylvia sat up, but she wasn't looking or listening to Ginny. "Wow," she exclaimed, "look at that guy Matt's talking to."

Ginny was too entranced with her scheme to pay attention to some guy she couldn't have, even if he was handsome. "Tomorrow, let's get everyone we can to imitate Marjorie. Sevun nyon nyon fyov. Wouldn't that drive them nuts?"

Matt brought the other boy over as she said it. "Sylvie, this is Paul Keller. Paul, Sylvie, and that one who wants to drive the people at the telephone company nuts is Ginny."

Paul appraised her in one long sweeping look. "She can drive me nuts any time." His teeth glistened when he smiled and his eyes glinted. He had to be at least six feet tall, nice and slim, with a tan the color of her mother's mahogany coffee table.

Matt patted him on the shoulder, "Easy, guy. She's got a boyfriend in the army." Matt motioned to Sylvia, and the pair jogged off in the direction of the water.

Still smiling at her, Paul shrugged. "A bird in the hand." He plunked down on the edge of her blanket.

Playing it cool, Ginny rolled onto her stomach but kept her face turned in his direction. Without his tan, Paul might be quite ordinary, but the contrast of dark skin, light hair, and pale greenish eyes intrigued her. Where did he find time for such a tan? Didn't he work? She raised her head slightly to ask. She hesitated for a moment but was too curious to let it go. "Are you in the service?" She tried to sound casual, just a matter of academic interest. So many times the question really meant, "Why aren't you in the service?"

Evidently unsure of her intent, he answered sharply, "Merchant marine." When she didn't react, he relaxed. "My ship's laid up for repairs. I managed some leave."

She raised herself onto her elbows to look him over. Manning those merchant ships was a risky business even though it paid well. "You must like to live dangerously."

He shrugged and accepted her surveillance as though he were used to girls giving him the once-over. "What was all this about driving people crazy?"

She turned onto her back again and stretched out. "Oh, I work for the telephone company. Long distance. I have a supervisor who really hams it up and I'd love to drive her nuts. She complains because I don't say fi-ov ny-on as though I had a New York cold. Do you suppose maybe we could get her to join the merchant marines?"

"Ah, you have a very sexy voice. Next time I call I'll keep dialing for the operator until I get you."

"Nyon to wonne. Fyov to nyon."

He smiled politely but looked as though he didn't understand.

"I work a split shift."

"Oh." He nodded. "Nine to one? Five to nine? That's why you can come out here and dazzle all us guys." His gaze swept along her legs then back to her face. "Is your boyfriend here in the states?"

"I wish. He was one of those guys who were supposed to be in for a year and ended up at Pearl. Combat engineers.

He's still in Hawaii, I think. I hope. At least his APO hasn't changed."

"Ah." His teeth glinted.

What do you say to "Ah," she wondered? He *did* have a nice smile! A bit like Eisenhower's. Open, friendly.

He said, "Looth lips think thips."

It was her turn to be puzzled.

His eyes crinkled at the corners, emphasizing the deep lines that must have come from squinting at the sun out on the ocean. "Being out there in the Atlantic on a ship with U-boats swarming around us, I have a built-in alarm that goes off when any location is given." His voice was light, but he threw a stone into the quarry with a quick hard movement. "Even one as innocent as you just said. Sorry, overreaction."

She looked at him curiously. He didn't seem like an ordinary sailor. Maybe he was an officer. She asked, "What was it you said before? Luth something?"

"Loose lips sink ships. Only I was kidding. It's a knee-jerk reaction."

"How long before you have to go back to your ship?"

"Two weeks, more or less."

"How'd you get so tan?"

"You ask a lot of questions. Are you a spy?" Amused, he cocked an eyebrow and answered her. "Radio operator nights. Long boring days."

"You don't talk like a radio operator."

He laughed. "How does a radio operator talk?"

She shrugged. "You just don't."

"I was going to MIT when the war broke out. I thought about going into the navy, then decided if I was going to get shot at, I might as well get paid for it. I need the money for school."

Matt and Sylvia came running back from the water. "Hey,

Paul. Sylvie wants to go to the USO on Saturday night. How about it?"

Paul gave Ginny a long, studied look, then shrugged as though he'd decided his idea was hopeless. "I don't know. Might not be worth the trouble I'd have. My uniform seems to attract the wrong kind of attention. I can hold my own, but I do get tired of trying to stay out of fights with you navy types. You seem to think we sail around for a lark." He picked up another stone and threw it hard. "I'd like to know where your blasted ships would be without us." His voice wasn't angry, but his mouth formed a grim line.

Matt said in a pacific tone, "It just makes the navy guys mad that the merchant marine's part of a union. After all, it's a war. And you do pull in a few more bucks. Then there's that story going around about how you wouldn't unload some supplies the navy escort needed. Kind of ticked them off." He smiled to show he had no personal stake in the argument. "I'll have my uniform on. If you're with me, it'll be okay." Matt was not only navy, he was huge and well liked among the guys who knew him.

Paul looked pointedly at Ginny. "I don't know any girls."

Ginny sat up, flirting with temptation. Dancing. Her ears tingled at the sound of the word. Her toes wiggled involuntarily. It had been a long time since she'd been on a floor. A whole year, in fact.

Sylvia plopped down beside her. "Why don'cha come along?"

Ginny considered. She'd give a month's pay to go dancing. She wavered and then said, "I really can't. Everyone will yap at me. I'd never hear the end of it."

"Jack wouldn't mind. It's not like it's a date—you'd be helping out at the USO. You'll probably never see the guy again." Sylvia glanced at Paul, but he hadn't seemed to hear.

Ginny pictured Carey sitting on her shoulder like a conscience, clucking her tongue. She didn't want to deal with the guilt, so she focused on Paul's half-turned back. Interesting. He had freckles under the tan when you looked closely. *Wonder what he looks like in a uniform. Don't think I've seen one from the merchant marines before.*

Sylvia wheedled, "Come on. It won't hurt, and you'd be helping morale. Jack wouldn't mind."

Ginny felt herself weakening. "It would be heaven to dance again." She hummed a scrap of tune that she suddenly realized was "Goodbye Dear", then sighed. "I don't know." If Sylvie said just one more word, she'd give in and go.

Matt interrupted. "It's almost four. We'd better head back." He turned to Paul. "Are you coming?"

"Sure, might as well."

The butterfly that had fluttered in her stomach when Paul had approached took flight again. She turned away. "We've got to change. You guys stay here."

The limestone quarry was surrounded by a large shelf of flat, gravel-covered ground with plenty of room for cars. The shelf of rocks rimming the water was now overgrown with vegetation and it gave the girls a precarious sort of privacy as they scrunched down in the back seat of the car to climb into their clothes.

As her head emerged through the top of her dress, Sylvia said, "Paul's a swell guy, isn't he?" She shook her hair. "I think he has a case on you. I can tell."

He had seemed interested, Ginny thought. She held out her hand and looked at the third finger of her left hand. The polish was chipped. She put her hand down quickly. Jack never did get the chance to buy her that ring. "I'll get you one as big as a dime when I get back. Promise." He'd said it as he kissed her the last time. Only they hadn't planned on the war.

She pictured Jack watching the girl in the green bathing suit dance a hula. A girl for his morale.

Well, if he needed a morale boost, so did she. "All right. I'll go just this once."

Sylvia nodded conspiratorially. "Sure. It's just for the morale of the boys. Jack shouldn't complain about that."

Nine

Carey paused at the doorway to her sister's room to give Ginny the once-over. "You're awfully dressed up. Must be going somewhere."

Ginny sniffed.

Carey walked around her humming, "Don't sit under the apple tree with anyone else but me!" Then she said, "You don't get that fancy *just* to go out with your girlfriends . . ."

Ginny lifted her chin and looked down her nose, then decided the wisest tactic would be to ignore Little Sister.

She surveyed herself in the mirror. Conservative enough. The neckline wasn't too low. She looped a button she'd missed and smoothed the front of the beltless moray taffeta dress. The long lines made her feel willowy, even at her not-so-tall five-foot-two. She paused as she fastened a rhinestone necklace. Was it too dressy? Perhaps she'd better change to pearls. Just so Carey wouldn't think she was trying to impress someone.

Carey took an insistent tone. "Where're you going?"

Ginny took a deep breath. Sisters were meant to be ignored, but this one was a pesky mosquito. "I'm going to the USO canteen just to entertain the service men, if it's any of your business."

"My, aren't you touchy? One would think you had a date."

Ginny picked up an ankle strap shoe from the closet floor and threatened her.

"Okay! I give up." Carey held up her hands and backed out the door. "What do you suppose Jack's doing tonight?" she tossed over her shoulder as she bolted for the stairs.

"Probably eating your cookies." Ginny stuck out her tongue and fastened her shoes. She ran her hands up the backs of her stockings, adjusting them, complaining to herself about twisted seams. Some girls always had straight seams. With her, one of them always managed to go right and the other left like soldiers in an Abbott and Costello movie.

Perfume? Her hand lingered over the atomizer of LeLong's *Indiscréte* Jack's mother had chosen for her birthday present from Jack. He claimed he'd had his mother pick out his presents because the mail from overseas was so impossible, but still she felt miffed. Mrs. Andrews was always pleasant, but there was a reserve that Ginny was sure meant she thought Ginny, or any girl probably, wasn't good enough for her son.

Ginny wondered if she'd feel that way about her son. She meant to have a boy who looked like Jack and a girl who took after her. Fathers liked that.

She didn't think she'd be like Mrs. Andrews. It might all have to do with the depression. A backlash of pride because they'd had a hard time.

Ginny put down the perfume, wishing anyone else, even some old girlfriend, had picked it out. Well, maybe not that, but even a late present would have been better.

She picked up a bottle of *Friendship's Garden* but decided it was too ordinary and went back to the *Indiscréte*. For some reason, it reminded her of Christmas. Not piney Christmas, maybe just romantic. She sniffed it again and reluctantly returned it to its place on the dresser. She wouldn't wear perfume tonight. The decision made her feel virtuous and calmed her restless conscience. This wasn't really a date, even if Carey was being snotty about it. She was just helping the morale of the troops. Still, she was excited. Just the thought of dancing set her toes tapping.

Carey's voice rose to her from the bottom of the stairs. "Gin-ny, your friends are here." She added slyly, "And your da-ate."

Ginny picked up her purse with a defiant swing and walked down, flashing a dirty look at her sister that Sylvia, Matt, and Paul couldn't see. She asked sweetly, "Mom and Dad gone?"

"Bridge." Carey said, then, with a needling grin of her own, added, "Have a good time."

"I won't be late."

None of them had said anything to Carey except to ask for Ginny when they came in. Now as they turned to go, Sylvia said, "You could come along if you want to. We can wait a moment for you to change."

"Thanks, but I thought I'd just stay home, listen to the *Hit Parade* and bake Jack some cookies." She glared at Ginny. "Can't have our boys without cookies, can we?" She hummed the first bars of "Don't Sit Under the Apple Tree" again.

Ginny glared at her, drew a deep breath, and took Paul's arm. Someday, she'd strangle the girl. But she couldn't bother to be angry now. She was going to dance.

By the time they arrived at the National Guard Armory, the place was jammed. They stood for a moment searching, but found no empty tables. A young ensign rose from his table. "You can join us if you like." He'd spoken to Matt, but his eyes were on Ginny.

She looked away, but not before she'd catalogued him: tall, not particularly handsome and a bit bookish with his wire-framed glasses. The girl with him was a classy-looking brunette.

Matt said, "Thanks. Appreciate it," and pulled out a chair for Sylvia.

Paul did the same for Ginny who, although glad to have a place to sit, was still a bit annoyed, thinking the ensign's glance had rested on her longer than necessary. Especially since he was with that pretty girl. Ginny barely acknowledged him. Was he going to be one of those rude wolves?

The corner of his mouth twitched, as though he fought and conquered a smile. "I'm Steve. This is Eileen Randolph."

Matt made the introductions for their group. Steve nodded indifferently to Paul.

Ginny frowned, remembering Paul's talk about the bad feelings between the navy and the merchant marines. She watched with approval as Matt maneuvered Steve, seeing to it that Paul was included in the inevitable navy talk. She decided that Sylvia should hang onto Matt. He was a special kind of man.

While the men launched into service talk, Ginny turned to Eileen, who had not yet spoken. She smiled brightly at her. "Do you live around here?"

Eileen nodded. "River Road." She paused for a moment. "Perrysburg, that is."

"Oh," Ginny sighed, envious. Maumee River Road was nice, but she wanted Perrysburg. "That's where I want to live when I get married." Her chin went up. Yes, just like the song, "Goodbye Dear", she would buy that cottage outside of town—in Perrysburg.

"I hostess here occasionally," Eileen offered.

Curious, Ginny looked over at Steve. "Then you're not with him?"

Eileen made an indifferent motion with her hand. "We met a couple of weeks ago. He was here when I came in tonight, that's all." The dimple in her right cheek deepened as she spoke. Her voice was low and musical.

Ginny regarded her with a bit of envy. Eileen was very pretty. The hair around her face was swept up into Rita Hayworth rolls, and the rest tumbled over her shoulders. Her clothes were expensive. Ginny had often wondered about the hostessing, about the kind of girls who did it, but Eileen was no floozy.

Steve interrupted her thoughts as he reached over, smiled an "excuse me" at Ginny, and led Eileen onto the dance floor.

Paul touched Ginny's hand and started to ask, "Shall we—" but she put in hastily, "I really want to, but if you don't mind, Sylvie and I want to freshen up. We'll be right back." She grabbed Sylvia's hand and tugged impatiently.

Paul and Matt looked at them with bemused expressions. "We can always find someone else."

They said in unison, "Don't you dare." Ginny added, "We'll only be ten seconds," and dragged her friend away.

The minute they were in the rest room, she blurted out, "Sylvie, did you hear where she's from?"

"Who?" Sylvia raised an eyebrow at her and nonchalantly touched up her hair.

"That girl. Eileen," Ginny said impatiently.

"Oh, yeah. She's from River Road. So what?"

Ginny wasn't interested in hair. "She said she hostesses here."

"So?"

"River Road! She's got money. That's what."

Sylvia giggled. "Are you planning to do away with her or hold her for ransom or something?"

Ginny sighed. "No. Don't you see? She's a nice girl."

"That's a stretch, isn't it? You mean if she's got money, she's a nice girl?"

"Oh, Sylvie, don't be dense. It's just that I didn't know they had regular hostesses here. And if I had, I would have figured they wouldn't be nice girls."

"Why not? The canteens don't take just anybody, and they have pretty strict rules. No dates, no nothing."

"Oh." That would settle Carey's hash and make her quit complaining about being unfaithful to Jack. Ginny gave the image in the mirror a smug look and patted her hair. "I'm ready."

When she got back to the table, she didn't bother to sit. She snatched Paul's hand. "Come on. I haven't danced for a year. I hope you're in good shape, because I don't intend to rest."

At her tug, Paul rose so quickly he almost knocked over his chair. He faked an exaggerated limp. "I can't dance. I'm wounded."

She gave him a shove. "Then hop, buddy. I'm dancing."

He held up his hands in mock fear. "Okay. I'm a dancin' fool." He held her close as the small band played "At Last", the new Miller hit. "T'aint old Glenn himself, but as long as I'm dancing with you, it'll do."

Ginny didn't bother to answer as she succumbed to the wail of the sax. For her, even the largest orchestra didn't matter except for the sax. Its mellow tones dominated the music and drifted over them, cloaking the barracks-like hall in a veil of romance. Ginny closed her eyes, thinking dreamily, *Heaven. This is heaven. I'm going to spend my time up there dancing. If I can't dance there, I just won't go.*

She imagined Jack's arms holding her, her face against his chest, feeling the firmness of his muscles.

Paul held her there for a few moments, then drew back to examine her face. "You're really beautiful tonight. It's just as well that I have to go back to my ship early. I might—"

"You have to go back early? I thought you had two weeks."

"I got notice today. I have to leave Tuesday. The repairs happened faster than originally thought."

"Oh." Just when she'd found someone to dance with! She was instantly ashamed of the thought. Here he was, going back into danger, and all she could think about was whether she'd get another opportunity to dance.

For a moment, neither said anything until Paul spoke, "As I started to say, it's just as well, because I might do something foolish, like fall for you."

She raised an eyebrow at him. "Me or Eileen?" She had seen the way he looked at Eileen, too.

He slanted her a sidelong glance and laughed. "Either one will do."

The remark pricked her pride but relieved her conscience. It just proved the date was impersonal, didn't it? She thought furiously, still trying to come up with a snappy reply when Steve tapped Paul on the shoulder. "Shall we trade?"

Paul didn't seem disappointed as he turned to Eileen.

Ginny shrugged and let Steve take her hand, trying to look him over without being obvious. His uniform helped, but Jack certainly had nothing to fear from this guy. Even Paul was better looking. But as they danced, she relaxed and began to enjoy herself. He was a good dancer, better than a book-worm should be. With those glasses, he had to be a brain. And not only that, he didn't try to hold her as though she were glued to his chest. It was a nice change not to have to constantly create space between them.

But his expression bothered her. Like right now. He didn't say anything, but every time she glanced at him, he looked like he had a secret joke he didn't intend to share. Silences could be comfortable, but she felt he was teasing her. When she couldn't stand silence any longer, she blurted out, "Where're you stationed?"

"Great Lakes Naval Base," he answered rather formally.

Damn him. She ought to just shut up and leave him in silence. She tried again. "On a ship?"

He pulled her a little closer. "No, I'm just another ensign doing the navy's nuisance jobs."

She was beginning to be comfortable in his arms. Only for dancing, of course. She forgot to be cross with his teasing. "Don't you like the navy?"

"Better than the army. I'd just as soon be home, but failing that, I'd like a ship with a little action." He leaned his head back and tilted it to look her in the eye, still with that amused look on his face. "I do get most weekends off," he said in a hopeful tone.

What was she supposed to say to that? Did he expect her to fall in his arms or something? She tried a little ice in her tone. "My fiancé's in the army. He was at Pearl Harbor."

His amusement changed to interest. "At Pearl? I'm impressed. Wish I was over there."

"Well, at Schofield."

"I'd like to hear that story from the horse's mouth. Must have been quite a day." He sounded wistful as he said, "I keep asking for a ship."

They paused as the song ended and the band switched into "Polka Dots and Moonbeams." *Dreamy,* but Ginny wished Jack were right here, right now.

Steve leaned his face against hers. He bent slightly, since her forehead only came to his chin. She didn't protest the nearness. Dancing cheek to cheek made the world cozy and full of dreams. Maybe he wasn't such a bad guy, after all. Curious, she asked, even though she knew the answer, "Are you and Eileen engaged or anything?"

She felt the muscles in his cheek twitch against her face. She leaned back to look at him and saw a glint of mischief in his eyes again. He drew her back against him.

"No, we just met a week or so ago. She has a guy on a ship, too." He pressed his face harder against Ginny's. "It seems like you all do. Have a guy, that is."

She hated for the song to end. Paul returned to claim her but the band went into "Boogie Woogie Bugle Boy" and he pulled back. "Not for me. Do you mind if we sit this one out?"

She was having such a good time, she didn't mind anything.

The rest of the evening passed in a glow. Paul hovered over both her and Eileen while Steve spent the evening looking pleased with himself, giving her that look, the one that said he knew a secret. It made her uncomfortable, like Scarlett in *Gone With the Wind* when Scarlett said Rhett Butler looked as though he knew what she had on underneath. Ginny didn't think the remark was a complaint from Scarlett, though.

She sighed when the band finally played, "Goodnight Sweetheart." It had been so much fun. The six of them lingered until almost everyone was gone, then walked out reluctantly.

As they drifted out the door, Steve hung back. In a bit of mock gallantry, he tipped his hat to her and said, "I hope I'll see you again."

"I don't know if we'll be back. This is only our first time here."

His eyes seemed to catch some of the twinkle from the

stars. They flashed at her. "Might as well come back. Pearl's a long way off and we poor servicemen need some enjoyment before we go off to war." He gave her a salute and started away, still watching her over his shoulder. He and his grin dissolved into the night like the Cheshire cat.

Ten

A Week Later

Ginny cringed as Marjorie plugged into the listening jack on the switchboard. Her prissy supervisory voice complained, "You and Sylvia have been doing far too much talking today. I suggest you save it for this afternoon when you're off."

Ginny counted to ten. Marjorie hadn't been around for a week. Ginny had hoped the woman had joined the WACs. Without replying, Ginny answered the next signal in Marjorie's syrupy tone. "Looong diisstaance." She repeated the customer's number three-a, four-a fi-ave nyon, and drooled, "Thaank youuu," and dialed. She bit her lip to keep a straight face. Sylvia averted hers.

Between calls she could hear Sylvia's "Looong diisstaance" and exaggerated numbers from down the board. She coughed to hide the giggle that rose in her throat. Just in time, a pair of relief operators appeared and released the two of them from their boards. From the corner of her eye, Ginny saw Marjorie head for the supervisor's desk.

In the relief room, Ginny got two cokes from the vending machine and brought them back to the table. The moment she met Sylvia's glance, the two of them erupted into laughter.

"You're going to get yourself fired," Sylvia warned.

Between fits of the giggles, Ginny snorted, "Good. I've never been so bored."

When they gained control, Sylvia gave her a smug look. "Matt says Paul has to go back to his ship. I think he's sweet on you."

"Me or Eileen?"

"He is a bit of a wolf, isn't he? But a nice one, I think."

"He's okay. He told me he was going back. The repairs didn't take as long as he thought." The idea of Paul being sweet on anyone wasn't all that interesting and her tone showed it.

"Don't you care?"

"He's not my boyfriend. Jack is."

"Natch." Sylvia gave her a conspirator's smile. "Only it's nice to have someone hanging around. We can use a morale boost, too."

Ginny made water rings with her soda. "It was fun to dance, but I wouldn't take him seriously even if I didn't have Jack. I think Paul just likes a pretty face. Eileen's, mine, or any other."

One of the older operators passed the table. "You two are really pushing it with Marjorie."

Ginny dismissed the warning. "They're too hard up for operators. Serves her right for being such a fake. That tone of hers is awful."

The operator shook her head and walked away.

"Guess we'd better cut it out." Sylvia lit a cigarette. "Want one?"

"No, I don't have the patience to smoke."

"Just as well. I stood in line fifteen minutes for these things. Then I got in another line for a couple of candy bars." She shook her head.

"I know. I got a sweet tooth and had to wait, too. Carey's

just about used up all our sugar making those damned cookies."

Sylvia chuckled. "I'm sure Jack and Ted like them, though." Sylvia tamped out her cigarette, then sighed and took out another. She didn't light it, but tapped it absently on the table and opened her mouth to speak, then shut it again. She took a deep breath and tried again, almost whispering. "Looks like I'll be sending Matt cookies. He's got orders for the *North Dakota.*"

"He's leaving? For a battleship, right?" She examined her friend's face closely. It hadn't occurred to her before that anything serious was going on. "Do you care?"

Sylvia pounded the cigarette so hard it broke. She dropped it into the empty coke bottle. "I've seen him every night since we went to the USO." She opened her purse and drew out a small box, caressing it with her fingertip. "He asked me to marry him last night." She looked up at Ginny shyly. "We went to the Commodore for dinner and he had this huge gardenia corsage for me. It was in a box with a satin lining. He had the ring box hidden under the flowers." She opened it.

Ginny gasped. A solitaire. And much larger than she would have guessed. "It's gorgeous! How come you're not wearing it? He's such a swell guy. Congratulations!" Ginny jumped up and hugged her. "Oh, Sylvie, I could cry."

Sylvia smiled weakly. "Please don't. And, anyway, I think congrats are for the guy. It's like saying I finally caught one."

Ginny laughed, "Well, you did land a good one. Oh, Sylvie, it's wonderful." She hugged her again and sat, scooting her chair nearer. "But you don't have it on, and you don't look excited. Didn't you say yes?"

"Yeah. I did. But I'm scared." She put the box back in her purse, then lit a cigarette.

"I know how you feel. It's been a year since Jack left.

Sometimes I feel like he's someone I knew in another life. It's hard to be stuck here with the guys gone." She put her hand on Sylvia's. "But this is so romantic."

Ginny envisioned the amorous scene at the Commodore, the soft lights, sparkling glass and silver, the sweet scent of the fragile gardenia. Ooooh. Just the way she'd wanted Jack's proposal to be instead of his hurried question over the telephone. But at least he had asked her over again.

She squelched an unreasonable feeling of envy. Besides, with Sylvia engaged and Matt off at sea, maybe she'd have someone to spend her evenings with. Sylvia was always busy now.

Sylvia rarely chain smoked, now she lit a another cigarette. "But you're only engaged. You can still change your mind if you want to. Matt wants me to marry him next Saturday."

Ginny gasped and nearly let the coke slip from her hand. "Next week? Wow. He's not wasting time." She squeezed her friend's hand. "He's a very special guy. If it were anyone else, I'd worry. But not Matt."

Sylvia sat up straight and squared her shoulders. "Will you stand up for me?"

Ginny squealed. "I'd love it. What did your mom say? Have you told her?"

"I didn't call her yet." She looked down and smeared the rings from the bottle. "I just don't want to hear those hard luck stories, all about her heart and all, and how lonesome she is down there by herself. Except, of course, for a whole county full of aunts and uncles and loads of kissin' cousins, natch."

She nodded her head toward the door. "I asked them for my vacation. Matt only has the weekend, so I thought I'd go down and see her after he leaves. I know she misses the boys."

Marjorie appeared at the door and glowered at them.

"You girls are late. Others are waiting for their relief."

For once, Ginny apologized. "We're sorry." She looked at Sylvia. "Can I—?"

She shrugged.

"Sylvie just told me she's getting married next Saturday. I got so excited, I forgot about the time."

"That's good news. You have my congratulations. Under the circumstances, we can forget your tardiness, but you'd better hurry." Marjorie actually smiled, then frowned as they scooted away, leaving their empty cokes on the table.

"Sylvia, you're gorgeous. You make a beautiful bride. It's just too bad your mom and brothers can't be here." Ginny straightened the flared peplum on the back of Sylvia's white suit. "It was such fun to shop for this. I can't believe we found real silk even if it did cost a fortune. I think I'm jealous. Can't wait 'til I can get my own dress."

"Me, neither. I want to go with you when you get yours. Wish this horrible war would get over." Sylvia gave her a token hug, careful not to wrinkle her bridal suit. She picked at a microscopic piece of thread. "I do wish my brothers could've been here. I really miss them. Gosh, we had fun."

Ginny walked around her, inspecting for flaws. She fluffed up the bit of veil that almost hid Sylvia's tiny hat.

The bride stood directly under the only light in the dim hall. The suit glowed softly, light and shadow danced on it as she moved. The ivory accented the flawless tones of Sylvia's fair skin. In the pencil slim skirt, jacket with its tight waist, the slim sleeves puffed at the top, she looked like a porcelain figurine.

Ginny took the sprays of yellow roses from a box on the bench and buried her nose in them. *Heavenly. I'll have deep red ones for my wedding. As dark as I can find.* "There. We're ready." Reluctantly she handed the spray to Sylvia who gripped it as though it might disappear. Ginny gently brushed her silk shoulders. "Relax. You'll be all right. Matt's a darling."

Sylvia seemed to melt at the mention of his name. "Yeah, he is, isn't he?" She sighed, then looked down the hall. No one in sight. The contentment changed to panic. "Where are they? Do you suppose he's changed his mind?"

Ginny chuckled. "No, I can't see him doing that. He's . . ." She stopped as the men rushed around the corner of the courthouse hallway. Matt looked pale, almost green. Ginny was tempted to reach out, pat him on the back, and tell him, "It's okay." Her attempt at comfort was diverted by the sight of a flushed Paul, feverishly searching his pockets. He breathed a sigh of relief as he pulled out two small silk envelopes. "You girls are the ones who are supposed to be late."

Ginny's eyes filled with tears that were only partly from sentiment as she watched the look of adoration Matt turned on Sylvia. She struggled to bury her envy. Sylvia deserved Matt.

He took Sylvia's hands in his. "This is it. Are you sure?"

She glowed and looked up into his eyes. "I'm sure." Her hands trembled.

He turned them palms up and kissed them, then kissed her lightly, careful not to smear her lipstick. "I love you."

"I'm sure." She stopped trembling.

The emotion was so thick that Ginny and Paul backed away. For what seemed a long time, the only sound in the hall was the silence of lovers staring at each other. After a few moments, a woman in a matronly maroon dress and black oxfords opened the door to the judge's chamber. "Judge Stritch will see you now."

They stepped into a warm, sunny room glowing with mellow wood steeped in lemon oil. The scent mingled with the aroma of the bridal roses, sending Ginny's senses reeling with the bittersweet emotions of unfulfilled romance. Her heels sank deep into the pale blue carpet and for a moment, she forgot she wasn't the bride. The judge lined them up next to a shining mahogany library table on which a silver vase with a single American Beauty rose shared honors with a silver tea service. A bottle of champagne and cut glass stemware sat on the other end of the table. Best of all, the judge reminded Ginny of Andy Hardy's father in the Mickey Rooney movies.

Ginny beamed at Sylvia. This wedding in a judge's chamber was going to be romantic after all. Ginny had expected a bare closet that smelled like the hall near the men's room, where they'd hear an indifferent, mumbled ceremony. But this was really nice. Sylvia was beautiful and Matt could have been a handsome prince in his white uniform. The knuckles of Matt's hands as he held hers, were almost as white as his jacket.

The judge smiled and cleared his throat. The spinsterish secretary beamed at them with a hungry look in her eyes. The judge began, "My friends, we are gathered here today—" Ginny wondered if the hungry look was for the judge.

She turned to watch Sylvia's rapt expression and the adoration in Matt's eyes. Tears welled in her own. She tried to swallow her jealousy. Her throat hurt. Why couldn't it be her and Jack standing there?

She closed her eyes and Jack stood beside her. The judges's words, heard from a far place, were spoken to her, to him. "Do you, Ginny, take this man—" *Yes,* her mind whispered. "And do you, Jack—"

"I now pronounce you man and wife. You may kiss the

bride." The words brought her back to reality. A shiver sped down her spine.

Sylvia said, "Oh," and Matt kissed her tenderly.

Ginny sighed with both stardust and envy in her heart. She was glad for Sylvia. Glad for Matt. If only Jack . . . oh, well. She hugged Sylvia and kissed Matt on the cheek. "Be happy."

Paul clapped him on the back. "Congratulations, old man."

The judge beamed and opened the champagne. "So many of you have only a few days, I like to make this as festive an occasion as possible." He poured and lifted his glass. "Here's to you both and to a happy future."

Ginny nodded and toasted them with her first sip, "To happiness." Her second toast was a secret one for Jack and herself. "To us," she thought silently.

Paul took Ginny by the arm and shepherded them all out. She sighed dreamily as they reached the sidewalk, "I love weddings." But, she thought, as romantic as this has been, I shall have a church wedding with white Skinner satin as thick and creamy as any velvet—well, almost—her gown full of beading, with a train half the length of the church. I'll have six bridesmaids, a flower girl, ring bearer, and ten ushers. If only he comes back.

Dear God, please. Let him come back.

Eleven

Ginny caught the glint of blue V-mail among the envelopes on the hall table. She snatched the pile and shuffled them greedily, scattering the unwanted ones on the floor.

Yeah! Three! From Jack! And one was big and fat. White, for a change. Finally. It had been almost four weeks since she'd heard from him.

She ripped eagerly at the white envelope. The V-mails could wait—they were so small, just folded over pieces of paper like valentines she used to make herself. She hated them, even if they did save paper and money. If they were supposed to save work for the services, she couldn't see how. A letter was a letter, and at least a real one had room enough to say something.

A sepia photo fell to the floor as she pulled out the letter. She stooped and picked it up, still disregarding the discards. These brown snapshots always looked faded and old-fashioned, but at least it was a picture. Jack, Red, and Goat grinned at her from beneath a clump of palms. A bit of the ocean sneaked into one corner. All three fellows sported leis around their necks.

Ginny stared into Jack's tanned face and looked longingly at his lips, spread wide in a smile. She took a deep breath to

104

slow her racing pulse. Gosh, he was handsome with that tan. His hair looked almost white. Goat was tanned, too, but paled in comparison. Red looked like he'd never heard of sun, let alone been out in it.

She tried to decide if they were grinning for her or at someone or something there. A Hawaiian girl maybe, taking their picture or standing just out of sight. Some exotic, raven-haired beauty with a flower, an orchid, tucked behind her ear. The out-of-sight girl swayed her hips and the grass skirt swished like waves lapping a shore. For a moment Ginny considered tearing the picture in half. But Jack was way too cute. Maybe a pal was taking the shot.

She kissed his image and turned to the letter. This one had only two blacked-out passages, rather long ones, but he was getting better. It was dated August 21, 1942. Four weeks ago.

"Dear Ginny,

You have no idea how great it is to be sitting on my bunk in clean clothes. I'm still a bit damp from my shower, but I had to write. I know how you worry when you don't hear. We just came back from three days of maneuvers, a long hike with a full pack then a combat exercisexxxxxxxxxxxxxxxxxxxxxxxxxxxxxxxxxxxxxxxxx xxxxxxxxxxxxxxxxxxxxxxxxxxxxxxxxxxxxxxxxxxxxxxxxx xxxxxxxxxxxxxxxxxxxxxxxx. I lay for two nights under the stars, staring at the largest, biggest, brightest one in the sky, hoping that you would look up at it and see me staring at you. Gosh, I miss you so much.

We listen to the Armed Forces radio and wonder and wait. Guadalcanal is the big news. We all pray we win it fast. Everything here xxxxxxxxxxxxxxxxxxxxx xxxxxxxxxxxxxxxxxxxxxxxxxxxxxxxxxxxxxxxxxxxxxxxxx xxxxxxxxxxxxxxxxxxxxxxxxxxxxxxxxxxxxxxxxxxxxxxxxx

xxxxxxxxxxxxxxxxxxxxxxxxxxxxxx *At least we are beginning
to pick up the pieces. Red keeps telling the sarge he wants to
volunteer for Guadalcanal. The sarge ignores him, which is
just as well seeing he can't hit anything he aims at anyway.
He'd probably be a big help to the Japs.*

*I didn't tell you that Goat and I made Expert in rifle
firing. Red is furious. Everyone's laughing. They all know
he didn't even make a hole in the target. Sarge posted
it . . ."*

Ginny laughed. Great! At least there was one thing Private
Tarzan couldn't do! She'd finish the letter upstairs. A tear
welled in her eye. She didn't know whether to laugh again or
cry. She prayed Jack would stay in Hawaii, but fear haunted
her. Any day, they could send him someplace like
Guadalcanal. She closed her eyes and held her breath. *Dear
God, bring him back. In one piece, too. Please.*

She tucked the two blue V-mails under her arm and
stooped to pick up the mess on the floor. One was for Carey.
From Ted. She put them on the table, went up to her room,
and threw herself on the bed. She smoothed the crumpled
page and started over, savoring each word. She read the letter
twice and then finally got around to the V-mails. They were
older than the real letter. With their black cross-outs, not
much was left of Jack's messages. Remembering Paul's
words, she laughed. *Looth lips think thips.*

At the thought of Paul and the USO, she paused guiltily.
Jack's sharp-tipped writing seemed to stand up on the page
and point a finger at her. She flicked the paper and brushed
over the letters, smoothing over her pangs. Nothing had been
wrong with her night at the USO. Passing ships.

"Oh, you're home." Carey observed from the doorway.

Ginny turned. "Mm, I saw you got one from Ted. How's

he like the air corps?"

"He says it's the toughest thing he's ever done, but he loves it. Can't wait to get his wings. But that'll be a while." She waved the envelope in dismissal. She still wasn't comfortable about Ted.

Carey looked from the letter in her hand to the pages scattered on her sister's bed. "How's Jack?" anxious to know, yet dreading to hear. It wasn't fun being stuck on your sister's fiancé.

"Just got back from a three-day maneuver. He said he made Expert with the rifle, whatever that is."

Carey raised an eyebrow. "That's pretty darn good. I know some guys from Camp Perry where they do a lot of that stuff. So many shots lying down, kneeling. The whole bit. Not many make it."

Ginny cocked her head at her sister's enthusiasm. What with that girl in the grass skirt, this was getting to be too much. She asked sarcastically, "Sent them any cookies lately? Jack didn't mention getting any."

Startled, Carey snapped, "You could always make them yourself. You seem to have lots of time to run around and I do have school, you know."

Ginny reddened. Carey was right. She rose and put her arm around her sister. "I'm sorry. I know Toledo U's keeping you busy. It's great of you to make all that stuff. The guys love it and I just hate baking cookies and my fudge is always runny."

Carey hugged her back. "Waiting and worrying isn't easy, is it?"

For a moment, another of those ubiquitous tears welled in Ginny's eye. She'd think about it all later. Right now, it was time for the news. She put an arm around her sister's waist. "Let's turn on the radio."

They went downstairs together, each holding their letters. As they tuned the radio, H. J. Kaltenborn's distinctive voice, serious and authoritative, was saying, ". . . grim total of twelve freighters and one destroyer were sunk in one Atlantic convoy alone. Of the thirteen German U-boats in the attack, only one is known to be damaged." Ginny paled and clicked off the radio.

Carey looked at her curiously and turned it back on.

Ginny ran to the telephone and dialed. Her finger slipped and she started over. It rang.

Sylvia must be there, she was supposed to be back from her honeymoon today. When the ringing stopped, Ginny didn't wait for a voice. "Sylvie?"

"Ginny?"

"Did you hear Kaltenborn just now?"

Sylvia's voice on the other end of the line said, "I was just unpacking. Didn't have the radio on."

Ginny gripped the phone. Her knuckles were white.

Sylvia demanded, "Why? Is something wrong?" There was a deep intake of breath. "Not with Jack?"

Jack? Oh, no. Not Jack, Paul. A moment of guilt over her loyalties made her pause, but it passed quickly. "Kaltenborn just announced that a whole lot of freighters were sunk in the last four days in the Atlantic. I thought of Paul and I panicked."

Sylvia's voice came back calmly. "Ginny, the Atlantic's a big ocean. There's lots of ships out there."

She sighed, "I hope so. This damned war. I wish the guys were all home. I didn't mean to worry you." Then she brightened. "How's the old married woman? How was your mom?"

Sylvia's voice carried a smile as she said, "Matt's great. I just wish he hadn't had to leave so soon." She added wryly, "Mom was fine when I left. After she finished having her spell over everything. A couple of days was plenty of time with her."

Ginny nodded her head as though Sylvia could see her. It would be tough having a mother who made you feel guilty all the time. She shifted the phone to her other ear and said, "Well, at least Matt's on a battleship. It would take a lot to sink one of those things."

"Yeah. You're right. And he's not in the Atlantic. I miss him so much, and it's only been a week. Listen, I'm beat. The train was jammed and I had to sit on my suitcase half the way home, then practically on some guy's lap the rest of the time." She started to hiccup and then laughed, "Must be guilt for the flirting. But it was fun, anyway. I don't think I've ever had so many passes made at me. A uniform brings out the wolf in them, I guess. But they were just having fun. Didn't mean it." She yawned. "I'll see you at work tomorrow. I'm ready for bed."

Ginny jerked awake and sat upright. She didn't know whether she'd screamed aloud or not. She'd dreamed Matt and Paul were on a toy boat out on the ocean in a big storm. Then there was a fire.

When her heart slowed its thumping, she rose. Shivering in the cool room, she knelt beside her bed, something she hadn't done in years. *Dear God, keep them safe. Jack, Matt, Paul.* She stayed there for a moment, willing, consigning her words to the heavens. It had been almost two months since the wedding, and Matt would be back in action. But she didn't believe in omens and dreams, did she?

Depressed, she headed for the bathroom but the door was locked. She could hear Carey humming.

"Carey, Hurry up. I'm going to be late!"

The door opened and Carey emerged, loaded with her makeup.

Ginny took the rollers from her hair and tossed them in the sink. When she had her own house, she was going to have a bath for every bedroom.

The telephone rang twice downstairs. She heard her mother pick it up and answer.

That's another thing, she thought, I'm not going to have any darned party line, either. A line of my own with no neighbors listening and trying to hurry me up. I'll talk and talk as long and as often as I want.

"Ginny! Telephone. And hurry up. Your breakfast's getting cold."

She ran the comb through her hair for the last time and let the rollers lay. *Let Carey pick them up. She has time.*

She hurried downstairs and picked up the phone. "Hello?" Who would call this time of morning, anyway?

"Ginny—" Sylvia's voice was strangled by great heaving sobs.

Ginny could barely understand her, but a huge lump of pain rose in her throat as Sylvia choked out the words. "Ginny, he's—" She couldn't finish.

"Paul? Was he on one of those ships?"

"Oh, Ginny. Not Paul. It's—"

She didn't have to say it. Ginny turned to stone. *Dear God, NO. It couldn't be. Please don't let it be Matt.*

"It's Matt. He's dead."

"Sylvie, no. It's a mistake. He's on the *North Dakota*." She shook her head. "It's a battleship. They can't sink a big thing like that."

"They just said he's dead. Got killed. I got a telegram." Sylvia's telephone hit something with a loud crash. Ginny could still hear the sobs.

"I'm coming, Sylvie," she yelled, "I'm coming." *To hell with the telephone company. They can do without me today.*

Twelve

December 1942

"Ginny? Paul's home for a couple of days. A bunch of us have reservations at Ken Wah Lo's for New Year's. Would you and Sylvia like to come?" Eileen hurried on before Ginny could object. "With you two, there'd be eight. Not pairs, really."

Ginny frowned at the voice on the telephone. It was bad enough that Eileen was so pretty, but did she need such a deep, sexy voice, too? *No wonder Paul called her and not me.* Her conscience reprimanded her. She was engaged. Paul shouldn't be calling her.

The invitation, though, sounded great and it would be nice to do something for a change. She debated for a moment. Finally, she said, "I don't think Sylvie'd go for it. It's only been about six weeks and she's still down in the dumps. She won't even go to a movie with me."

Eileen commiserated. "Poor girl. I'm really sorry. Well, listen, we don't seem to be there on the same weekends, but I still hostess at the USO sometimes. Next time I'll call you and maybe we can get together. You still go, don't you?"

She opened her mouth to answer but Eileen didn't wait. "Paul's here. He says hello. I've got to run. I'll call." She hung up with a loud click.

"Yeah. Do that." Ginny slammed down the phone, her

111

jealousy returning. It wasn't Paul. It was just that Eileen seemed to have it all.

She glared at the offending instrument. Old cyclops stared back. She reached toward it. Maybe she should go. Her hand paused over the receiver and then clenched into a fist. Paul says hello? Who'd Eileen think she was, anyway?

Then again, Paul wasn't her type and she really had no claim on him. She was engaged to Jack. But what about Eileen? That sailor she was supposed to be waiting for? At least, that's what Steve had said.

Steve. She hadn't thought of him in months. A smile pulled at the corner of her mouth as she saw him in her memory—tipping his white hat and grinning at his secret joke. Mmmm, the dancing . . . it all came back to her. She smiled dreamily and danced a quick turn. She wanted to go back again. Steve probably wouldn't be there.

Shoving temptation aside, she turned to the stairs. She ought to pick up her room. All her last-minute bits and pieces of wrapping paper and ribbon still lay strewn about the floor. But she didn't feel like it. It was Christmas night and she didn't have to work.

She turned and crept into the dark living room. Pine from the Christmas tree filled the room. She closed her eyes. The last picnic with Jack! They'd gone to Oak Openings! She could almost hear the pine needles crackle under her feet, feel the crunch.

But that was then, and this was now. She picked up one of the larger cones on the mantle where it nestled among the pine branches in front of the fat red candle. She'd brought the cones back from the park that day.

She replaced it, turned on the Christmas lights, then switched on the radio. She dialed through the stations hoping for carols, but she stopped at Walter Winchell's voice barking out his greeting, "Good evening, Mr. and Mrs. America, and all the ships at sea." Compared to Kaltenborn's measured tones, Winchell's voice conveyed the excitement of an old, hard-bitten reporter, like Pat O'Brien or Jimmy Cagney in the movies. Of course, Winchell's column had Hollywood and Cafe Society gossip, too, something Kaltenborn wouldn't do.

She held her breath and listened as Winchell snapped out his words, "On the western front, Marshall Petain accuses the Free French of betraying French Africa to the Allies. The Soviets continue to hold the encircled German Sixth Army and Fourth Panzers at Stalingrad. In the Pacific, bitter fighting continues at Guadalcanal."

She swallowed and tuned him out. She hated the news, even Winchell. It frightened her, but she couldn't stay away from it. If only the war would get over. It seemed like it was going to drag on forever. And why couldn't Jack get a leave? The army gave leaves even in the Pacific, didn't they? If he'd been in the navy, maybe he'd have come home sometime.

She reached for one of the Christmas ornaments hanging precariously from a drooping limb, moved it farther back, then looked about restlessly. Her mom and dad had gone out for a walk to enjoy the neighbors' Christmas lights. Carey was in the kitchen again.

She turned back to the radio. Winchell still droned. Except for him, everything was gloomily quiet. Even Carey wasn't banging pots and pans. Ginny dialed the Bakelite box until she managed to find carols, then closed her eyes, summoning a Christmas mood. After a fruitless moment, she gave up. The tree lights glowed hopefully and silver tinsel glittered with flashes of red, blue, and green like miniature kaleidoscopes. But the fairyland in her living room failed to enchant her.

A plate of Carey's cookies sat on the table. Christmas boxes of them had gone out to Jack and Ted months ago. Would they have them yet? Would they be eaten or stale? Or would the boys devour them even if they arrived as nothing but crumbs?

With the Germans holed up at Stalingrad, the North African victory at Alamein, and the Jananese defeat at Midway, the allies were at last making progress, but how long would it all take? How long would Jack stay in Hawaii? Was he there right now? The last letter had been two weeks ago. She picked up the terrible pink-fringed pillow with *Sweetheart* scrolled on it. Jack grinned at her from the picture he'd pinned to it with the note, "I'll see you in my dreams—this is for dreaming of me." Pretty romantic for him! These gosh-awful pillows showed up everywhere. She sighed and hugged it, then brushed a fallen tear from the gaudy satin. Why wasn't anyone home? And poor Sylvia. She must be feeling awful. *I'll call her after a while.* If only she'd go somewhere, do something.

She tossed the pillow on the sofa just as Carey came into the living room. Carey picked it up. "Pretty awful, isn't it?" She toyed with the fringe and regretfully tossed it back, wishing the ridiculous thing were hers.

Ginny pointed to the flour on Carey's blouse and asked, "Are you making cookies? I might as well help."

"I've got some in the oven. Jack said in his letter that he couldn't get enough. That sweet little Mrs. O'Hara gave me some of her sugar rations. Said she doesn't use it all."

"When did you get a letter?"

"That day you got those other two. Mostly thanks. He told me all about their maneuvers. Nothing special. I would have passed it on, but you were reading and I had to go. Then I forgot about it."

"I'd like to read it." Ginny tried to sound nonchalant.
Carey shrugged. "It's upstairs somewhere."

A week after the New Year, Ginny sat in her car outside
the USO watching the servicemen hurry inside. She hadn't
gone with Eileen and the gang to Ken Wah Lo's. She wished
she could have, but she had Christmas off so had to work
New Year's Eve. When Eileen had asked her yesterday to
come tonight, saying they would be short-handed after the
holidays, she'd quickly agreed.

Well, for better or worse, here she was. No use wasting
gas. She turned off the motor. She'd really been glad when
Eileen called, yet now stupid guilt nipped at her like a little
dog. She told herself for the hundredth time, it wasn't like she
was going on a date.

Startled by a tap on the glass, she jumped, then turned and
breathed a sigh of relief. She rolled down her window. "Steve!"

"It's a bit cold to stay out here for long, isn't it?"

"Mm-hm. I'm coming." She rolled up the window,
opened the door and got out.

Steve closed it behind her. "I have a feeling you were sitting there wondering what Jack would think."

She gave him a quick look. "What are you, a mind reader?
A gypsy or something?"

He shrugged innocently but the corner of his mouth
wouldn't cooperate. "As a matter of fact, my grandmother
was a gypsy. Cross my palm with silver and I'll tell all."

She was about to reply, but Eileen met them at the door
and led them to a table.

Ginny had barely set her purse down before a short,
freckle-faced kid in bell-bottoms approached. "May I have
this dance?"

Well, that's what she was here for. She smiled. "Sure."

Steve raised an eyebrow. His eyes sparkled.

Wishing some tiny, four-foot-eight girl would ask him to dance, she held out her arm to the kid. *Well, we are here to entertain the troops.* This one seemed extra shy, so she broke the ice. "Do you come here often?"

"No, ma'am. I'm on leave." He held her at arm's length and concentrated on each step, counting the rhythm under his breath as he plodded, stiff-legged, across the floor. He didn't have time for conversation.

When the tune ended, he squared his shoulders and started to say, "May I—" but a tall, skinny private with freckles and big ears managed to get his words in first. "May I have this dance?"

She looked apologetically at the little sailor who walked away with his chin on his chest.

She turned her charm on the soldier. He placed his hand on her waist with a slap, grasped her other hand firmly, and started to pump in time with his two-step. She groaned inwardly. This wasn't exactly what she came for, but duty first. She looked for Steve but didn't see him. As the next song started, a beefy sergeant claimed her. At least he was a good dancer. When he gave her the final spin she could honestly say, for a change, "I enjoyed that."

As the band swung into "In the Mood," she saw the shy owner of the bell-bottoms weaving toward her again. She moved quickly toward her table. Enough. She'd had enough. She managed to get as far as the edge of the floor when a hand clasped her shoulder. *Oh, no!* Turning, she started to say, "I'm sorry, I'm—" then finished with a glad "Steve!"

He whispered, "I thought you might need rescuing. After all, I'm a sailor sworn to protect my countrywomen." He told the diminutive sailor who still trailed her, "Sorry, son. This one's mine. For the rest of the evening."

She buried her head against his shoulder and sighed. "Thanks. Entertaining the troops is fine, but, that's a bit too much."

"Think nothing of it."

Why did he always look as though he were teasing her? Maybe it was only because he had those lines that crinkled at the corners of his eyes even when his mouth held no hint of a smile. For a wild moment, she thought of *The Night Before Christmas.* "His eyes how they twinkled, his dimples how merry." Steve's only dimple was a slight indentation in his chin. She looked at him through partially closed eyes and tried to add a round, fat face. It didn't work.

He drew back and squinted at her. "What's so funny?"

She giggled, "Nothing." Let him stew for a change.

He pulled her close and pressed his cheek against hers as the band drifted into "I'll See You in My Dreams."

She pictured the pink satin pillow under her Christmas tree and stiffened. The muscles in his cheek moved against hers. Was he laughing again? Must he always laugh at her?

To divert him, maybe sting him a bit, she asked, "Where's Eileen?"

His eyes were as innocent as St. Joseph's in the church statue. "She's playing chess with a major in the other room."

Oh. Was that why he showed up so suddenly to save her? "Don't you want to rescue her?"

He never missed a beat. Just kept on dancing cheek to cheek. "Nope."

"Oh."

The muscles in his cheek moved again.

Damn, he could be annoying. Thankfully, the band broke into "Choo Choo Cha Boogie." "Why don't we sit this one out?"

"Not on your life. I've been waiting for a chance to break loose."

To Ginny's surprise, he jumped, sprang, bounced, and put on quite a show. She could hardly keep up and was terrified he might try to pick her up and throw her over his shoulder, or maybe slide her through his legs. It looked easy enough, but Ginny was sure she'd land ungracefully on her seat. When it was over and she hadn't spun into some stranger's arms or fallen into the lap of someone unlucky enough to have a ringside table, she sighed with relief. The band settled into a version of Dorsey's theme, "Getting Sentimental Over You." She relaxed against Steve, feeling warm and happy.

He sang the title words and pulled back just enough to gaze into her eyes for a moment, then drew her close again.

Only twice during the rest of the evening, when a tune held a special memory, did Jack's image come to her. Ginny managed to brush it aside both times. This USO dance was just for one evening. She needed to feel alive again, to do something besides listen to war news or go to a movie with a war theme. When the band wound down with "Goodnight Sweetheart," they dawdled as they had before. She was the last to get her coat, hating to waken from this dream.

When she went out into the night, she gasped at the blanket of shimmering white that lay before her. Great flakes of snow tumbled lazily, as though reluctant to settle.

Groups of servicemen stood about smoking and joking, waiting for a bus. Steve took Ginny's hand and said, "I'll walk you to your car."

Her heel slipped and she fell against him. He reached out and grabbed her and held her close. When she looked up to thank him, he leaned over and gave her a long, testing kiss.

He pressed his face against hers for a moment, then released her.

She took a deep breath. Her insides were on fire and her mind churned in confusion. It had been a long time since she'd been kissed. That's what it was. It wasn't Steve, she told herself. She turned in consternation and almost bumped into a black Ford. The windows were rolled down and a man leaned over from the driver's seat. "Hello, Ginny."

She looked into the face of Jack's best friend. When she found her voice, it didn't sound natural. "Hello, Tom. What are you doing here?"

She hadn't seen him inside the armory and he was a civilian. Could he be spying on her? Had people talked? She wanted to explain that the kiss had been an accident, but her tongue stuck to the roof of her mouth.

Tom's expression told her nothing. "I promised to pick up some friends. They needed a ride home."

Steve put his hand on her arm protectively. She introduced Tom. "Steve, this is Tom Gordon, a good friend of Jack's."

Steve barely acknowledged the introduction. Nor did he take his arm from her as he led her to her car. Giving her his "I've got a secret" smile, he tipped his hat and closed the car door.

Thirteen

May 1943

Carey laid down her pencil and got up to fix a cup of hot chocolate for Ginny and herself. "Ted wants me to fly to Kelly to see him get his wings. He even offered to buy the ticket."

"Well, if you're worried about your reputation, you can always say you went to visit the Alamo."

Carey scowled. "Be serious."

Ginny grinned and went over and hugged her. "Really, I hope you're going." Then, her moment of sisterly love over, she looked askance at the welter of books scattered on the kitchen table. "Do you think you have enough room?" But even as she said it, envy tweaked at her. Perhaps she should quit the telephone company and attend college herself. She shoved the books and papers aside, but her hand lingered on the biology text. She leafed through it and quickly put it down. If she did, it certainly wouldn't be for that. Anyway, when Jack got home, it would all be a wasted effort. She wanted that vine-covered cottage.

Ginny picked up her mug and stirred so vigorously it splashed on Carey's paper. In answer to her sister's dirty look, she said, "I'm sorry. But you are going, aren't you?"

Carey shook her head and Ginny threw up her hands. "I

swear, you're not normal. You're going to end up an old maid, all alone in the world, no husband, no kids."

Carey dismissed the barb. "Finals are next week, but I've been thinking about going to summer school."

Disgusted at her sister's stubbornness and sure that Carey was laughing at her, Ginny scowled. "Even a brain like yours needs a vacation. Besides, it's Ted."

When Carey didn't bite, Ginny gave up and changed the subject. "This stuff looks like dirty milk. How can you water down perfectly good chocolate? I've been dying for some and there wasn't even a decent candy bar in the drugstore."

"Well, do you know what my psychology professor would say about a craving like that?"

"I don't think I want to hear about your psychology. Anyway, what are you going to do about Ted?" Ginny studied her sister. How could she pass up a nice guy like Ted? She wondered how many other opportunities Carey turned down at school.

Carey's look was comical. "You're determined to pick an argument with me, aren't you?"

Ginny sighed and then grinned back. "I just don't understand you, that's all. I don't think you're normal."

"Because I don't want to marry Ted?"

"Because I don't think you care whether you marry *anyone*."

"Look around, Ginny. Women are doing just fine without men to hang onto." Her eyes lit. "I've seen a lot of men who could make me say 'hubba hubba'." She grew serious, almost sad as she continued, "But first, I intend to be able to take care of myself, not wait for Prince Charming." She stopped and then added grimly, "His Highness might not make it home."

Hurt even though Carey didn't mean Jack, just men, Ginny lifted her chin and straightened her shoulders. Jack

121

was coming home. He had to. She turned the focus back to Ted. "That's silly. Anyway, you haven't answered my question. I think all this is just to avoid the subject."

Carey reached out and touched Ginny's hand affectionately. She shook her head. "I hate to disappoint Ted. But then, if I go, he'll just be encouraged. And Ginny, I don't love him." She sighed and pushed her cup away. "I like him a lot. I always have. But it's not enough."

"He's a nice guy. Maybe you should quit worrying about things you can't have and settle for the possible."

"Settling for half a love would hardly be fair to either of us, would it?"

Ginny looked steadily at her sister. "Half a love on whose part? Ted loves you."

"That's the trouble. I'd settle for second best and he'd get nothing at all."

"Who's first best, then?" She didn't say, "Jack," but the name lay between them. Even though she considered Carey's crush to be kid stuff, that little green imp continued to prick her with jealousy. But even if it were true, she couldn't really be angry. Or could she?

They never talked about it openly, nor had they even hinted at the possibility that Carey might not have outgrown her feelings for Jack. Ginny thought she probably had. Other than cookies and the occasional friendly letter, Carey never showed any signs except for her extraordinarily protective attitude when she thought Jack was being neglected. But she was just as protective of Ted.

Carey rose and went to the stove. "Don't worry. I'm not out to get your precious Jack. If I do get married, it has to be someone I love desperately, someone who loves me deeply. Anything else would be a consolation prize. I won't settle for second best."

She turned to face Ginny. "Besides, as you complain, I'm not sure I want to get married. At least for a long time. I'm thinking of taking up medicine. And I don't mean nursing, either." Carey's face was serious, but her tone was amused.

Ginny stretched. "It's your life."

Carey's voice acquired a defensive edge as she asked, "By the way, do you think you're being fair to Jack with this USO bit?"

Ginny looked Carey straight in the eye. "There's nothing to it. I just help out."

"Mm-hm. Have you seen Tom lately?"

Ginny caught her breath and a flush of guilt suffused her face. Why should Carey ask that?

Ginny shoved at the books, sniffed and said, "What's Tom got to do with it?" But it was a half-hearted try. Tom had seen Steve's kiss. Well, she hadn't asked Steve to do that. It wasn't her fault. But had Tom said something?

Carey looked at Ginny accusingly but reassured her, "Don't worry. Tom won't say anything to Jack. I just happened to run into Tom and he asked about you." Carey came back to the table. "And about the USO. Just idle chatter for the most part."

Ginny gritted her teeth. "Tom should mind his own stupid business."

"He will. But you have to remember, he and Jack grew up together."

"Everyone's out to protect Jack from me, is that it? You, Tom, and certainly, his mother. Heaven knows who else."

Carey took Ginny's hand in both of hers. "He's been gone for two whole years, and it looks like it'll be a lot longer. We know you're both lonely. We just don't want anyone to get hurt."

A tear fell into Ginny's cup and disappeared in the chocolate. She sniffed and pushed the cup aside. It tipped, spilling the dregs onto the table in a small brown puddle. "I can take care of myself, thank you." She didn't bother to clean up the spill. Without even a look at Carey, she marched upstairs and threw herself on her bed. The tears she had held back downstairs began to flow and after a time, she cried herself to sleep, but not before she decided she was tired of being lonely. Steve would be at the USO on Saturday. She didn't care what anyone thought.

Fidgeting with her dress and hair, Ginny watched eagerly from the window for Eileen's car, trying to suppress her excitement. She couldn't. Tonight she didn't care what anyone thought. She intended to dance until she fainted.

When the black Buick finally pulled to a stop, she didn't wait for Eileen to get out. How could Eileen afford to keep the thing filled with gas? It had to use a month's ration in a week. She clambered in and breathed a sigh of relief. "Wow. Am I ever glad to be out of there." She giggled as though she'd pulled a fast one. "Carey's not home yet. I didn't want to get into it with her."

Eileen raised an eyebrow and half her cheek disappeared into the dimple. "A little family squabble, hm? You look nice. Those the pearls Jack gave you for your birthday?"

Ginny, still feeling smug, smoothed the moray taffeta skirt and ran her hand over the wide satin straps at her shoulders. "Yeah. His mother picked them out. She made a fuss about whether Jack would be pleased. It didn't matter if I was or not." She put her hands to her throat and rolled the pearls.

"You're going to break them if you do that much." Eileen cast her a quick look of sympathy and turned her head back to watch the road. "I take it you're a little upset tonight."

For a moment Ginny wanted to give in to her self-pity, but

she was determined that nothing was going to spoil the evening. She shook her head in an effort to shake off her devil. "I just get so tired of everything. And of everyone trying to tell me what to do." And people spying on me, she thought. Tom had better not say anything. She sat up straight and steeled her nerve. "I'm not doing anything wrong, and I'm not going to let them bother me."

Eileen pressed her hand. After a moment of silence, she changed the subject. "Well, it's time for the good news now." Her throaty laugh sounded nervous. "I'm going to marry Doug."

Ginny crowed in delight and threw her arms around Eileen.

The car swerved and for a moment, Eileen's arms flew like a symphony conductor's in an attempt to straighten the wheel.

Ginny bumped her shoulder on the door but ignored the pain as she exulted, "Eileen! That's swell. The Major, you mean?"

"Who else?"

"I've always wondered about you and Steve. You know, I didn't even know his name. We never called him anything but 'The Major'."

By the time they arrived at the USO, Ginny not only knew all three of his names but his confirmation name, too. Douglas William Michael McInnis. That and a good bit more, such as the brand of his socks. She was almost relieved to see Steve waiting for her by the door.

He looked over his shoulder, then kissed her quickly on the cheek.

The woman with the guest register pushed it toward them without looking up. Her face looked a little red. She brushed a thin, nervous hand across the bun on her neck.

The kiss wasn't allowed in the canteen but that had been more of a peck. Might she be in a bother because Steve and Doug spent their free time here? It was obvious, Ginny thought, from the frequency of their visits that they weren't passing through, and they didn't look very needy in the date department. A couple of officers would normally be taking girls out to nice restaurants and other places.

The woman straightened her sharp, bony shoulders and sniffed. "Back again?"

Steve tried to imitate Cary Grant's charm. "Your doughnuts are the best in town, didn't you know?"

Her expression didn't change. Ginny decided she must not like Cary Grant, an unimaginable feat.

Ginny wanted to say something but hadn't quite figured out what. Steve took her elbow and led her away. "She has no reason to cause any problems. Let's not give her any."

The Major appeared and spirited Eileen away to the card room.

Steve frowned at their backs, then shrugged and put his arm around Ginny's waist. "Let's dance."

The magic word pushed her questions about the woman's frown far from her mind.

They threaded their way onto the dance floor and he drew her close, murmuring in her ear, "I've missed you. You haven't been around."

"I know." She didn't want to explain. She wasn't going to justify her actions to him, either. She motioned at the band, "That's a new group, isn't it?" Six young, pretty women occupied the bandstand.

"Amen," Steve said and nodded appreciatively. "They started last week." His eyes crinkled at the corners. "When you weren't here, I went out with one. That'll teach you to stay away."

She snapped, "Oh. Well, I won't dare miss anymore then, will I?"

"Feeling rebellious, are we?" He laid his cheek against hers and held her tight.

She relaxed and let herself be carried away by his comforting nearness. The alto sax filled the dim room with the melancholy strains of "Stardust." She listened dreamily, thinking it had to be the most romantic song ever written. "Goodbye Dear" might be *their* song, Jack's and hers, but "Stardust" was her all-time favorite.

They danced quietly, letting the mellow tones work their magic. After a while, Steve began to sing the lyrics softly until he ran out of words. "That's all I know of it," he apologized, but he continued to hum.

Ginny, her eyes closed, half-listened to his sexy baritone. It wrapped her in a warm, fuzzy cloud and transported her to a dream world where she could dance on and on, floating forever in her man's arms.

Her mind wandered lazily through the fantasy, happily dreaming about the men in her life. Funny about them. Jack was unromantic, but so sweet and so handsome. Sometimes he surprised her, but mostly he just accepted feelings like love. Steve, rather ordinary looking, definitely was romantic. Only he could be irritating, too. She bristled a little, thinking of that ever-present laughter. It left her confused and never quite sure what he really thought. Oh, well. To heck with trying to figure him out. She intended to dance and dance. To heck with the war and all of them, too. She felt light-headed, almost drunk with happiness.

When they finally sat down, Eileen and Doug emerged from the card room and took the floor. She turned excitedly to Steve. "I forgot to tell you. Did you know that Eileen and The Major—I mean *Doug*—are getting married?"

Steve's eyes clouded over. He only said, "Mmm. He told me."

Surprised at the chill, Ginny searched his face. Did he still like Eileen? Had he ever? He hardly mentioned her name. The first time she and Sylvia showed up, he'd said he and Eileen weren't together and she had a sailor somewhere. He hadn't seemed interested then but she was always around.

Ginny hadn't the nerve to ask. She glanced back at Eileen and Doug. "What happened to the sailor?"

He searched his pocket as though he hadn't heard the question, then said, "Excuse me a minute. Be right back." He left and returned with a pack of cigarettes.

"I didn't know you smoked. Give me one."

"Nor I, you." He smiled briefly, pushed one up for her and lit it. "I don't, usually. Right now it's either a cigarette or an ulcer." He took a long puff, blew three smoke rings, then made an annoyed face and stubbed out the cigarette. He looked at Eileen on the dance floor.

Ginny followed his gaze, unaccountably jealous. "You didn't answer my question. What happened to the sailor you said she was waiting for?"

He frowned and pulled another Chesterfield from the pack. He didn't look at her as he tried three times to light a match. "He shot himself. Guess he couldn't take the Dear John bit."

Ginny blanched and choked on the smoke from her own cigarette. She threw the stub into the ashtray. "Excuse me. I want to comb my hair."

Her insides cramped as if caught in a vise. For a moment, she thought she might be sick and leaned over the sink until the nausea passed. She raised her head and stared at herself in the mirror. A Dear John letter. Now she knew that was what Carey fussed about, that she'd meet someone else and give

Jack the heave-ho. But she wouldn't. Never.

She stared at the girl in the mirror and asked herself, What am I doing here? What if I really fell for Steve? I wouldn't. But Jack is so far away. I do love him, though, and I couldn't ever leave him. She splashed cold water on her face. Anyway, if she did write a letter like that, and she never would, Jack wouldn't do anything so stupid. He wasn't the type.

But was he? She pictured him the night he'd dropped her off and run after the fire engine. No. He wasn't the kind who couldn't live without his love. Even when he'd proposed, he'd never said anything romantic like, "I can't live without you. Will you marry me?" He'd just backed into the question and had been surprised when she'd said yes.

She looked again at the pale woman in the mirror and took out her rouge. She needed color.

All her life, she'd dreamed of marriage to a guy like Jack. She'd dreamed of being in love and living happily ever after with The One. But this damned war made everything so hard.

She put her comb and makeup back into her purse. Besides, if this Major was really the one meant for Eileen, well, no one could help that. It happened.

She put on a final dab of lipstick, pinched her cheeks, and returned to the table.

Steve looked concerned. "Are you okay?"

She took his hand. "I'm fine. Let's dance."

But the glow had gone from the evening. They danced close together but the warmth wasn't there. Her heart had turned cold. Long before the orchestra played "Goodnight Sweetheart," she was ready to leave.

Steve walked her to Eileen's parked car and opened the door. She turned to get in, but he put his hands on her shoulders with a firm grip and turned her around. She looked up at him and he leaned over and kissed her, a long, yearning kiss that seemed to seek her soul. He pressed her against him with such power she winced.

She tried to push him away but he held her firmly and continued the long, commanding kiss. She melted and responded hungrily. She wanted to cry.

He finally loosened the embrace but he kept his hands on her shoulders. His voice was husky. "I've wanted to kiss you like that for a long time. I should have. I just didn't want to frighten you away. Now, it's too late."

Her heart sank. What more? "What do you mean, 'too late'?" She wanted him to kiss her again, but the thought of Jack and the fate of Eileen's sailor came back to confuse her. Her heart said, "Kiss me," but her mind said, "Get in the car and go home."

He stroked her hair, caressing it gently. "I've been assigned to a ship. An anti-sub in the Pacific."

She put her face against his chest and her arms around him. "Oh, Steve. When?"

"I'm leaving tomorrow." He cradled her and asked longingly, "Are you still going to marry Jack?"

She began to cry. "I don't know. I don't know anything."

She pulled away and flung herself into the car.

He held the door open and put his head in. He smiled his odd smile, but she could see the pain in his eyes this time. "Will you write?"

"Where?" She sniffled and nodded and fiddled with her purse, searching for a tissue.

He leaned over, kissed her on the cheek, and handed her a slip of paper on which he'd already written his APO. His hand brushed hers. He gripped it and held on tightly. He said again, "Write. I need you."

She nodded.

Fourteen

October 1943

Bemused, Jack watched the luau scene before him. Goat, standing not a hair over five-foot-five, sitting beside a five-foot-nine Dorothy, reminded him of the Mutt and Jeff cartoon. The combination had to be one of Red's practical jokes. The redhead had masterminded their dates for this luau. The Company Commander had thrown it to celebrate the men's two years on the island.

Red himself was busy leering at Bev, a short, gorgeous WAC who, surprisingly enough, he'd picked for himself— surprising in that she was short. With his six-foot-three build, he usually liked them willowy. Jack decided Red had traded her lack of stature for more provocative assets like the copper hair that almost out-flamed his own, sea-green eyes, and a figure that rivaled Lana Turner's.

The outnumbered WACs had only been on the island about a month. What could the odds be, with the WAC-to-GI ratio, that Red could commandeer three of them? The guy definitely had some unexplainable charm women liked. Even now, Bev had her arms wrapped around his neck while he kept right on spearing fruit from a pineapple shell.

Jack turned to his own date who just happened, according to Red, to resemble Ginny more than a little. Another of his

131

jokes, probably. Emily wore her hair short and curly instead of in a page boy, but it had the same reddish tones as Ginny's, maybe a bit lighter.

Even the disapproval on Emily's face as she watched Bev nibble Red's ear reminded him of Ginny. He supposed the look-alike was supposed to be some sort of a fidelity test in Red's mind. It could hardly be a coincidence.

Deliberate or not, the resemblance made him both glad and uncomfortable. Distance and time were taking their toll on his memories of Ginny. Last night, he'd tried to envision her face, but it wouldn't come to him. He'd gotten up and gone into the latrine, with the only light around, to look at her picture. He'd stared as though it were a hypnotist's amulet, and tried to burn the image back into his brain.

He found himself poring over her letters again and again, straining to hear her voice, listening for its cadence, trying to evoke her laughter, hear it ripple up from the page.

He wondered if Ginny were sitting with someone right now, just as he sat with Emily. His conscience prodded him, even though he didn't consider Emily a date, just welcome company. Red constantly badgered him to go out, and he occasionally went just to keep the man quiet. But he didn't trust Red's motives.

So far, it hadn't been too difficult to be true to Ginny. The island mamas maintained a close watch on their good-girl daughters. Until the WACs arrived, few nice women were available. Mostly, he just played pool or got into a craps game where he'd become a legend with his nineteen passes. The story went that if you got him down to his last penny, he'd clean you out. He found himself with a lot of backers and few opponents.

But Ginny was at home in the good old U.S.A., and here he sat with a strange WAC and a great feast.

Emily turned from her disapproving surveillance of Bev and smiled sympathetically at Jack. "Two years is a long time to be away from home. Are you very homesick?"

Jack lapped up her concern. "Well, it started out for a year. You know, 'Goodbye Dear.' But here we are, fish and poi and all that stuff." He poked his fork into a stray piece of pineapple. "What I wouldn't give for an Ohio tomato."

She contemplated the remains of the lavish food. "I didn't know a company commander would or even could arrange a celebration like this. It's great."

"Yeah. The cook told me he said to pull out all the stops and lay out the most impressive feast he could come up with. I think he followed orders just fine."

The aroma of the now-barely-recognizable pig in front of them had tormented the men's growling stomachs all day as it roasted over the open fire. In gleeful revenge, they'd laid waste to it, along with huge mounds of fruit, rice, chicken luau, and baked sweet potatoes, like kids loose in a candy store. Crumpled fragments of two bathtub-sized cakes, one decorated with the company insignia and the other a painting in icing of Diamond Head, added to the look of a pillaged land.

The fellow across from him burped. It sounded as though it had come all the way from his toes. Jack cracked, "Amen."

Before the soldier could enjoy Jack's appreciation of the quality of the emission, a hoarse snort, followed by the whoosh of sucked-in air, and more snorts like the braying of a donkey, distracted him. He swiveled his head sharply to the left. The rasping came from a red-faced Dorothy who shook with laughter. Goat had been spinning tales to Dorothy about the tricks they'd played on Red. He tried to finish with, "He was out like a light and—", but the sound of Dorothy's laughter collapsed him into a helpless heap.

Red wasn't amused. He leaned over and grumbled, "Yeah, you guys are regular clowns," then turned back to Bev. "What do you say we blow this joint?" Her arms still encircled his neck as he rose, pulling her up with him. He grabbed her waist. "I know a nice, lonely bit of beach . . ."

She turned pink, giggled, and said, "Oh, Red!"

Sparks flashed as Emily glared at her again.

"I'm game, too." Dot took off her shoes and unfolded her long body to tower over Goat. He looked up at her like a stranger gaping up at the canyons of New York's Wall Street, then, grinning, rose to a kneeling position. When she turned, he followed, still on his knees. She hooted and joined him. They struggled along for a moment together, then still braying and chortling, they clambered to their feet and ran off holding hands.

Emily and Jack followed at a distance. She laughed at the picture Dot and Goat presented and nodded approvingly, "She's a real nut, but she's okay." She sent a flight of invisible darts at the retreating figures of Red and Bev.

Jack wondered at her strong disapproval. Was Emily a prude? But thinking her a prude wasn't fair. What his mom called *good girls* had to be careful of their reputations. Both his mom and his dad drilled into him that guys might have fun with fast girls, but they didn't marry them. He tried not to smile as he remembered the times he'd tried to unhook Ginny's stockings, how she'd put him off using that line, "I have to watch my reputation." Maybe Bev wasn't always fast. He said, "Red has that effect on girls."

She looked up at him with a curious expression on her face. "I'm glad you're not like that."

He supposed she meant that as a compliment, but there were times when he wished he could lose his good-guy image and act like Red. He couldn't keep the envy out of his voice as he said, "Yeah, but he sure manages to have one darned good time."

With the luau far behind them and the others far ahead, they had the beach to themselves. Emily gripped Jack's shoulders and spun him away from her. "Turn your back, okay? I don't suppose Hawaii has poison ivy, does it?" He could hear the rustling from the clump of palms as she kept talking. "Can you believe these orange flowers? I'd pay a fortune for this stuff at home."

"Mom grows a lot of plants in . . ." He turned without thinking and blushed at the sight of her thigh as she unsnapped her garter. He turned back quickly.

Emily laughed. "It's okay, you can look now."

At least men don't have to worry about rolling up their trousers, he thought as he piled his shoes and socks with hers. They waded hand in hand along the water's edge where the shoreline stretched to forever before disappearing into the horizon.

He tightened his hold on the small, soft hand and wished it were Ginny's. His mind drifted back and forth between the two girls as they strolled. To keep himself in the present, he asked, "So what are you doing in the WACs?"

She shrugged, "What are you doing in the army?"

He raised an eyebrow at the flip response, but decided to answer her question. Maybe she didn't want to talk about her reasons. He said, "I was so flattered by my personal greeting from the President, I didn't have the heart to say no."

"Yeah. Well, I just thought it seemed like the thing to do." She picked up a broken shell and tossed it. "I was bored with school."

He wondered if the undertone of anger he thought he heard meant a man had been behind the decision.

"Da-aarn," Jack exclaimed, suddenly hopping around

holding his foot and yowling in an exaggerated bid for sympathy. "I broke my foot. See? Ooh, ooh." She laughed at him and he gave her his famous silly grin and bent over to examine his toe. "Ow. I really did hit this ingrown toenail." He dug in the sand for the cause of his pain and brought up an empty wine bottle.

She snatched it. "Oh, I want that!"

"An empty? I'll buy you a full one if that's what you want."

She smirked and looked around in the sand. "No, this is just what I want." She unscrewed the black cap then fished in her shirt pocket and brought out a pencil stub. "Got a piece of paper? I've always wanted to do this."

Plucking the pencil from her hands, he examined it as though it were a work of magic. "You're as good as Tom Sawyer. Do you just happen to have a bit of string and an apple core with you?"

One dimple on her right cheek flashed at him. "You're talking to a Girl Scout, and a good scout is always prepared." She patted her pocket and her hips, "But I just failed the test. I still need a piece of paper."

Jack reached into his pocket and, after a moment of regret for the loss of a page from his precious brown notebook, he tore out a sheet and handed it to her.

She snatched it eagerly and grabbed the little brown book to use as a pad. She scrawled a note, rolled and stuffed it into the bottle, and put the lid on. She lobbed it as far as she could into the ocean.

Jack whistled. "That's quite an arm you've got there."

"That's what comes of playing baseball with three brothers. Heck, I played better than they did, and then someone pointed out I was only a girl."

"Yeah, boys do get touchy when they realize there's a difference. Luckily, we pass through it." He tilted his head and looked her over critically. "And you definitely qualify as one of those girl people."

His emotions flip-flopped as he said it, the longing for Ginny translating to hunger for Emily, then guilt. He tried to stifle his rising desire with talk. "By the way, what'd you put in that bottle?"

"Why don't you swim down to China and find out?"

"You don't throw that good." He waded in after the bottle but it bobbed tantalizingly out of reach. He knew he couldn't swim for it; it would be dark in a couple of minutes. Even now, the setting sun glowed on the horizon, sending great magenta tongues and orange-tipped fire that inflamed the ocean.

"I'll never get used to this Hawaiian sunset," she breathed in awe. "I hardly ever see a whole sunset at home. Sometimes the sky's pink, but that's about it."

"Where do you come from that you don't see a sunset? We get them in Ohio."

"Manhattan."

She strolled back to the dry sand.

As he watched her walk away, that hunger returned. She sat on a low rise with her face turned toward the huge red ball, almost sunk now into the ocean. The reflection painted her with a pink glow. An early evening breeze wandered past, teasing her hair like a love-hungry gypsy. *Like some love-hungry* GI, his conscience repeated. The first of the evening stars came out and winked as if to say, "Go ahead. We won't tell. The islands were made for romance."

He dropped down beside her, wanting Ginny, needing someone, needing Emily. He drew palm trees in the sand to distract himself, wondering at the same time what Ginny was doing right now. Probably working.

Emily leaned over to see what he was doing, then joined him, her arm brushing his, sending tingles of excitement up his arm. She drew a line of water behind his trees and added a sailboat. He drew a wavy shore line and their fingers touched where the shore met the horizon. Jack looked up into eyes that looked almost chocolate in the dusk. Desire overcame him and he reached out to embrace her.

For a moment, he thought she would respond, sure that she felt the peculiar chemistry between them. But she'd never know how much she resembled Ginny.

But she did know there was a Ginny. She pulled back. "You've got a girl. Remember?"

He dropped his arms. "How'd you know?"

She sat back, but not far. "All the girls know everything about you, but I don't think I should repeat what they say. You'd just get conceited."

"What do you mean, they know everything?" He knew she was laughing at him. He tickled her in the ribs. "Tell me what they said."

Emily coiled away from him, giggling. "Okay. Not everything. They know who you are and they all think you're a dreamboat."

Jack blushed. Still, it was nice to know. "I thought it was Red they liked."

"Yeah, well, they do in a way. He's kinda sexy. But they all think you're sweet."

"Sweet! I think I resent that. Sweet, I'm not, but then what do they know? And who are *they,* anyway?"

"Remember the time you brought the colonel that message from the sergeant? Sheila said you looked like Robert Taylor, only better."

Jack lay back, smug and gratified. So the girls all liked him, thought him handsome, huh? But Robert Taylor? He'd rather look like George Brent or even Gary Cooper. "And what did *you* say?"

She became serious. "I wasn't looking at guys just then." Pain clouded her face like an Ohio thunderstorm. Seeing her so vulnerable weakened the last of his reserve. He stroked her cheek with the back of his hand. She closed her fingers around his.

Overwhelmed by loneliness and desire, he drew her down on the sand and put his arm around her. He caressed her neck for a moment, touched his fingers to her lips, crying for Ginny within himself. He looked at her lips hungrily. He couldn't. He mustn't. He bent toward her.

Emily stirred under him. "Jack. Don't."

He let her go.

She had tears in her eyes. "I'm afraid to get involved with you."

Relieved and disappointed, he shrugged and touched her tears. "It's okay. Don't cry."

She kissed his hand quickly and let it go, picking up a handful of sand, letting it sift through her fingers. She looked up at him, her eyes large and luminous. "I wish you weren't engaged."

"I'm sorry." He put his hand on her shoulder. "I lost my head, I guess. Thanks."

"Ah-hem." From behind them, Goat cleared his throat. "Hey you two, we're going into town for a movie. Want to join us?"

Jack looked around, red-faced and feeling guilty. How long had he been there?

Emily brushed the sand from her blouse.

Goat and Dorothy stood smirking at them. In his hand he held an empty wine bottle by the neck. She held the cap.

Emily flushed and put her hand to her mouth.

Jack took it from him. "Where'd you find that?"

"Up the beach a-ways."

Dorothy waved a small piece of paper. "I found this mash note in it." She laughed and looked directly at Emily, put one hand on her heart, flung the other in the air, and panted, "I think I'm in love."

Jack took Emily's hand, gave it a squeeze, and rose.

Fifteen

October 1943

The mail had provoked a flurry of exclamations up and down the room.

"Geez, you'd think with all the dough I been sendin' her, she'd have enough," one of the fellows griped.

Goat flourished a new pin-up of Betty Grable and her million-dollar legs. "Hey guys, look at this." Wolf whistles and laughs answered him.

Jack sorted his mail and whistled happily at the haul: a manila envelope, a letter from Ginny, a shoe box package and a letter from his buddy Tom. The mail was waiting when the men got back from an overnight hike into the mountains.

The barracks hummed, mostly with sounds of pleasure.

Except. He glanced nervously at Dick Young, a burly corporal with hash marks for length of service almost to his elbow. Dick, a sometimes-sergeant, had been temporarily busted to corporal. Temporarily because it wasn't the first time, and chances were he'd get his rank back quickly. He housed a private demon that showed itself periodically, but Jack liked the guy. Now Dick sat quietly on his corner bunk, staring at a sheet of paper.

The corporal clenched his jaw, raised his head, and looked around, lost and trapped by the laughter of his friends. He crumpled the letter, squeezing it in his fist.

Jack put down his mail and leaned over. "You okay?"

Dick hurled the crushed letter at him. Jack straightened the page. The few lines addressed to "Dear Dick," really meant "Dear John."

He wanted to say, "There are others," "She wasn't good enough for you," "It's better to find out now," or any of those lines. But he couldn't. Those words suggested, "Oh, well. It's not important," as though the hell of heartbreak were a mere feather on the wind that would blow away if you huffed at it. Jack put his hand on his friend's shoulder and said nothing.

Dick brushed off Jack's hand and rose. His jaw could have been stone. His eyes were just as cold and hard. "What the hell. She might as well marry someone else. I'm not coming back."

"Sure you will."

"I said," he looked past Jack and spit out the stony words, "I'm not coming out of this alive," and left the barracks.

Jack stared after him. Dick's coldness worried him. The man should have been angry. And what an odd thing to say. Jack didn't believe in people who had so-called premonitions. Naah. They were silly. Dick was probably just depressed over the girl. Maybe she had been his demon all along. Well, the brass kept all the guys hopping these days. Maybe he'd be so busy he wouldn't have time to mope. Dick would get over it, in time. They all did.

He went back to his bunk and picked up Ginny's letter. Dread twisted his guts. What would he do if Ginny wrote him that she'd found someone else? The fat envelope reassured him—but if not this time, what about the next? Life at home had to be dull, and she liked to dance and go places. What *does* a girl do when she doesn't have a boyfriend? Ginny had always been a fan of those romance stories. He ought to know. She made such a fuss, telling him he wasn't romantic. It wasn't as if he never said "I love you." He did, in every letter. But he supposed girls were like that, always expecting someone to be a Charles Boyer. Maybe he should try a French accent and speak in a deep voice, say things like *Je te de l'amour* or even *Zhevrolet beaucoup,* or whatever Frenchmen really said.

Smiling to himself, he rubbed his thumb across her name on the envelope. Since he wasn't supposed to be a romantic, reading her letter could take second place to the cookies. The moment he started to tear at the paper, he found himself surrounded by hungry buddies.

"Cookies!"

"Hope she baked those oatmeal ones."

"How 'bout peanut butter ones, Jack?"

Jack snatched three of the cookies and a smaller white box inside the larger one. He abandoned the rest. Good thing other guys got some in the mail today, too, or he'd have been flattened in the crush.

He knew the little box had to be fudge and stashed it under his pillow. He bit into one of the cookies and picked up the manilla envelope, closing his eyes, willing the contents to be the photo she'd promised.

Gingerly, he drew the hand-tinted eight-by-ten from its envelope. He drew a deep breath and studied her features. Jack had always thought of her as beautiful, but time made it harder and harder for him to visualize her, to remember sometimes just how fragile that beauty was. She gazed up at him from tinted brown eyes that couldn't begin to compare with the warmth of her own fiery sienna. Her smile and her eyes seemed to say, "I love you," better than any words. Goat's poster of Grable would never compete with this.

Overwhelmed with loneliness and intense sadness, he

scrutinized every feature. If only he could hold her again, re-assure her that he missed her and be reassured that someone else didn't hover in her background, waiting to wear her re-solve down, take his place. She'd signed it "I love you, Ginny." He hoped it was still true. He put the picture back into its envelope and slipped her letter under his pillow, saving it for last, like dessert.

He opened the letter from Tom. Funny how Tom's hand-writing didn't match his personality at all. It ought to be neat and controlled. Instead, it looked like the impatient scribble of a kid.

September 30, 1943

Dear Jack,

Sorry I haven't written before this, but my schedule has been very hectic. I finally did it, though. I graduated Magna Cum Laude. *Mom cried, of course. (She says hello.) I am the first in the family. You can imagine how she felt. I'm working on my masters now.*

We all missed you. We've had such fun together that it's a shame we can't share our small triumphs. But war is hell, as they say. Even in Hawaii, I guess, although somehow the concept of that island paradise and Hell don't mesh. I pic-ture you lolling on the beach, bathed in a tropical sunset, with three nurses (an area where you're well qualified and, incidentally, I saw Penny last week—she said "Hi" too). I can just see one nurse on each arm and one at your feet. But seriously, I know being over there away from everyone can't be a picnic.

I ran into Ginny one day. Went down to the USO to pick up Bob. He came home on leave from the air corps. It looks like they'll be shipping him out soon, probably to

England, which makes me jealous. Ginny looked good.

I seldom see her, but I do run into Carey on campus. She's quite a dish these days. If I didn't have Kathy . . . well, anyway. Carey and I had a long talk in the cafeteria. Says she wants to be a doctor, not just a nurse (like Penny and Marge). Speaking of them, I always think it's too bad I don't have a second appendix. Remember that masquerade? We did have fun, didn't we?

Carey is very different from Ginny. She's so level-headed. Carey, that is. That sounds like a criticism of Ginny. It's not, but I think the older sister is the younger in this case. It's too bad you and Ginny didn't get to spend more time together and really get to know each other. It must be hard for a pretty girl to stay home and knit.

Jack frowned as he finished the letter, then reread it. Tom wasn't usually so subtle. If something were really wrong with Ginny, he normally would have come right out with it and made some sort of crack. Which might mean anything. Of course, Jack thought, he doesn't know that I know she goes to the USO.

Jack picked up Ginny's photo again and studied it. Her eyes still glowed softly and innocently at him. The thought of her being around all those guys did worry him, but so far, things had been okay. Even Carey had written to him before, "Don't worry about Ginny. She's fine and waiting for that dream cottage in Perrysburg."

He shrugged. It would be okay. He retrieved Ginny's letter from beneath his pillow and held it, almost afraid to open it. He turned back to the photo, silently willing her to wait for him. Say something, Ginny. Tell me you're still my girl. Her eyes promised something, but did they promise, "I'll love you forever"?

That evening, Jack wrote a letter on real paper. She hated those blue things.

October 25, 1943

Dear Ginny,

Your picture is swell. It has all the guys drooling and they took a vote over whether they'd rather date you or Grable. (Goat came up with a new poster of Grable which set them all howling.) You won, but before your ego gets too big, you only won by one vote—mine. Anyway, a tie with Grable should make you happy.

Tell Carey her cookies are all gone and I'll write and thank her soon. My buddies crawl out of the woodwork when I get a box. They know it's from her. I'm keeping the fudge for Goat, Red, and myself. The others don't get any of that.

Dick Young (you remember, I told you before about the sergeant-sometimes-corporal), well, he got a Dear John today. He usually is pretty testy but he's so quiet I'm worried about him. He's too okay.

I also got a letter from Tom. Says he runs into Carey regularly (said she's quite a dish). Tell her to send me a picture, I'd like to see this grown-up dish. I still picture her as that cute little runt.

He also said he ran into you at the USO. I suppose he doesn't realize that I know you go there. I have to admit I do worry about you, but I know it must be awfully dull for you there without the light of your life around to keep you happy and take you to places like the Purple Cow. Just don't get hung up on any of those guys, even if they dance better than me. I suppose most of them are on short leaves, so I don't worry too much. As the song goes, "Don't Sit Under the Apple Tree."

We had a big anniversary celebration last week. The company commander threw a luau on the beach for us. You wouldn't believe the army could put out food that tasted and looked like that. Roast pig, yams—it was really swell. The only thing missing was you. What I wouldn't give to have you here on the beach with me.

Jack put his pen down and stared out the window. USOs, luaus. Would he and Ginny be able to hold onto each other? He'd really been tempted with Emily that day. Funny how much they resembled each other. If Goat hadn't interrupted, what would have happened? He hadn't seen Emily since the party, and he hesitated to call her, afraid of his loneliness and her nearness.

But maybe, just maybe, he should find some excuse that would take him to company HQ. Emily had said the WACs thought he was sweet. Sweet wasn't his favorite description, but if that's what the girls thought, he'd live with it. He wondered what "sweet" acted like. Probably a damned fool.

Now that he thought about it, a lot of WACs usually did appear each time he had an errand there, all with urgent messages. Unconsciously, he squared his shoulders and sat up straighter.

He stared down at his unfinished letter to Ginny. If she went to the USO, couldn't he take a girl to a movie without having a guilty conscience?

He picked up the pen again, but it had lost its magic. No words came. He carefully folded the half-written letter. Later.

Sixteen

November 1943

USS Starfish
October 10, 1943

Dear Ginny,

Here I am aboard this decrepit old tug. It's hot and crowded and I work like a dog, but I love it. At least I'm not up in the freezing North Sea.

Too bad it took me so long to get away from Great Lakes.

The only thing I really miss is you. I know you don't want to hear it, don't want me to say it, but I fell in love with you, desperately, hopelessly and forever. If you won't throw Jack over and marry me, I'll stay on this tug for the rest of my life and become a crusty old tin-can captain. Then, when I'm too old to sail the world, I'll retire to some old sailor's home. How far is the Sandusky Veteran's Home from Toledo? Then on Sundays, when the home lets me loose, I'll come over to your place and hobble around the sofa trying to catch you.

You really wouldn't want me in that kind of life, would you? Just think how terrible you'd feel every time I sent you a letter to remind you how I suffer alone, neglected and for-

gotten. I'll be like your Heathcliff, from Wuthering Heights, forever calling "Gin-nny, Gin-nny". Or since Sandusky is on the lake, I'll be Poe mourning for his Lenore.

Well, if that isn't enough, then at least send me your picture. I'm the only one on the whole ship who doesn't have some sweetheart or pin-up. There's always Dorothy Lamour, but when I remember you in that black dress, dear Dorothy is a washout.

The food is tolerable, but you keep talking about Carey and her cookies. If you won't bake, talk her into sending me some, too. Tell her I'm a lonesome sailor on a lonesome sea, that ought to get her. Or you.

Gotta go, the Captain's calling. Probably wants to resign and let me run the ship.

Your lonely, languishing lover,
Steve

Ginny laughed and tucked the letter under the lingerie in her drawer. He was full of it, but the letter was fun. The envelope hidden in her drawer instead of in the box with the rest added an element of dangerous romance to her dull life.

November 2, 1943

Dear Carey,

I got your cookies about a week ago and today your letter turned up. Can you figure that?

I meant to write and say thanks before this but they've really been keeping us hopping. Gosh those cookies are good. They go so fast I have to hold the guys off while I grab a couple real quick, or else I don't get any. But first I stash away the fudge. That has to be the best stuff I've ever eaten. Anyway, we love your boxes and thanks.

For a kid, you ask some pretty good questions. When anyone asks how I like being in the army, I always say I hate it. It stinks. And it does. I'm bored and lonesome, stuck here away from Ginny and Mom and Dad, and Littlebit, that precocious little monster of a sister. Next to Ginny, I think I miss her most of all.

Loneliness and boredom are the big devils in the army. I wish I were back drawing milk bottles.

But as much as we all gripe, I think the funny thing about it, if you don't count things like heat and bugs and being pushed 'til you'd give anything for a fifteen-minute break, well, it's kind of interesting. Have you ever seen the picture in the Toledo Art Museum of an Indian standing all alone on a cliff, looking out over the hills, with a mist hovering in the background? You should take a good look at it next time you're there. (I miss the museum, too. I love that picture.) And sometimes when I'm out there on maneuvers with the guys, I think about that Indian and the old Indian-cavalry wars, especially since war then was so much different from the hell today. Death is always hard, then or now, but maybe there's a part of every man that hankers for that special kind of adventure.

And then, there are these guys. Some of them, like Goat and Red, seem like the brothers I never had. Their friendship makes me value all my friends more. Especially Tom. You tend to take people you've known all your life for granted.

But playing soldiers in maneuvers is one thing, and the real war out there is something else.

You never talk about your school or your dates, but I'll bet all the boys are lined up clear around the corner from your house. Do you go with anybody special? Are you really going to be a doctor? Tom said you're thinking about it.

You know the old saying goes, "The way to a guy's heart is through his stomach." What you have to do is take some of your fudge to school. Red and Goat both are in love with you. Of course, Red is in love with anything in skirts.

Gotta go, but thanks again—and keep up the good work! Ha! Ha!

Love,
Jack

Ginny appeared in the doorway just as Carey folded her letter. "How come he's writing to you?"

"Just thanking me for the cookies." Carey studied her sister for a moment. Ginny's question sounded a bit accusing. "I didn't get a letter."

"I told you, he's thanking me for the cookies. Telling me about what it's like to be in the army. Really romantic stuff!"

"Well, if he's got time to write to you, he should have time to write to me."

"Look Ginny, he probably wrote this the same time he wrote yours. It just got lost in the shuffle. Don't worry, I'm not after your boyfriend." She held out the letter. "Here, you can read it if you want to."

Ginny was ashamed of her suspicions, but still so jealous she wanted to tear the letter up. Her conscience told her to be nice. "I know. I really appreciate you sending all that stuff. I hate to bake cookies." In a bid for sympathy, she sighed as she took the pages. "Guess a letter to you is better than nothing." She unfolded it. Cookies or not, it had better be a kid-sister kind of letter.

Seventeen

The guard at the camp gate barked, "Passes?"

Jack cussed under his breath. "Hell." It wasn't his pal.

"I said, let me see your passes."

Red cleared his throat and kicked the heel of Jack's shoe.

Goat tried to look soldierly. It took some effort. He and Red were both pretty close to the staggering point.

Jack stood at attention and asked, "Is Mays around, sir?" His buddy usually had the dawn shift at the base gate.

The MP gave him a jaundiced look. "Transferred. Now, with that little detail cleared, I'd like to see your passes."

Jack's heart dropped. Not good! He turned, hoping Red hadn't had so much to drink he wouldn't catch on. "Got 'em, Red?"

Red was nothing if not seasoned at this game. He made a big show of searching his pockets. "Gosh, I must've lost 'em when I had that friendly little tuthle with the marine."

The MP scowled and barked, "You mean you were fighting, too, private?"

Goat moved to the front, "Well, you see, shir. It was like this. He made sevral slandruss remarks about the sexual pershuasion of the army, sir. Called us pantywaisths and said anyone but a sisshy would have been a marine."

152

Red drew himself up to his full height. "And I ain't gonna take that from no damn jarhead." He tried to salute smartly but the motion proved too much for him. He swayed against the guard.

The MP jerked away.

Jack fastened his eyes on the brass buttons on the guard's shirt and kept them there. Red always seemed to swagger through life without serious consequences. Perhaps the most powerful guardian angels were assigned to the hard cases. If that was so, Red's angel had to be no less than the supreme Archangel, Michael himself.

The guard must have swallowed the story of the marines and struggled to keep his look of disapproval. "Who's your lieutenant?" He turned his back and picked up the phone.

"Grimshaw, sir." Jack winked at Red. They were home free. He'd known the looey back in the real world. They'd even gone to the same high school, although Grimshaw had been two years ahead of Jack.

The guard turned and spoke into the phone, "Lieutenant, three of your men are up here without passes."

The guard scowled at the three. "Names?"

Red and Goat tried to stand smartly. Jack relaxed a little as though he knew they had done nothing out of line and expected corroboration. "Andrews, Carter, McCann."

"Andrews, Carter, McCann, sir. They say they lost their passes in a friendly discussion with a marine."

The MP glared at them over his shoulder as he listened. "Yes, sir." He snorted and put the phone down with a loud click. Turning back to them, he could barely make himself say the words. "Okay. You guys are clear." He wore the grin of a hangman who enjoyed his work. "This time. If I ever see any one of you without a pass again, I won't be calling any lieutenant. Got that?"

"Yes, sir. Thank you, sir." Their acknowledgment came so perfectly timed, it sounded like one loud voice. They walked away in their best parade ground manner, but as soon as they felt safe they started to run. When they reached the haven of the barracks, they broke down and howled.

Jack held up his hand. "Shh. Watch it! Don't wake the sarge."

Inside the barracks, everyone was fast asleep, or so it seemed. The three men took off their shoes and stumbled toward their bunks, tiptoeing past the morning duty officer. He snorted like a cornered pig as they slipped by and Jack jumped. When he could breathe again, he crossed his fingers and hoped Red's arrangement was in place and working.

They lay down fully dressed and threw a cover over themselves. At least they'd be on time and dressed for roll call.

At breakfast, Red downed his plate of powdered scrambled eggs and six soggy pieces of toast, then dumped the untouched delicacies from Goat's plate onto his own. "Ain't you guys eatin'?"

Goat looked at him in disgust and got himself another cup of black coffee.

Jack managed to finish his breakfast. He hadn't had nearly as much to drink as the other two and found himself surprisingly hungry. As the last crumb disappeared, Lieutenant Grimshaw approached. "Been looking for you, Andrews. Come to the office when you're done."

"Yes, sir." Jack searched his face, wondering if they'd finally pushed their luck too far. Neither Red nor Goat looked up from the table.

Before going to the office, Jack slipped back to the barracks, got into fresh clothes, and combed his hair. He squirted extra toothpaste onto his brush and scrubbed everything in his mouth he could reach except his tonsils.

At the desk in front of the lieutenant's office, his heart stopped at the sight of the red-gold hair.

Emily raised her eyes from the typewriter.

Jack reddened. He hadn't seen her since the luau. He'd made a point of staying away. He'd come too close to forgetting his determination to be faithful to Ginny.

Emily greeted him as though they were old-shoe friends. "Hi, Jack. What've you been up to?"

Was it the light in here or had her eyes sparkled? Had she noticed his red face?

She nodded in the direction of Grimshaw's office. "The lieutenant told me to send you right in."

He wondered if he looked as silly as he felt, but she seemed okay, not mad or anything. He took a deep breath. One down, one to go. The casualness of her greeting seemed to hint that the looey might be okay, too. He opened the door and saluted.

"At ease." Grimshaw studied Jack as though he were trying to make up his mind how angry he wanted to be. He frowned but spoke softly.

"Okay, Jack. I know you guys were just having a bit of fun after the mill you were put through. But—" He let the word hang in the air, then his voice picked up authority. "But you're going to have to knock it off. You know things are heating up around here." He fingered some papers on his desk then raised his eyes to stare Jack in the face. "There's a lot going on and security's going to be tight. Don't repeat this, understand? It looks as though we're going to be tapped for a Marine Corps operation. So, no more of your extra-curricular activities."

Jack knew when he was well off. "Yes, sir."

Grimshaw relaxed and his mouth curved a little. "I said, at ease." He sat down and stretched his legs, then motioned toward a chair stuck in a corner. "Sit if you want to."

Jack sat and waited.

"Got a letter from my brother at Camp Perry. Says he met your girl at the USO."

Jack raised his eyebrow. That was pushing coincidence, wasn't it? He opened his mouth to speak but Grimshaw waved his hand and cut him off.

"I'd mentioned that an old school buddy was in the battalion here. He stopped at the armory with a buddy and asked one of the girls to dance. In their conversation, she mentioned that her boyfriend was over here. So he asked who, and well, the pieces just fell into place." He opened a pack of Chesterfields and offered one to Jack, who shook his head. "He said they had a great evening and he thinks you're a lucky guy."

Jack tried to read Grimshaw's face. Did he mean what he said, or was there more to it? Since that letter from Tom, Jack was edgy.

Grimshaw gave Jack another of his thoughtful looks, as though measuring him. "My wife helps out at the Red Cross. Maybe she could call Ginny and they could get together. Maybe they know each other already. They're probably the same age—might have been classmates." He turned an eight-by-ten silver frame around so Jack could see the picture. "Used to be Claire Harcourt."

"Where'd she go to school?"

"Ursuline Academy."

Jack shook his head. "Ginny went to DeVilbiss."

"Give me her number and I'll get Claire to call her." Grimshaw stubbed out his cigarette and rose.

Jack wrote the number, then looked up. "Look, sir, I know Ginny goes to the USO."

Grimshaw gave him a brief nod and moved from behind

his desk. "Has to be hard on the women. At least we've got something to do besides wait and wonder."

The interview over, he nodded. "Dismissed. But remember what I said. And don't repeat anything."

Bemused but relieved the interview was over, Jack wondered what it had all really been about. True, the purpose of the meeting had been the warning, and for an officer, Grimshaw was probably as decent as they came, but the bit about Ginny? First Tom, now him.

Preoccupied, he passed Emily's desk without looking at her.

On the veranda, he paused to watch storm clouds roll in from the horizon. He had the uneasy feeling they gathered especially for him, what with Ginny and her USO, Emily's hair that reminded him so much of what he'd left behind, and the coming invasion.

A couple of weeks ago he'd seen the film, *The Mortal Storm* with Jimmy Stewart and Margaret Sullivan. During the credits, storm clouds gathered for the Jews as Hitler rose to power. His own storm clouds were gathering for him now, up there in his own sky.

"Jack?" Emily came out, holding official looking papers.

Feeling unaccountably guilty about everything, he turned and tried to smile. "Hi, Emily. I, uh, meant to look you up, but we had this long hike." Stupid thing to say. The luau had been almost three months ago. He cleared his throat.

Amusement materialized in her eyes again. "It's okay. I understand. You're engaged and you're a nice guy." She shrugged it off and held out some papers. "The lieutenant told me to give you these for your sergeant."

Disconcerted, Jack's collar got tight. He moved to stretch it.

Emily wore that isn't-he-cute expression his mother sometimes wore when he did something she thought was *dear*.

He wrestled with an urge to ask her out again. Her warm, brown eyes held little fires that danced. He'd give anything to have Red's aplomb right now, instead of this urge to dig his toe into the dirt. What harm could there be in taking her to a movie? He took a deep breath and ignored the warning voice in the back of his head. He blurted out, "Look, Emily, I'm pretty sure I can get a pass. Want to go to a show Saturday?"

She looked pleased. "Sure. You know it's Abbott and Costello, don't you? I love them. Even after six times."

"Great. I'll pick you up at your barracks." He waved and ducked into the shower of giant raindrops. USO, movie. What's the difference? If Ginny was bored and lonely, well, so was he.

Eighteen

The familiar hum of mail call reverberated through the barracks as soldiers pored over their letters. A large batch of delayed mail awaited them after another three-day training ordeal on Maui.

Jack tore open his letter. Ginny had written it the day before Christmas. She sounded like she had the blues and it both disturbed and pleased him. She missed him, at least. What he wouldn't give to hold her and comfort her, comfort himself, for that matter.

Red sat on the bunk next to him, engrossed in a bright pink letter from Barb. Barb always used pink. Red grinned from ear to ear.

Jack couldn't figure the guy out. Obviously, Red cared for Barb, but he certainly didn't bother to be faithful. But that was Red's own business, wasn't it?

Jack went back to his own letter, then waved it at Red. "Ginny says she'd been feeling lonesome and called Barb. Says they had a good cry together." Then he asked cautiously, curious but not wanting to start an argument, "What are you going to do about Barb, Red?"

"Barb's doin' just fine. Sent her one of those shell things for her ankle. Said she was tickled pink." He waved the pink

159

envelope and chortled over his humor. He read it a second time and put it away. "That gal sure does have nice ankles."

Goat stopped reading long enough to comment sarcastically, "I'll bet she just went wild. Must've been what she wanted more than diamonds or anything."

Jack shot Goat a warning look. Everyone was on edge these days, expecting to be shipped out at any moment. Fights had started over a lot less.

Goat continued his sarcasm. "You going to marry her or what?"

Red ignored the tone. "Sure. What else?"

Goat just muttered, "Lucky gal," under his breath.

Jack coughed and shook his head. He regarded Red with a mixture of envy and dismay. *Didn't anything bother him? Did he have any conscience at all? Must be nice. I feel guilty just because I went to a movie with Emily.*

Torn between disapproval and affection, Jack watched Red's smug face as he opened another pink envelope. The guy was a good pal, lots of fun, and could be counted on in a tight spot—unless you needed him to shoot a gun straight. The memory of Red's practically unscathed rifle targets gave Jack a moment of guilty satisfaction. At least the guy wasn't good at everything.

Jack put the letter from Ginny in his locker. He'd read it again later. Too many thoughts jostled for position in his mind. The looey had said two weeks at the most and they'd be off. The whole island seethed with rumors and felt like a volcano about to erupt. Everyone was jittery.

Grimshaw had said that Goat, Red, and Jack were about the best in the company. Well, if he ignored Red's shooting record, Jack supposed. But Jack didn't think he'd ever feel like a real soldier. Mostly, he felt like a man trapped in one long, bad dream. Not exactly a nightmare, more like a prisoner of unreality, like some of those Dali paintings. Too bad he couldn't be an Ernie Pyle, except instead of writing, paint the war. The thought made his fingers itch. Maybe he should get some watercolors. Maybe it was too late. They'd be shipping out soon. Someplace where watercolors couldn't go.

He opened his locker and took out the sketch book. Not much to show for two years in what should be a paradise. One good sketch of Diamond Head. A couple from their stint on Molokai when they'd temporarily worked at the base there. Not even a sketch of Emily. Maybe there'd still be time for that.

A mocking voice echoed the length of the barracks. "Jaackeeeee, it's a girrrl."

He put the pad away. He hadn't heard the phone ring. He ignored the barks and turned his back to the room. "Hello?"

"Jack? It's Emily. You told me to let you know the next pass I had. Well, I've got one for Saturday night. They haven't changed the marquee, though."

He hesitated. This would probably be the last chance in a long while to have any kind of fun. And it wasn't like he was going behind anyone's back. Emily knew about Ginny. He spoke quickly before he could change his mind. "Great. But I know that movie by heart and if I have to look at Costello's face again, I think I'll get sick. How about just mooching around?"

She paused a moment, then said, "How about some place to dance?"

Jack groaned to himself. Dance. Well, he didn't want to, but when a woman decided she wanted to dance, that's usually what a man ended up doing. "Okay. I'll meet you in front of your quarters."

Saturday evening they escaped the fences of the base and hopped a bus for Honolulu. Jack sought out a small bar patronized mostly by locals, its only claim to fame being an old juke box in the corner that played at top volume. Jack and Emily chose a dark corner booth but Jack still had to wave the cigarette fumes away. "This is like a London fog in one of those Sherlock Holmes movies."

A blond waitress with the proportions of Mae West approached and summoned what seemed to be her last reserves of energy to demand, "Whatcha want?"

Jack and Emily looked at each other and sputtered. Finally, he said, "Do you think you could manage two rum and colas?"

"Yeah. Gotcha."

Emily laughed and looked up at the smoke-stained ceiling. "Ugh. What are we doing in here? I thought the base was depressing!"

"Well, we're only a block from the beach. We can get a quick drink and run. Unless you want to dance. This is kind of out of the way, but I didn't want to run into any dogfaces tonight. I'm sick and tired of the army."

"I know. It's been a rough week and everyone's meaner than a New York taxi driver. Makes me feel right at home. Reminds me of Manhattan when it rains." She motioned toward the floor. "Shall we?"

"It's on your head. The smart girls find something else to do if I even suggest dancing." Thank goodness it didn't happen often.

Their only options on the dance floor were to sway in one spot or bump into other couples. After a few minutes, Jack lost what little enthusiasm he'd managed to muster. When he stepped on her toe, he gave up and mumbled, "Let's get out of here and go down to the beach."

The waitress glared at the half-finished drinks in their hands as they headed toward the door and called in a bored tone, "Not allowed to take those out."

Jack gave her his most charming smile. "Okay."

She walked away and they slipped out laughing, glasses in hand.

The hulk that was Diamond Head rose like a paper cut-out against the night sky. Drawn by its centuries-old secrets, they picked their way toward it through rustling grasses and waving hibiscus.

Jack had explored this part of the island before, but at night, it made him feel like a kid in one of those magical, never-never land stories. An eerie sense of being haunted by sloe-eyed gods crept over him, of being under the spell of Hawaii's dark, primitive side.

The ocean breeze ruffled Emily's red-gold hair and set the palms murmuring restlessly, whispering to themselves, their breaths echoed and fortified by the eternal swash of waves. Jack half expected Pele, the goddess of the volcano, to appear. Or Fletcher Christian. Or maybe some wild, painted natives with spears. But those were in Africa, weren't they?

Emily took his hand and pulled him down. "All it needs is Lamour and Jon Hall."

He put his arm around her and looked out across the ocean, Captain Cook's ocean. "You feel it, too? I just know one of those outriggers is going to come along, snatch me off to some island where the natives think I'm a white god, ply me with sweet potato brandy, and lend me their best young maidens for a little frolic."

"Or throw you in a volcano to appease the gods. Then I can have Jon Hall." She put her arm through his and lay her head on his shoulder. "The moonlight's missing. Nothing works without moonlight."

Her nearness unsettled him. He leaned forward and began to draw in the sand. She teased him, "Do you always do that when you get nervous?" Reaching past him she poked holes in his sky. "We have stars, though."

The weight of his loneliness for Ginny plus Emily's nearness, his yearning for comfort and the conflict of two women in the wrong places pressed in on him. In the darkness, Emily's hair took on a deeper tone, her resemblance to Ginny uncanny. If not for the style . . .

The starlight warmed her face, accentuating her sunbronzed skin, deepening the contrast against her white blouse. The neckline, low and round, barely covered the curve of her breast, revealing bare golden flesh.

He took a deep breath and tried to shut out the stars and the waves. He asked, "What are you going to do when you get out of this war?"

"Doesn't seem like we ever will, does it?"

"I've been away from home so long that my other life seems almost as fantastic as the story I just made up about being kidnapped and turned into a great white god."

She nodded. "Maybe I'll stay in the army. Most of the WACs'll go home, and maybe the ones who stay can get somewhere."

"Don't you want to get married?"

She gave him a funny look. "No."

He grinned. "Don't like men?"

She shrugged.

"Oh?"

At the bemused tone of his "oh", she laughed and explained. "I should say I don't like most men. I was going with this fellow, and when I said I wanted to join up, he had some nasty things to say about my reasons." She reached into his pocket and took a cigarette.

"Yeah, well, a lot of guys say that most of you are just looking for a good time or a man to marry."

"You don't really believe that?"

"No. I don't think they do, either. It gives them a good excuse to fool around. They might not have the nerve to do it otherwise."

Emily drew an island on the horizon of his sand drawing and added a sailboat, then rubbed out the picture. She said, "My next-door neighbor in Manhattan was a nice Jewish fellow. He worked with an organization that tried to get some of the Jews out of Germany. He had some awful stories." She drew a picture of a swastika then pounded it viciously with her fist. "When the chance came to join, I did."

"What about your boyfriend?"

"He's not my friend."

"What about after the war?"

"I told you, I'm staying in. I like it here."

"You really don't ever want to get married?" He hadn't believed her the first time. Every normal girl wanted marriage, didn't she? As soon as he thought of it, Carey's face came to mind. Carey wanted to be a doctor more than just marry. Certainly she was normal. Still, he thought most of that was bravado. Of course they wanted to.

Emily sighed and looked at him, her face placid and mysterious. Then she said softly, "That's the second time you've asked. Is that a proposal?"

He blushed.

She changed the subject. "What are you going to do after the war?"

"Get my job back." He hesitated. "Get married."

She ignored the last part. "You should move to New York. You can't get very far working in advertising in Toledo."

"That's a thought." He rose and held out his hand to help her up. "It's too late to go up Diamond Head. Pele might get us." They turned toward the beach. "If I get back, that is."

She stopped him and kissed him on the cheek. "You will."

He squeezed her hand but kept walking. Her hand felt warm and soft and he absently stroked her palm with his thumb. The faces from home pushed and shoved forward in his mind, leaving him with a desperate ache to get back to them. Involuntarily, his ache escaped into a long, slow sigh.

She seemed to read his thoughts. "Don't worry. It's like they say, only the good die young."

"You said I was a nice guy, remember?"

Emily reached out and turned him to her, then took his face in her hands and kissed him gently. "I remember. But I've waited long enough for you to stop being a nice guy. I hope to fix that tonight."

He felt her softness, ached for it, but shame spoiled the moment. He mustn't. Not while Ginny waited. But he didn't move away. Emily's nearness held him. Her luminous flesh offered its own snug reality, while the shadow of Ginny crossed his mind from a long distance away. That held little warmth to carry into the coming darkness, the darkness of the invasion which he was sure lay ahead.

Emily led him back to a clump of trees and pulled him down beside her.

He touched her shoulder, tentatively at first, then slowly pressed her down on the sand, hungrily stroking her bare, warm arms, moving his lips along the rise and fall of her collarbone, tracing a finger along the line of her blouse to the hollow between her breasts.

She pressed her hands to his temples, raised his head, and gazed deeply into his eyes, as though trying to reach and release the soul that hid behind them.

He stroked her hair. In the starlight, it looked so much like Ginny's. Except that this hair was short. He sighed and rolled over. Why must he always feel guilty? Thousands of guys all over the world were taking advantage of situations just like this, probably right at this moment. Like Red. The thought of Barb would never cause that guy to hesitate. Yet here was this warm, willing flesh, this lovely, yielding girl. He sat up and rested his head between his hands. "I can't, Emily. I'm sorry. I want to. I just can't."

Nineteen

February 1944

Jack squeezed his eyes shut, trying to ignore the lurching of the landing craft. He held his breath, desperately hoping he wouldn't throw up on himself and his buddies. Puddles of vomit already spattered the bottom of the boat.

Jammed into the metal hull of the landing craft, Jack's outfit waited for the great jaw to drop and evacuate them into the hell of Kwajalein. Jack wasn't sure which was worse, the stench of fear or the reek of those puddles, his present misery or the horrors that awaited.

The clumsy landing craft dipped and bobbed, a toy lost in the Pacific. The bitter contents of Jack's stomach bounced to his mouth and dropped to his toes with each wave.

Desperate for a distraction, he got out his tattered brown book and worn stub of a pencil. He began to write, "Tuesday, February 1, 1944. Kwajalein," but could only clench his teeth and put the book away. *I won't throw up. I won't. I won't.*

The guns of the ships behind him belched their dragons' breath, and shells roared toward the island in a constant roll of thunder.

Seven battleships and hundreds of air missions had pounded this island and the other Marshalls for three days.

The acrid smell of spent ammunition, of uncontrolled fires and dust filled the air.

Grimshaw had told them that the Fourth Marines had landed on the islands of Roi and Namur yesterday. In a few moments, this clumsy boat would unload his own battalion. Yet in spite of his fear, he could feel adrenalin coursing through his limbs. Worse than the fear of dying was the fear that he might freeze, might not be able . . . *Dear God, give me the guts . . .*

He looked at his buddies, all combat engineers. They were in the third wave to land on the island, but that didn't make it any easier. His artist's eye observed the taut muscles of his friends' faces, jaws tight, clenched teeth. He felt their fear and dread on his skin as sure as he felt the hot sun.

When the gate dropped, could he fool himself into believing this was just another practice maneuver like so many when he'd crawled belly down in the dirt? He hoped their training had amounted to something more than just amusement for the officers. Those maneuvers were supposed to turn men into soldiers, but Jack didn't feel much like a man at that moment, and not at all like a soldier. He wished he were home, cleaning the garage or fixing the lawnmower, anywhere but right here, right now.

This would be their first taste of battle. Pearl didn't count—that had been a one-sided mayhem with little chance to fight back. This one counted.

Nausea rose again as the metal monster bucked and dipped. For a moment the sickness almost crowded out his fear. Good thing he'd never signed for the navy. He'd never have survived. He was always seasick. On that trip from Frisco to Pearl, he'd wanted to throw himself overboard and get it over with. He clamped his mouth shut and swallowed the bile. He'd almost prefer the battle.

Once more on the side of the angels, Red didn't even have the decency to look green. He squatted, grim-faced, beside Jack, his jaws clenched. He claimed he was never seasick. Did Red worry about his manliness or was it death? Occasionally, Red raised his head and stared as if trying to see through the big iron ramp in front of them, their bridge to the inferno. Hardly anyone spoke.

Goat looked as miserable as Jack felt.

Precisely at noon, the monster opened its jaws and spilled its guts.

Red yelled, "I ain't supposed to be on no island. I ain't no virgin." He stood and prepared to run for the beach.

Jack took a deep breath and gave Red a weak grin and yelled back. "Next time tell 'em you want the Atlantic. You're in the wrong ocean." He hauled himself to his feet and scrambled down the ramp. The barked orders, shouts and chaos around him sounded in slow motion like a stuck reel at the movie theater. He concentrated on willing his legs forward, forcing them on through the warm Pacific waters. Part of him wanted to sink, hide under the waves, anything, go back, go back. He moved forward, slogging onward with his buddies under the spell of some strange security that reduced him perhaps to a dot too small to be picked for death from so many.

Jack's ears already hurt from the noise of the shells. By the time he neared the beach, the smells of ammo and dust burned in his nose and chest. He waded on, ducking the spurts of water from the enemy artillery. Mentally he protested with Red, "I ain't supposed to be here." *Dear God, me neither. If I ever get out of this . . .*

Now the water was only up to his knees and he poured all his strength into moving forward. In front of him, only ankle deep, Goat and Red ran full speed. Red's rifle suddenly flew high in the air and he fell forward. Unaware, Goat ran ahead. Jack threw himself forward and plunged into the water.

Red snarled, "I'm okay. Shoulder." He grimaced. "Get out of here." The red stain of his blood was quickly lost in the blue-green water but Jack thought he would never forget the sight of it. But Red always won, didn't he? He couldn't be hit. Then Red picked up his rifle. "I'm coming. Get out of here."

They stumbled forward, Red trying to keep up. Jack saw other bodies plunge into the water or drop to the sand, but his brain refused to acknowledge the sight. Time expanded and collapsed, running fast and slow in a wild frenzy. A record player wound by a madman.

Keeping one eye on Red, Jack threw himself onto the beach. Goat had already reached a couple of fallen palms about ten feet ahead. Jack and Red dove for them, dropping with long gasps of relief.

Red's ashen face contorted in pain. He pressed his hand over the wound, trying to stanch the bleeding. Jack yelled, "Medic!" sure no one would hear. Miraculously, someone did.

The medic crawled over and looked at the wound. "Not good, but you'll live. I'll fix it up for now. When things slow down and we get a station set up, get yourself down there. You're not going to be much use here."

Jack found Red's canteen, gave him a drink of water, and reassured him, "You were never much use, anyway. Can't hit the broad side of a barn." He watched the medic work, repulsed but fascinated. Funny how the sight didn't make him sick. He'd never seen anything like Red's torn flesh and bone. Goat looked at anything except the patchwork being done on Red.

Sweat ran down Red's forehead and he gritted his teeth under the medic's work. When it was over, the bandaging

171

done, he managed a weak grin. "When I get out of this son-of-bitch hell-hole, I'm going to round up every whore on the island and take 'em all on, one right after the other."

The medic nodded, humoring him. He probably heard that one all the time, that and promises never to whore again. He grunted, "Okay, guys. That's it. You'll be okay." He scanned the beach, patted Red on his good shoulder and scrambled away in answer to the next call of "Medic! Over here!"

"Hey, guys. Pass the word. Sarge says dig in."

Jack shouted down the line. "Sarge says dig in. Pass it on." He looked up at the sun, wiped his brow. "Let's volunteer for Alaska." He got out his shovel. Shells from Japanese guns sprayed stinging sand that bit into skin like grains of glass.

Goat grunted. "Looks like this is going to be one damned long day."

"Sorry I can't help you guys." Somehow Red managed to look smug.

"Yeah, I know you are. You must have one hell—uh, heck of a guardian angel." Somehow, saying a "helluva" guardian angel didn't seem right.

Hours later, as they lay in the hole they'd scratched out of the sand, Jack realized how much his arms ached. "Dammit, Goat. Next time I'm gonna lose my shovel and let you dig."

From their right, a voice came, "Looey wants to know if you guys are okay and if anyone's missing."

"No one's missing. McCann's hurt."

From down the line, someone called, "Young's dead."

Jack's head popped up. "Young? Aw, shit." He tried to feel something—sadness, anger, regret—but he felt only exhaustion and emptiness and a cold curiosity. After that *Dear John* had come, Dick said he wouldn't be going home. Had despair made a promise the corporal had kept? Jack wondered how he would feel if Ginny sent him one of those letters.

Dear God, I want to get out of this. I want to see Ginny and Mom and Dad and Littlebit again. He closed his eyes against the war and the fear. He had survived so far. Maybe he would make it.

He turned to focus on Goat, who was opening a box of C-rations and asking Red, "Whatta ya want? Steak, French bread, or chocolate cream pie?"

"Water."

Jack gave him a drink.

Goat unwrapped crackers and laid them on Red's chest, then opened his own rations and announced in disgust, "Crackers, Spam, and chocolate wax. Yum!"

"What'd you expect? Maybe you'd rather eat shingles!"

"I really think I would." Goat sniffed and threw the chocolate back in the pack. Between mouthfuls of Spam, he asked, "You sorry you didn't go back for OCS that time they asked you, Andrews?"

"Nuts. I don't want to be an officer. I'd just be on another island doing the same thing with a bunch of guys I didn't know. Besides, I don't want to be responsible for someone else."

It was true, Jack thought. These were his buddies, his lifeline. Their need today had forged a special bond that would never be broken, not by years, not by absence. Their feelings might weaken with time, but Jack knew that in fifty years he would still recall their names and faces and kinship.

He tried to stretch, but the foxhole was too small. He picked up his helmet, smashed some weird looking bug that crawled across his path, then leaned against the wall of his makeshift home. "What I wouldn't give for a bottle of beer!"

The sun seemed to take forever to drop near the horizon

and Jack sat in the narrow foxhole, feeling as if he were inside a straight jacket. Ginny's image tried to push into his mind, but he rejected it. He couldn't think about her now. He hadn't the strength to face the longing, the homesickness. Better to think of the here and now, keep busy. In desperation, he picked up his shovel. "Give me a hand, Goat. This mouse hole is driving me nuts."

"Good thing it's only sand. You should try digging in some of the clay back home."

"I should be so lucky. I'd dig granite with a spoon if I was home." They managed to scoop enough to stretch out a little and they huddled, pinned down by Jap shelling. Would it go on all night?

Goat rubbed his sleeve across his forehead. "I could sure do with a swim."

Jack looked out at the ocean. It was quieter but the island guns still sprayed shells at the landing ship tanks shuttling back and forth to the transport ships. "You know, when we unloaded and were running in, I was so scared I think I pissed my pants."

Goat grimace. "Yeah. I know what you mean. Good thing we were in the water." He took out his comb and covered it with a piece of leaf. "Didja ever do this with tissue paper when you were a kid?" He blew against it, producing a thin, reedy sound.

Red had nodded off. Now he woke and grumbled, "That supposed to be music?"

Goat looked affronted. "Yeah."

Jack tried to stretch. "Well, how about 'Goodbye Dear, I'll Be Back in a Year'?"

"Boy, that crap, *just for a year* was about the biggest whopper I ever heard."

Jack squirmed some more, trying to get comfortable for

what he hoped was the night. "Yeah. Hey, you can sit up all night if you want to. Me, I'm going to sleep. You okay, Red? Want anything?"

"Yeah. I wanna spray the lawn."

Jack raised his head out of the hole and looked over the beach. "Me, too. I'll join you." An occasional shell hit the sand and sent it flying, but darkness had brought relative quiet. The ships had moved as close to the island as they dared and their guns sounded a monotonous chorus, megaton frogs croaking a lullaby.

The night, with its own demons, was worse than the day. Memories, regrets, and hopes emerged from their hiding places, forming the parade in his mind that he had rejected in the daylight. Ginny in his arms, swaying to Miller, Ginny kissing him, Ginny laughing. Ginny in the arms of a soldier at the USO. Emily in his arms.

He moaned aloud. Goat stirred but didn't wake.

"Dear God, get me out of this," Jack prayed.

Exhaustion at last put an end to the parade of his past and he fell asleep. He dreamed he danced with Ginny at Luna Pier on Lake Erie. Some girl he didn't know offered him cookies.

At first light, Jack and Goat delivered Red to the aid station and settled once more into their foxhole. By mid-morning, the sun made sure their stiff, salt-drenched shirts were soaked with sweat. The beach was littered with shells and dead bodies. A sickening stench of decay and gunpowder smothered everything. It filled their lungs, cloaking them in a heavy, invisible syrup both inside and out. The men had to shield their rations from the flies before they could take a bite.

Each new day yawned with the promise of lasting a month. Jack's outfit stayed in its foxholes perhaps because they were an engineer outfit, more useful later. Other troops had moved inland, and the beach became quieter. On the fourth day, the sarge crept by ordering, "Okay, guys. Patrol." The danger of being shot at by Japs seemed less of a threat than the boredom.

The unit's patrol route led them into a jungle of palms and thick, green vegetation. Goat slapped at mosquitoes and glared enviously at Jack, who didn't have to. Goat whispered, "According to the girls, you're the sweet one. Why the hell are they biting me and not you?"

"Too tough."

Goat, a few feet ahead, stopped suddenly and raised his hand.

Jack peered into the green curtain. He shook his head. He hadn't heard anything.

Goat motioned to the left and held up his hand, mouthing "Wait," then mimed, "Cover me."

Jack raised his rifle.

Just as Goat disappeared into the shadows, Jack heard a snapping sound behind him. He whirled, rifle ready.

A bedraggled boy in a too-big Jap uniform, looking like a kid playing at war, stood frozen, his rifle at his side where he held it carelessly, near the bayonet. His fingers twitched but he didn't move his hand. His dark oriental eyes widened into enormous circles.

Jack held his aim on the target, his finger ready to squeeze the trigger. The boy stared at him, his mouth open as if to speak. He took a step backward. For a second, Jack's finger tensed. Then he lowered the rifle a few inches. The boy dropped his gun and ran.

Goat heard the rustle and saw the fleeing shadow. He fired into the jungle. Jack reached out and pushed Goat's gun barrel down.

"What the hell?"

"He's just a kid. Must have gotten lost."

"Yeah! Right! Too young to pull a trigger ain't he?"

Jack flinched. "Dropped his gun."

The rest of their zone was clean. They reported then dropped back into their foxhole. Jack tried to sleep but the frightened eyes of the boy stared at him again. He stirred restlessly. *I should have fired.*

He turned his back to the wall of sand. God, he was tired. Tired of the heat, the smell of death. How the hell could he shoot a kid? For a moment, his eyes stung with unshed tears, but finally, they closed in sleep.

The boy stood again in the jungle. This time, rifle ready, he aimed at Jack. The heavy gun wavered. The kid pulled the trigger. In slow motion the bullet tumbled into solid flesh. Goat's throat.

Twenty

"Okay, guys. Get ready. We're moving up. Hop to it," the sarge commanded.

"About time." Jack kicked the walls of their foxhole, sending the sand flying, destroying the neat nooks and crannies dug into the sand to store their rations and gear. "Glad to get out of here."

Goat jumped on the sand castle he'd built in one corner. "Hell, Sarge, just got my room fixed up."

"We got a big fancy suite up ahead, just for you."

"Should'a told us."

"Yeah, well, the maid didn't get it ready until just now. Let's move it!"

The island had been quiet for days. Most of the battleships and destroyers had moved out and the men heard only occasional gunfire in the distance.

The squad now stood in front of the sergeant, kibitzing and waiting for orders. "Where we goin', Sarge?" "Can we go home now, Sarge?" "I'm ready. Been ready for a year."

He ignored their remarks and yelled, "Squad column!" When they had moved into formation, he said, "Fighting's 'bout over. We got engineer work to do. Corporal?"

"All here, Sarge. Ready."

The squad moved out.

The men grumbled about the heat, the bugs, and the load, but Jack knew they were as glad as he was just to be moving. It would be great to have real work for a change.

For lack of any better amusement, he decided to join the chorus of griping. "Cripes, I could use a bath!" He'd have given anything for a dip in the old quarry at home. He sighed wistfully at the thought. Wonder what Tom's doing right now? He pulled out his little brown book and licked his pencil. "What day is it anyway, Goat?"

"Y'know, that drives me nuts when you lick that pencil! You're gonna die of lead poisoning."

Jack flicked him a side-long look and laughed at the incongruity of the words. "Yeah. One kind or another!" He was feeling pretty good about his chances of getting out of this one alive.

Goat hadn't missed the joke, but decided to ignore it in favor of complaining.

Jack licked the point again. "I don't know why I do it. Gives me inspiration, I think. Ginny kids me about it, too. Hey, what day is it?"

Goat grunted. "Saturday, I think."

"Saturday, what?"

Goat thought for a moment. "I figure the twelfth."

Jack counted on his fingers. The last entry read, "Tuesday, February 1, company landed on Kwajalein Island, third wave, twelve noon. Plenty of action." He added, "Saturday, February 12th. Company moves up island after spending eleven days and nights in foxholes."

He said, "You know, for all the good we did in that foxhole, we could have stayed back in Hawaii for another week."

"Weren't takin' any chances on the Jap, I guess. Maybe it went better than they thought and they didn't need us up there. Engineers are valuable merchandise. Don't want us to get shot 'til we have to." Goat grabbed the book, looked at the entry, turned a few pages, then flipped the book upside down and shook it. "You mean that's it? Couldn't you have even mentioned the 'roar of the cannon, the pregnant odor of death, hell and all that good stuff'?" He tossed it back. "I think you need a new pencil. Ernie Pyle don't need to worry about you getting his job."

"I wouldn't mind being able to write like that. He's a hell of a guy."

"Yeah, he could've had a cushy job in the office of *Stars and Stripes*, but he gets right out here with us guys."

"And he doesn't muck up to the generals, either. He's okay."

The sarge passed them in line. "Get a move on."

"I'm tired, Sarge," Goat whined.

"I'll order a jeep. Pick up your feet."

When the sarge was gone, Goat lamented, "You know, that Red has to be about the luckiest bastard I've ever seen."

"Sure. That's why he got shot."

"Only his left shoulder. He gets a Purple Heart. And anyway, I'll bet he gets out."

The wound hadn't looked too bad to Jack, but from its location, he figured the arm would be pretty stiff. Red probably would get sent home, and he was a lucky SOB on a lot of counts. In the first place, since he couldn't hit the broad side of a barn, he just would have been in the way. And in the second place, there were all those women. Wolf that he was, he'd only gotten crabs once. It hardly seemed like the kind of thing guardian angels, especially archangels, ought to be taking care of.

Maybe Red would see Ginny when he got home. But with his talents, maybe that wasn't such a hot idea. That time in

Virginia when Ginny had danced with Red, she'd come back with a rattled look on her face, and kept smoothing her skirt like she was nervous. But hell, he knew Ginny didn't approve of Red. She'd told him more than once.

He bit his lip. Trouble was, according to most women, Red was one hell of a Romeo. But the guy was a good friend. Wasn't he?

The image of the torn skin and bone in Red's wound rose before him. Lucky or unlucky, who knew? At least he wasn't dead. "Goat?"

"Yeah?"

"Do you think you killed anyone back there?"

"You mean with the field gun?"

"I don't know. With those big guns, everything's so far away, it's like shooting at targets, not at a guy with a rifle. You don't know if you hit anyone. It's easier. No, I meant when we were out on patrol."

"You thinking about that kid?"

"Yeah. I'm glad I didn't shoot him. But when I had guard duty, I fired a couple of times. I keep hoping it was just shadows. I don't know how I'd feel when it came to shooting a real soldier, face to face."

"I did, one night I was on guard duty. You just do it. It's sort of automatic when you see the threat. It's you or them. You think later."

"I remember seeing that pilot fly over the day Pearl got hit. I wanted like hell to shoot him. I'll never forget that grin when he passed over and I was lying between those barrels. I wanted to shove my bayonet in his mouth, the bastard. But most of the time I wonder if the Japs want to be here any more than we do."

"That pilot sure looked like he was having fun."

"Yeah."

Tired of struggling with emotions, they fell silent, trudging mindlessly along with the pack. After a while, Goat launched into his gripe routine again. It took their minds off their weariness. "Damn, I want a shower."

By late afternoon, they arrived at their new bivouac, conquered and domesticated by the marines. Goat came out of his longed-for shower with the look of a well-fed baby. "Damn. I may just have to apologize to these marines for calling them jarheads."

"They got us into this."

"I said I *may* have to."

The next morning, the sergeant picked Goat and another guy for a TNT detail. Goat glared at Jack and mumbled under his breath, "Why me? You're the dynamite expert. I'm just an old taxi driver."

For a moment, the sarge looked like he was going to eat Goat, but instead, he barked at Jack. "Andrews, you got a party of Japs to take down the road for a digging detail. You get to play Mama and Papa. Don't let 'em out of your sight, or else. Got it?"

"We allowed to work 'em, Sarge?"

"Fighting's over. We do it where it's safe."

"Okay, Sarge." At least this time, he'd be watching someone else dig.

Jack was assigned to five Japs. One, a big man built just a little smaller than a Sumo wrestler, had insignia on his uniform that looked like maybe he was a noncom. He might be good to put in charge. Jack figured the guy could easily wrap most men around the nearest palm if he decided to. It might be smart to keep his distance from this one.

"Any of you guys speak English?"

The big wrestler nodded.

Jack raised his voice and spoke slowly. "Okay. You

foreman. Foreman number one man." He held up his index finger. "Number one. Boss. Okay?"

"Okay, Joe." Then he added in flawless English, "I understand perfectly. Thank you for the honor."

The man bared his teeth in a smile and for a moment, Jack saw again the joy in the pilot's face as he strafed the field at Pearl. Jack's grip tightened around his rifle.

The big man read Jack's confusion and said, "A year at the University of Minnesota. It was a good year for me."

"What's your name?"

"Takeo. Takeo Tagama."

Jack stared at him. His clashing emotions played a game of tag in his mind. He pictured himself a prisoner. The horror stories of Jap prison camps were plentiful, yet when he looked at this crew, he saw only men like himself, and one of those men liked the University of Minnesota. It was easy to hate a pilot who grinned as he fired on you, but for Jack, anger had always been a fickle emotion, constantly soothed by the normal, the familiar. Or like right now, sometimes even degrees of understanding. He couldn't bring himself to smile back, but his finger relaxed on the trigger.

The men worked well and the big man made it easy. Jack wanted to ask him about himself and Japan but kept his distance. Finally, on the fourth day out, when the men had stopped for lunch, Jack offered him a cigarette.

Takeo took it eagerly. "Thanks."

Jack finally got the nerve to ask, "What work do you do in Japan?"

"In Osaka, I teach children." He nodded at a skinny young soldier. "They aren't much younger than he is." He frowned at the kid who sat glowering at his food. "I wanted to be able to reach the minds of the young ones. They are new scrolls ready to receive the strokes of the teacher's brush." He sighed and shook his head. "But in his eagerness, the teacher can apply the ink too heavily and turn out an unbalanced work."

Jack had noticed the sullen look on the kid's face before and it made him uncomfortable. He always sat alone and seldom talked or laughed like the others. Yet, he'd done everything he'd been told without even a flicker of rebellion.

As he watched, the young man turned and looked at him. The noon sun blazed directly down, so that his face under his cap was hidden in shadow. For an instant, his eyes disappeared into that darkness, then he opened them wide and smiled. Again, Jack saw the teeth of that pilot.

By late afternoon, Jack figured the men had completed their job. He inspected it with Takeo, who indicated he wanted to relieve himself. Jack kept his hand on his rifle even though he could see Takeo's head above the broad green leaves where he squatted. The young soldier called something to the big man, and when Takeo nodded, he trotted toward the clump of weeds, walking around behind it. He stooped for a second, then took off running. Takeo tried to stand but couldn't.

For a fraction of a second, Jack stared in disbelief, then swiftly raised his rifle. "Halt!"

The figure kept running.

Jack fired.

The young soldier fell.

Jack yelled angrily at Takeo, who had managed to get his pants up. "Get him." He turned his rifle on the others, but no one made a move. "Pick up the tools." He motioned with the rifle and nodded his head in the direction of the camp.

Takeo carried the dead soldier back. Jack glared at the man, angry that these grinning Jap bastards had made him do this. For a few moments, he wanted to shoot Takeo, too.

The big man shook his head. "He wanted you to shoot.

There was no place to run. He wanted to die honorably rather than return home with the shame of having been a prisoner."

Takeo cradled the boy against him.

Jack lowered the rifle but kept his hand closed on the stock, his finger on the trigger. He clenched his teeth. Takeo must have known all along that the kid wanted it. What had he said about teachers turning out unbalanced work?

He blinked hard to keep back the tears.

Twenty-One

May 1944

Ginny grabbed the mail from the hall table and shuffled through it eagerly. Bills. Oh, good. One from Steve. She tucked that under her arm. A letter for Carey. From Jack? She stiffened. Even before she saw the name she'd recognized his writing. It always looked like he was at war with his pen.

And now, when she hadn't heard from him in ages, he writes to Carey? On regular paper? She slapped the envelopes onto the table.

A little blue V-mail dropped to the floor from the middle of the pack. She snatched it. For her. He writes me a V-mail and Carey one on real paper? For a moment, she was tempted to tear Carey's up or maybe take it and read it, just to see what it said.

She looked at the V-mail and decided she'd get to Carey later. Steve, too. She settled into the straight chair next to the table and ripped at the seal, tearing the corner in her haste. She hated these dumb blue fold-over sheets. What were they supposed to save, anyway? Paper, space, what? If it was postage, he could have spent an extra nickel for a real letter. Like Carey's.

Sunday, April 16, 1944

My darling Ginny,

What a beautiful name. Music to my ears. Ginny—Ginny—Ginny—I wasn't sure for a while if I'd live long enough to write it again. But I did, and I'm here to say it, darling Ginny.

I guess the censors will let me tell you by now that we were in that big battle on Kwajalein. We're out of it now. Plenty of action. Red got hit in the shoulder and is probably home and maybe getting released from the army. He promised to look you up, but if he does, tell him you're out of circulation. Goat is still here and still complaining.

Remember Dick, the corporal who got the Dear John letter? He got himself killed on the first day on the island. The first hour, actually. The guys said he just stood up, yelling and firing. When he got that letter, he'd said he wasn't going to make it. I guess he meant to do it.

But thank God, I am still here and maybe the gods will continue to smile and I'll make it home. I miss you so much. It seems like I've been away forever.

Grimshaw's wife was supposed to look you up, did she? Maybe you would like working with her at the Red Cross. Grimshaw's okay.

Well, it's mess time and this page isn't very big. Tell Carey to send some of those cookies. We'll be back where we came from pretty soon and I'll write again.

Love,
Jack

Love Jack? Ginny made a face. He must have been in a big hurry to eat. Couldn't he at least have taken the time to say "I love you"? She smoothed the page as though she were smoothing his hair. His letters certainly weren't the most romantic she'd ever seen, not compared to Steve's. But, at least he'd begun with "darling Ginny" and he did miss her. Maybe being scared had done that. She folded the blue page and held it for a moment against her cheek.

She put it aside, and smiling in anticipation, opened Steve's letter. Even the opening line was funny.

April 10
My Dearest Cruelest Ginny,

Laughing, she put it down and went to the kitchen for a cup of tea. She'd love to have coffee, but it was so hard to get. She sat back down to read the rest of Steve's letter.

This is the first chance I've had to write. Been up where all the action was. I don't know why, but I'd rather have been a soldier about that time. Water makes a cold grave. But now again, I'm glad I'm in the navy.

Anyway, all's well that ends well. We've got the Marshalls and we're on our way and now we've heard the Russians have begun to win some of their battles.

I don't think I'd like to be a defeated German there.

At least we can begin to hope again, although I guess I never really doubted that once we were in, we'd win eventually. It's the eventually part that costs so much, isn't it?

As for me, I'm as fit as ever except that I sometimes despair of you. Why couldn't I have met you first? You are constantly on my mind, sometimes like a beacon in the storm and sometimes you are the storm. Oh, Ginny. I told myself I wouldn't tell you all of this, and I won't again, I promise. Perhaps it's the aftermath of battle that makes me weak. I don't know. I know that I love you desperately.

I could tell you a lot of things about yourself that you don't know, about why I love you, but you'd never believe me. I just hope you find them out before it is too late.

Well, my darling, cruel Ginny (for love is cruel), I shall now revert to character and tell you all about my last leave which I spent at the library at Honolulu. Of course, it is almost totally staffed by gorgeous wahines wiggling their little fannies off all day long. One of them followed me back to the ship and threatened to throw herself into the volcano if I didn't desert and live with her. Notice I said most of them were gorgeous. The problem was, this was the one who wasn't. She was fat and lumpy and must have been about sixty.

If she'd been just a little younger, I might have taken her up on it, considering your continued resistance to my proposals.

Goodbye, cruel love. I'll write again, if I can resist throwing myself into Mount Pele in despair of you.

Listen and you will hear me sing as I go, Goodbye, goodbye, gooooood byyyyeeee.

Ginny wiped away a tear. Had he been in the same battle as Jack? Wouldn't it be funny if they'd met? But that would never happen—Steve was on a mine-sweeper.

She reread the last line and laughed. Steve was such a nut. Sometimes she did wonder if she could ever love him. Maybe if she'd never met Jack . . .

She looked again at the V-mail and at the one for Carey and tapped them on the arm of the chair. Actually, he didn't write to Carey much. And he had said, "Ginny, Ginny, Ginny." She could almost hear Charles Boyer's voice saying those words.

She took her letters upstairs, went to her closet and pulled out the shoe box. Pretty full now. Jack's pile wasn't much bigger than Steve's. She picked up the fat one Jack had written when he'd first gotten to Hawaii. He'd told her all about the camp, the beach, his friends. He'd been thrilled to be on Waikiki Beach. She wondered if grass skirts had much to do with that. Of course he'd said "I miss you," "I love you." He hadn't been gone long enough to forget it.

She touched another, but didn't bother with it. They weren't as long these days. Those darn blue things. A tear fell on the new one as she started to put it in the box. She hesitated, then stretched out on the bed and read the words over again, "Darling Ginny, Ginny, Ginny."

Sniffling, she reached for a tissue and blew her nose. It's so hard to be in love when you've been apart for three years, separated by what, 4,000 miles?

She put his letter with his others, then picked up Steve's, still lying on the bed. She added it to his stack, and put them all back in the box. She clung to it for a moment, hating to put them away and yet depressed at the sight of them. She closed the lid and put the box back in the closet.

"Ginny?" Carey put her head through the doorway, then jumped when Ginny moved from the closet. "When I didn't see you, I thought maybe I was hearing things."

Ginny gave her an icy stare. "I didn't hear you come in."

"Oh. Well, I was downstairs reading Jack's letter." She waved the envelope in her hand. "Did you get one, too?"

Ginny glanced up at the box and sniffled. "He was in that invasion of Kwajalein. Just got back. That's why we haven't had any letters."

Carey nodded. "He said he's back in Hawaii now. I hope he stays."

Ginny reached up and plucked out her letter. "What's the

date on yours? He was back when he wrote mine."

"May 1st."

"Mine was April 16th." Maybe that was why he'd only sent her that blue thing and Carey a real one. Her jealousy was assuaged a little. He had written to her first, of course. She looked enviously at her sister's letter.

Carey chose to ignore the look and said, "Gotta dump this stuff," and went down the hall to her own room. She piled her books and papers on top of the small oak desk, opened the drop-front, and tucked the letter in the pigeonhole with her "to be answered" collection. She started to close the front, then took the letter back out of its cubbyhole.

She held it for a moment, thinking that he had held it too, then shook her head and sat down to read it again.

May 1, 1944

Dear Carey,

Just got back from Kwajalein and your cookies and letter were waiting. You have no idea how great it is to get one of your boxes. They always make me think of coming home from school and raiding Mom's cookie jar.

We all get so homesick around here. Hawaii is better than Kwajalein, but "there's no place like home." So your cookies give us a big lift. Thanks again.

I let the guys have most of them—not that I could stop them, anyway. But it's really sort of a diversionary or tactical maneuver. It keeps them busy while Goat and I eat the fudge. Red isn't here any more so Goat and I have more to eat. Red got hit on Kwajalein and was sent back to the states. He's okay, though. A shoulder wound.

As for Kwajalein, I'm sure glad to be back. Battles are strange things. When it's time to go in, you're so scared you don't even dare think about being scared. You just move. If you stopped to think about it, you'd either freeze or drop dead of fear. But as awful as that was, the after-the-battle part is even worse, because you can see what happened. Then the soldiers, ours and theirs, turn into real people.

Carey stopped reading to wipe her eyes. When he'd started talking about the battle, his writing got smaller and smaller. She could hardly read the last line.

She smoothed the page and read the rest of it.

Well, I won't bore you with all that.

Your school sounds swell. I hope you're having lots of fun and there is at least one good-looking guy around for you.

It's great that you want to be a doctor, but it must be hard work. Of course, you can always get some fellow to help you, even if you don't need help (from what Tom tells me, you don't). Girls used to ask me the dumbest things and it took me a while to figure out what they were up to.

I don't know any women doctors, but it must be difficult doing that and raising a family, too. But maybe you'll have a maid to do your work for you.

It's about time for mess so I'll sign off for now. Take care of Ginny for me. You sure are swell to keep sending those boxes.

Thanks, "Sis."

Carey folded the letter. She didn't know whether she wanted to kiss him or kick him. Get some good-looking guy to help me? He's seen too many Andy Hardy movies if he thinks that's all girls go to college for these days.

Then her head got the better of her emotions. A lot of girls did still go to college thinking it was just fun-time while they found a man to marry. The thought angered her, though. Maybe the war would make them grow up and teach them they couldn't always depend on some man.

She, for one, could jolly well be a doctor if she wanted to. Her husband, if she ever decided on one, could just put up with it. She was not about to empty bedpans. God gave her brains and she intended to use them.

Ginny appeared at her door. Her arms were crossed and her voice wasn't exactly sisterly when she asked, "What did Jack have to say?"

"He thinks I'm little Betty Co-ed." Carey grimaced and held out the letter. "Go ahead and read it." She resented giving it up, but supposed if Jack were hers, she might be a bit jealous, too.

She watched Ginny as she read it, thinking how odd it was that the two of them were so different. Even their rooms were opposites. Ginny liked blue fussy things and mahogany, her own room had bright colors and slick, modern stuff. Funnier still they should both fall for the same guy.

Ginny handed the page back to Carey. "Oh. Nice letter. He's right, you know. How are you going to be a doctor and have a family, too?" She walked away humming.

Carey tapped the letter against her forehead, and put it away with the others.

Twenty-Two

May 1944

Ginny bounced onto her operator's stool and plugged in her headset.

Sylvia gave her a questioning look. "You look like you just won the Irish Sweepstakes."

Ginny chortled. "Sylvie, guess what I've got tickets for?"

"President Roosevelt's next inaugural?"

"Sure. No, really. Benny Goodman's going to be at the Trianon Ballroom and I've got four."

"Four dollars, four dates, four o'clock?"

"Oh Sylvie, don't be dense. I was at the Red Cross with Claire Grimshaw and she had them and can't use them. She just *gave* them to me. Can you imagine?"

"Who's Claire Grimshaw?"

"Oh, I've told you before. Jack's lieutenant's wife. She used to be Claire Harcourt. She had a brother in my class." She sighed. "She said that her brother-in-law met me at the USO. From the way she lectures me, I think they're trying to keep me busy and away from there. Want to make sure I'm true blue."

Sylvia answered a light on her board. After she made the connection, she said in disgust, "That's silly."

Ginny looked smug in return. "Yeah. Well, anyway, I have four Goodman tickets. You're coming, aren't you?"

"I don't think so. I'm still out of it. I haven't a date and I don't want one."

"Sylvie, it's time you started going out again. I feel terrible about Matt, too, but it's been, what, a year and half now? You need to get back in the swing. You can't cry for the rest of your life."

"One year. Seven months." Sylvia blinked back a tear. "I don't cry much any more."

Marjorie walked up behind Ginny and plugged into the supervising jack. "Good morning, Virginia. Perhaps you'd like to answer some calls."

Ginny raised her eyes to heaven.

Sylvia turned her head away but not before she made a sound that could have been a hiccup.

"If you need a drink of water, Sylvia, I can take your board for a moment." Marjorie sounded concerned.

Sylvia pulled her plug and almost ran.

When Sylvia returned, Marjorie moved back to monitor Ginny. "Virginia, you are going to have to watch your conversations. Our answer time was up last month. We must do better."

"Yes, ma'am."

"All right. And watch your inflection. You still don't put enough life in your voice."

Ginny held her breath and counted to ten. Marjorie disconnected and walked away just in time.

Ginny released her breath slowly and looked over her shoulder. "All clear. Sylvie, no one has dates. Like Bette Davis says, 'They're either too young or too old.' We'll get Carey to go. She needs to get her nose out of her books. Maybe Eileen, if Doug's not in town."

"Speaking of him, have you heard from Steve lately? His letters are wild."

"Yeah, I did." Ginny sighed. "He writes such great ones, so romantic. And he's funny, too. I didn't know how to take that last one, though. He really came on strong. But he ended up kidding, as always. I can't believe he really loves me like he says he does. I think he's just fooling around."

She answered a couple of calls and said, "I finally got a letter from Jack. He was in that big battle on Kwajalein. Actually, I think Steve said he was there, too."

"Oooh! Was Jack scared? Did he say?"

Marjorie walked up behind them and said with an exaggerated patience. "Virginia. Sylvia."

They looked at each other from the corners of their eyes and got busy with calls.

As they left for the day, Sylvia said, "I do love Benny Goodman. I guess I would like to go."

"Swell. I'll talk to Carey and Eileen."

Carey threw her books in the air and yelped, "Beat Me Daddy, I'm a Flat Foot Floogie with a Jersey Bounce."

"I guess that means you'll go."

Carey gave a little hop and spun around. "I'm 'In the Mood,' daddy-o. Try and stop me." Singing, "It'll Be a Hot Time in the Old Town Tonight," she ran to her closet. "What are you going to wear?"

Ginny thought for a moment. "I guess the navy one. The place will be jammed and it's the coolest thing I have."

"Yeah. A cool dress for a real cool cat. I can't wait till ol' Benny gets here!"

Eileen was slightly less exuberant, but since Doug was out of town, she said she'd love to go. She volunteered to pick them all up and drive them home.

On the big evening, the four of them gently but firmly elbowed their way to a ringside table. "We'll have to keep a guard on this one," Carey laughed. Ginny plunked down on her chair with a sigh of satisfaction and lit a cigarette. Soft lights concealed the bareness of the room and warmed its half-darkness. She sized up the large dance floor that gleamed with wax. "How'd you like to have to polish that?"

Carey looked it over. "If it was the only way I could see Benny, I'd do it."

Sylvia shook her head. "Look at this crowd." She started to cough and wave futilely at the already-dense cigarette smoke. "We just got here and I can hardly breathe. I can't imagine what it'll be like by the time the evening's over."

"When they start to dance, there won't be so much smoking," Ginny stopped abruptly to watch the first members of the orchestra take their seats. The room buzzed with excitement and sporadic clapping turned into a roar as Goodman finally entered. The crowd exploded.

He put his clarinet to his mouth, stopped and smiled, then blew the first note of his theme, "Let's Dance." The crowd rose as one and gave him a standing ovation. When it petered out, he replayed the introduction. No one stepped onto the floor until he was almost finished.

Sylvia fairly bounced in her seat. Carey grabbed her hand. "Come on. With all these women, we'll never get a man to dance with us and I'm not going to miss one single note."

Ginny stayed in her seat and tapped her foot as the notes of "Stomping at the Savoy" then "I'll See You Again" rolled from the famous black clarinet. She groaned, "I wish Jack or Steve, or just anybody, were here. I feel like an old woman sitting here without a date."

Amusement tugged at the corners of Eileen's mouth. "Yes, you're all of twenty-four, aren't you?"

"Doesn't it bother you to have them all away?"

Eileen smiled and about a quarter of her right cheek disappeared into her dimple. "Well, Doug isn't gone much, you know."

Ginny watched that dimple and felt sure she'd turned green. Eileen had taken her hair down from the rolls that usually framed her face, letting it fall in a shiny light brown curtain that covered half her cheek. Like Veronica Lake. It wasn't fair, and she had Doug around, too.

Ginny's bout with envy was interrupted by a man's voice at her back. "May I have this dance?"

The voice sounded familiar. Startled, she turned, gasped, then squealed, "Red!" She almost knocked her glass over.

He turned from admiring Eileen and crowed, "Ginny!" He pulled her to her feet and hugged her as though she were a stuffed bear. Then he kissed her firmly on the mouth. "That's from Jack!"

A hot finger poked her in the pit of her stomach and the heat spread. Surprised, she stepped back and put her hand to her mouth. "What are you doing here?"

"Aren't you going to introduce me and ask me to sit down?"

She blushed. She knew he hadn't meant that kiss, but it had burned. That magnetism still attracted her. Why should it? She didn't even like him. Why should his touch affect her so? Her mind traveled back to that evening in Virginia, remembering the electricity when they danced. The vibrations had fairly crackled between them. She'd wondered if Jack had noticed how nervous she'd been.

Embarrassed but delighted to see and touch someone who'd been with Jack, she blurted out, "Oh, I'm so glad to see you. When did you see him last? Where's Barb? Is she here? Jack said you were hurt. Are you okay? How'd you get here?"

Red backed up and held up his hands, then turned the full wattage of his charm toward Eileen. "Whoa. First introduce me to this pretty lady."

Exasperated, Ginny glared at him. "Eileen, Jack's buddy, Red McCann. He got hurt at Kwajalein."

She didn't give them time to acknowledge. "Are you out?" He wore sergeant's stripes. That figured. "How long've you been home? How's Jack? You haven't said." Her voice was almost frantic.

Red grinned at her. "Slow down. We've got all evening." He turned to Eileen. "I'm very happy to meet you."

Ginny knew a lost cause when she saw one and continued the introduction. She snapped, "Mrs. Major Douglas McInnis," emphasizing the *Mrs.* and the *Major*. She wanted to hear about Jack. She didn't want him wasting the evening dancing with someone else. Besides, Eileen was her friend and this guy was lethal.

Eileen's dimple deepened again, but evidently she'd read the signals right and only nodded.

Ginny grabbed his left arm and pulled. He winced. She paid no attention. "Let's dance. I want to hear all about everything." She tugged harder. "C'mon." He looked apologetically over his shoulder at Eileen and laughed. "Sorry, but I'll be back."

As they danced, he told Ginny about the battle, keeping it light. Then he asked, "Have you heard from him? Is he still there?"

"He's back on Hawaii. He and Goat. I thought you were supposed to get out. Or are you? You're still in uniform."

"I talked them out of releasing me. I'm at Camp Perry."

"Jack said you were crazy."

"It hasn't been hurting much." He opened his mouth in a silent scream and elaborately removed her hand from his arm near his shoulder where she'd been hanging on. "At least until tonight."

She covered her mouth. "I'm so sorry. I didn't realize."

"It just left me with a limp," he whispered in a hoarse voice, then pretended to wobble.

"Oops, sorry." She giggled. "Jack was right. You are crazy. But what are you doing at Camp Perry?"

He threw back his head and roared. "Typical army screw-up. They have the worst shot in the army teaching marksman-ship. They think my bad aim is just a little stiffness."

Ginny tried not to look too amused, but she couldn't resist rubbing it in just a little. "Yeah. I've heard how awful you were. Jack got every medal for marksmanship there is."

Red didn't answer and they danced quietly through a couple of slow tunes. After a while, he began to talk of Jack again and drew her close. She was so busy enjoying herself, she didn't notice how close. He reminisced, "Remember the weekend you girls came down to Ft. Belvoir?"

"Yeah," she said dreamily. Then wondering what he was getting at, she added, "That was a long time ago." She felt his nearness. Just like that night in Virginia. Her blood raced.

"Yeah." He put his cheek against hers.

She blushed and wondered if he could feel the heat. She pulled back. She mustn't let him get to her.

The orchestra stopped. Goodman leaned toward the mike. "Ladies and gentlemen, Miss Peggy Lee is here to sing, 'Why don't you do right, and get me some money, too.'"

Ginny stopped dancing and took Red's hand, pulling him toward the crowd that circled the orchestra. They listened and watched, swaying with the beat. "She has a great voice, hasn't she? So sultry."

Red leered, "Yeah, she's pretty sexy, too."

Ginny frowned and touched her hair. Maybe she should

get a new style—maybe even become a blond. Peggy's pale hair glowed in the spotlight like cream satin.

He wasn't paying attention. He leaned over and whispered, "Isn't she great?"

The crowd agreed with him. They wouldn't let her leave the stage, and their applause turned into a stampede of sound. She turned and looked at Goodman. He gave the downbeat and she whispered the torchy "Jim" in that breathless, sexy voice. She followed with, "Don't Get Around Much Anymore," and earned another ovation.

Red held Ginny close, swaying as he listened. His fingers pressed into her waist.

Once again, his touch sent electric currents buzzing through her. But she mustn't. She didn't like him. He was a big, bad wolf. With a sigh of relief she spotted Carey standing not far away. She took his wandering hand in hers and led him to where her sister stood with Sylvia.

"Carey, this is Red. Jack's friend. You know, the one from Ft. Belvoir. He got wounded at Kwajalein and was sent home."

When Ginny said, "The one from Ft. Belvoir," Carey's smile froze. She looked him up and down and nodded curtly.

"The cookie and fudge lady! Jack never told me you were so gorgeous." He reached out and grabbed Carey's hand. She pulled it back. His eyes glinted for a moment. He executed a deep bow. "I am in your debt. You have no idea how great they tasted."

She turned to Sylvia. "C'mon Sylvie, let's dance."

Before Sylvia could reply, Red laid his hand on Carey's waist and took her right hand in his. "May I have this dance?"

She pulled away and turned her back. "Sorry. I'm busy."

He raised an eyebrow and a quick glint of surprise flickered briefly in his eyes. He bowed again, then led Ginny back to the dance floor.

Ginny glared at Carey's back muttering to herself. What was that all about? A sinking feeling in the pit of her stomach told her she knew the answer. She'd made remarks about how Red treated Barb, and, too, Ginny suspected that Red's personality had set off an alarm. Annoying, though, since Carey's instincts were usually on target, especially when Jack was concerned.

Ginny turned her attention back to Red, but she felt restless. The joy of dancing and the discomfort of his presence warred within her and she finally gave up. "C'mon on, let's sit. Eileen's all alone."

They didn't make it to the table. Goodman began to play "Goodnight, Sweetheart" and everyone crowded the bandstand to applaud. They kept it up even as the musicians began to put away their instruments.

Ginny turned to the others, who had found their way to her side. "Wasn't that wonderful? I hate to see it end."

Red hugged her and looked in the opposite direction. "Gotta find the guys I came with. I'll call you. I've lots of stories to tell you. Give me your number."

"Call me tomorrow." She grabbed a matchbook from the nearest table, wrote her number on the cover, and handed it to him.

Carey gave her a dirty look.

Twenty-Three

Monday

Carey frowned and looked her sister up and down deliberately as Ginny slipped into a green silk dress. "Do you really think you ought to do this?"

Ignoring the implied criticism, Ginny did a pirouette. "How do you like it?"

Obviously unwilling to say anything agreeable about the evening, Carey shrugged. "You always look good in green. Why a new dress tonight? Trying to impress Red?"

Ginny straightened the seams of her stockings as she considered whether she'd bother answering. She tried for a distraction. "Boy, I wish I could buy more nylons. They're so much nicer than silk."

"Where'd you get nylons?"

Ginny gave up and sighed. "Okay, Crabby Carey. What's your problem?"

"Jack is my problem."

Ginny tried a white fabric flower in her hair. She didn't want to quarrel.

"That looks stupid."

Ginny sat down on the bed and folded her arms. Evidently Carey wasn't going to let it drop. "All right. Let's argue, if that's what you want. First, Jack is *not* your problem. He never was." She paused and finished the sentence through clenched teeth, "And he never will be. Period. End of paragraph. Over and out."

Carey stopped glaring and lowered her gaze. She spoke in a low voice. "No. He isn't mine, but I still don't want to see you get involved with his friend."

"Red? Just because I'm going to dinner . . ."

Carey lifted her chin and met Ginny's stare. "Yes, Red. And it isn't just dinner."

She threw up her hands in a gesture of futility. "Carey, we're only going out to talk about Jack. It isn't even a weekend night. You're being silly."

"You're awfully good at kidding yourself. That man is the biggest wolf I've ever met. Can't you see that?"

"I know it. I don't even like him. You don't need to worry. We're going to be at the Hillcrest, though. I have to look decent." Ginny made a final check in the mirror. She patted a strand of hair that wanted to stand up by itself, then turned and put her hand on her sister's shoulder.

Carey wasn't placated by the touch. "I hope he isn't coming here. I'll slam the door on his foot. Or better yet, his bad shoulder."

Ginny sighed. Who was the old Greek god of patience? It had to be a woman. Athena? Well, the one for wisdom would do. She took a deep breath and looked up at the ceiling. *God, save me from little sisters.* Having just been in communion with Him, Whom she looked to for a little help here, she resisted the temptation to shout. "He's sending a cab for me. He got a room for the Goodman dance so he's staying over. Honestly, Carey, you can't expect me to go looking like a rag-picker."

"You ought to be glad I'm getting out. I never get to go anywhere but lunch with the girls. I'm so bored I could scream." Ginny slipped into her pumps. A tear flirted with her eye, but she refused to give in. "You ought to get out yourself. You look tired and all you do is study. How can you stand it?"

"I'm not tired and I have things to do. Maybe you should go back to the Red Cross with Claire. Stay away from his room." Carey turned to go. The argument had lost its steam when Ginny mentioned the Hillcrest. She saw herself there with Ted the night before he went away and was cast back to her own problems. Ted. She'd have to stop being nice and just tell him there was no hope for the two of them. He had to stop dreaming and get on with his life. But wouldn't it be a dirty trick to write him there in London? What if he went on one of those bombing raids and didn't come back? That would be awful.

Ginny, not realizing Carey had lost interest, snapped, "Maybe I'll just spend the night."

Carey whirled, "Ginny! You wouldn't!"

"Oh, Carey. What's the matter with you? Of course I wouldn't. But I don't want to go back to that Red Cross, either. They're all so prissy. Especially Claire. She always gives me that smug look of hers."

Suddenly tired and annoyed, Carey looked back at her sister. Why was she standing here arguing with Ginny about Jack? It wasn't her business and she'd better take care of her own messes first.

"Forget it, Ginny. I should mind my own business. Go with Red, but if you're smart, you'll keep that man at arm's length." She walked out of the room, turning back only to say, "Even if he doesn't care about his girl, he still has one, you know."

"Of course I know!" Ginny hurled at her back. "We're friends." Sweet little Barb. She felt sorry for her. The girl was too nice for her own good. No one should be such a pushover.

Anyway, she didn't have any desire for Red. She only wanted to hear about Jack and all the trouble the three of them had gotten into. According to what Red said last night, they were constantly up to something.

Red, with martinis waiting, was already at their table when she arrived. She pushed the glass farther from her reach. "I wish you hadn't ordered one of those. They're so strong."

"Shall I get something else?"

"Well, I hate to waste it. I guess it's okay. I'll just drink it slowly."

He nodded. "Pretty nice hotel." He nudged Ginny's drink in her direction.

She traced the foot of the glass with her finger. "You haven't been here before?"

"I usually end up at Port Clinton, or if I get the time, maybe Kelly's Island or Sandusky for seafood. You should try it if you haven't." He smiled confidentially at her.

As she watched him smile, her heart sank to her toes. Carey was right, she shouldn't be here. In his dress uniform, his sex appeal screamed and howled at her. His hair was no longer short from the regulation army haircut and it flamed even more brashly than it had in Virginia. It lay untamed, in disarray on his head. She'd never read *Peck's Bad Boy*, but Red had to be a grown-up Peck.

She unfolded her napkin and carefully spread it on her lap. Perhaps if she talked about Barb, she'd calm down. "Where's Barb these days?" At least it would remind him that she knew he had a girl, that neither of them was available.

"She's in Columbus. She's fine. But you didn't come here to talk about me and her, did you? It's that little old Jackie-boy you want to hear about, maybe about Emily and the WACs. She looked like you, you know."

She thought she heard a sneer in his voice, and she bristled. "He told me about her. You must have thought you were funny."

"Don't worry, he didn't fall for her." He laughed and lifted his glass. "Here's to the great romance. May your dreams come true." He waited until she picked up her glass, smiling slightly. Better to eat you with, my dear. But that was silly.

Flustered, she took a bigger sip than she meant to. Did he mean to make her jealous? Even if he didn't, he had a way of making her nervous by doing nothing. She tried to focus on his sergeant's stripes. Jack had refused officer's training. They hadn't asked Red, but she supposed you couldn't have a private teaching rifle. Jack should have taken that promotion. He would look great as an officer.

Not caring that the question was an abrupt change, she asked suddenly, "Jack said he was offered a promotion. How come he didn't take it?"

"He's not competitive enough. Too easy going."

Not competitive? Enough? The idea surprised her. Jack was pretty easy to get along with, but it never occurred to her he might not be ambitious. But then, an artist didn't have to be, did he?

Red opened the menu. "Shall we have T-bones?"

Steak. Just the word made her mouth water. She could almost smell it. A real T-bone. Nice and juicy. "Ooh. It's been ages since I've had one. Our rations don't stretch that far."

He laid the menu down. "How long's it been since you heard from Jack? Not much of a writer is he?"

"Mm-hm." She fingered the martini then drank. "I get these little V-mail things. Ernie Pyle he isn't." She thought she saw a twitch of amusement at the corner of Red's mouth and instantly regretted the implied criticism.

"Did I ever tell you about the time we went out without a

pass and they changed the guard on us?"

Before she could answer, he signaled the waiter and gave their order.

Impressive. He certainly didn't let a little thing like money worry him. After the waiter left, she raised an eyebrow and asked, "What are you, independently wealthy or something?"

He laughed. "Eat, drink, and be merry, and all that good stuff."

He talked then, about himself, Jack, and Goat, and didn't stop with his stories and jokes until after dessert. The dinner slowed him down only a little.

Ginny wiped her eyes. "Red, you're crazy." She laid her napkin down beside her empty plate. Her mother used to say a lady didn't clean her plate like that. It made her look like she couldn't afford food. But the steak had melted in her mouth. "I need a break. I'm going to powder my nose."

In the room, she stared at the girl in the mirror. What was her problem? All those stories had her doubting Jack, had her thinking how funny Red was. But then, Jack didn't need to be aggressive or competitive, did he? She was being silly. Red couldn't help being funny. Jack was sweet.

When she came back, two fresh martinis stood on the table. She eyed hers speculatively. She wasn't sure, had that one drink lasted all through dinner? Was she lightheaded from drink or excitement, confusion, maybe? A martini was probably the one drink most likely to put her under the table, and if there were any man she didn't trust, Red was the one. She decided just one more tiny sip would do.

He sat facing the dance floor, his chair turned slightly from the table. A sax, bass, and piano trio were playing on the tiny platform. A set of drums and a trumpet lay nearby, but no one played them. Red tapped his fingers with the thrum of the bass. "That Peggy Lee was sure something the other night, wasn't she?"

"Mmm. I love Goodman, but I think I like Miller better."

"That old licorice stick's sure hot and mellow." He began to nod and bounce. "These guys aren't bad. Can't stand it. Gotta dance." He jumped up and held out his hand.

At the touch of his hand, the butterflies, waking from their gin-drenched sleep, stirred in her stomach. Damn, not again. She reached back as they started toward the floor, snatched her martini, and took a big gulp. Just to quiet her butterflies.

When he made no attempt to crush her against him, she began to relax and enjoy the smoothness of his movements. Wolf or no, he danced like a dream. They danced to everything, to "String of Pearls," and even "Boogie Woogie Washer Woman." The floor was almost empty and small as it was, they had plenty of room. They slowed for "The Very Thought of You" and she floated on a satin sea. He could have been a prince wooing the enchanted swan, his princess. She wished she could go on gliding in dreamland forever, but the song ended and the group took a break.

She glowed as he led her back to the table. "I'd rather dance than eat."

He gave her a curious look. "Yeah. It takes me back." He took a long drink and stared pensively at the glass, his silence a sharp change from his previous mood.

A strange discomfort crept over her. Had she said something wrong? Maybe the dancing reminded him of Barb. Had she misjudged him? Did he miss Barb after all? Maybe he was all show.

She fiddled with her own drink. Was this the same one or a fresh one? She took a sip. Maybe he'd just run out of stories. It wasn't like him to be quiet. She squirmed nervously and finally, to make conversation, asked, "What do you do at Perry?"

He shrugged. "Not much."

"You have to do something."

"It's boring. You don't want to hear about it."

"Do you write to Jack?"

"Me?" He snorted a laugh.

"Oh."

She searched her mind. Why had he dried up? He didn't look upset. He sat leaning away from the table with one leg crossed over his knee. Must have been the dancing. He and Barb were so good together, maybe he'd been disappointed. Or maybe he just missed his girl. "Do you get to see Barb much?"

He shrugged and looked off into space. "Yeah, enough."

She was becoming annoyed. She took several big gulps of her drink. "A penny for your thoughts?"

"I was just thinking what a lucky guy Jack is." After an enigmatic look, he rose and went over to the piano player who had returned to his seat. After a whispered conversation and what looked like money passing hands, Red took the empty drummer's chair. The leader nodded and the group began "Drum Boogie." Sweat stood out on Red's forehead and the sticks flew like hummingbird wings.

Her emotions in turmoil, she watched him, impressed by his drumming, but confused. He'd said, "What a lucky guy Jack is." He couldn't have meant that the way she took it. But now he sat there smiling and looking at her as though she were *the* woman in his life. The band began, "I'll See You in My Dreams" and he handed the sticks back.

She wanted to escape and go comb her hair, anything, but she stayed, sipping her drink, feeling like a fool and trying to still the butterflies roused again by his remark, "What a lucky guy Jack is."

When he returned, he was his old talkative, joking self,

giving her fits of the giggles.

The liquid in Ginny's glass lowered faster and faster, but somehow, the glass never emptied.

Finally, Red looked at his watch and stretched slightly. "It's getting late. Let's have one last dance." When they reached the floor, he drew her tightly against him and put his hand on the middle of her back, massaging in a slow, sensuous motion. She melted into his arms and pressed her cheek against his chest, dreaming of Jack. It had been so long since Jack's arms had held her. Her head swam and a pleasant warmth took over with thoughts of Jack's strong grip. Her legs seemed to belong to someone else.

Many dances later, Red spoke into her ear, his lips brushing her skin. "Time to go home."

His breath was hot on her neck. She drew back a little. She mustn't fall for his tricks.

He led her back to the table. A fresh martini stood ready. She drank half of it in two gulps.

He reached over and took the glass from her hands. "Time to go." He pointed her toward the lobby, talking softly just behind her ear.

She picked up her purse and it slipped from her fingers.

Red retrieved it. "You may need this."

She giggled. Red was the funniest person she'd ever known.

"You're in no condition to leave right now. You need a little rest. We can go upstairs and you can sleep it off for an hour, then I'll see you home."

An alarm tried to penetrate her fog. She saw Carey's disapproving face. Ginny blinked. "I can't." She meant to add, "Mom'll worry if I don't get home," but somehow it didn't come out. Her tongue felt thick and lazy. She was too tired.

"You'll be okay. I'll have some coffee sent up and you can

rest. Then I'll get you a cab."

Strong, black coffee sounded good. She knew something was wrong—coffee and sleep? But she didn't really care. If only she could rest for a few minutes.

He led her to the elevator. "Seven, please." With a sly grin, the operator pushed the button and the door slid shut.

Through her fog, Ginny saw a man across the lobby pick up his crutches and rise from his chair, but then his image evaporated.

Twenty-Four

"Hi, Tom. Want company?" Carey set a loaded cafeteria tray down on his table, taking a "yes" for granted.

Tom pushed away his coffee cup and smiled. "Actually, I was hoping I'd run into you." He raised an eyebrow as she unloaded half a dozen dishes: beef stew, cornbread, fruit Jello, lemon pie, milk, and a candy bar. For later, she had promised herself. "Don't they feed you at home?"

She blushed. She didn't have to worry about her weight but she hated to have him think she ate like a horse. "I've been up since six and didn't get any breakfast. I'm starved." She arranged her dishes in a correct Emily Post pattern and tackled her food. Between bites, she managed to say, "I take it you're not expecting anyone to join you."

"No. I really wanted to talk to you." He looked at his watch. "I was at the library and I have an appointment with my advisor in an hour, so I came here on the off chance." He laughed. "I knew you liked to eat."

She blushed and changed the subject. "Mm. How's the thesis going? How do you like teaching those one-oh-one courses?"

Tom laughed. "Freshmen are babes in the woods, aren't they? I remember how adult and smart I felt that

213

first year! But we really need to talk."

Carey sized him up. Tom wasn't ordinarily the fiddling type but now he stirred his coffee, clanked his spoon and didn't know what to do with his hands. "Sounds serious. Something the matter?"

"I have a problem, and I don't know what to do about it."

"I'm not exactly an expert on problems, you know. I can't even solve my own."

"You mean Ted?"

"Mm-hm. He's in England, flying who-knows-where on missions. I want to come right out and tell him I'm not his girl, we're only friends, but it doesn't seem fair right now. On the other hand, this war's going to be over someday, and I hate to have him come home thinking I belong to him." It took her a while to spill all of her thoughts because she didn't want to stop eating.

"I'm sure deep down he really knows." He smiled a little and pointed at her plate. "Your dilemma doesn't bother your appetite any."

"I know, and I'm going to be as big as a horse."

"You?" He shook his head. "Do you have any idea how gorgeous you are, girl?"

She put her hand to her hair and preened for him. "Natch."

"I wish . . ." He frowned and tapped his fork, leaving the thought unfinished. Then he said, "I sometimes think Jack would have been better off with you."

She reddened and wondered what had brought that on. She'd never told anyone about her feelings for Jack, except Toni, of course. She'd never even admitted it to her sister, although she knew Ginny sensed, but resisted, the truth. She was about to dismiss the remark, then it dawned on her that maybe she wasn't as cool about hiding her feelings as she'd thought. Could he have guessed?

She defended Ginny. "You shouldn't say that."

Tom pressed his lips together and shook his head. "I like Ginny a lot. She's good fun. She's bright and pretty. But I just don't think she's right for Jack."

"Ginny has her head in the clouds. She truly cares for him. Maybe for all the wrong reasons, though. He's gorgeous and he has that wry humor." Carey pushed her empty plate away, suddenly bashful as she said, "He gets that silly look on his face when he thinks he's being cute. Like a little kid."

She stopped. As a diversion, she concentrated on her glass of milk, turning it in circles. Then she went on, more casually. "She complains he isn't romantic enough."

"She's seen too many movies." Tom watched her eat for a bit. "When's your class?"

"I don't have anything until two."

He nodded and fiddled with his cup again. He rose to fill it but she jumped up and got it for him. When she put it down, he fiddled some more then cleared his throat.

She pushed her plate away and leaned toward him. "Okay. What the matter?"

"I had a meeting at the Hillcrest a week or so ago. I'd just finished and was waiting in the lobby. One of the guys was going to give me a lift." He launched into a long explanation of the whys and wherefores.

She wanted to say, "Get on with it." Instead, she tapped her fingers. After a bit, she broke in. "Okay, Tom. What are you trying not to say?"

He picked up his spoon, stared blankly at it, then dropped it. "Ginny was at the Hillcrest that night."

"I know. An army buddy of Jack's got wounded and sent home. He's stationed at Camp Perry. They ran into each other at the Benny Goodman dance. That's all."

Tom frowned. "The one at the armory was a navy man," he said, referring to the time he'd seen Steve kiss her at the USO.

Carey figured that horse had already been beaten to death. "She writes to the guy but there's nothing between them and Red just took her out to talk about Jack and stuff."

"He did have red hair."

"So? What's the problem?"

"Ginny had more than enough to drink. He practically had to hold her up. But that's not the trouble. He took her upstairs in the elevator."

Stunned, Carey stared at him. Tears welled in her eyes and she rifled through her purse for a tissue. Her mother's voice echoed in her head. "There's only one reason a girl would ever go to a man's room. Good girls don't do things like that. It's asking for trouble." How many times had she said that?

Tom handed her a paper napkin.

She smiled weakly and blew her nose. "Sorry. I don't know what I'm crying about." She did know, damn it. She'd warned Ginny. Any fool could see Red was a damn Don Juan. Ginny knew it, too. Damn.

Tom voiced her thought for her. "What about Jack?"

"What about him?"

"Do we tell him?"

"We don't know if she did anything wrong."

"No, we don't. But then why would she go to his room?"

Carey shrugged. What could she say? Why would Ginny go? She knew better.

Tom repeated, "I think Jack ought to know."

"I'm sure if she has anything to say, she'll tell him."

Tom looked her in the eye. "Would you, if you were Ginny?"

216

"If it were me, I probably would. I hate deception."

"But Ginny?"

"I don't know." And she didn't. Ginny was good at kidding herself. She'd probably just find another excuse for this.

Tom brushed his hair back and scratched the back of his head. "The war in Europe doesn't look like it's going to last much longer. Maybe the Japs will give up when they know we can hit them with everything we've got. But it's not over yet, and I'd hate to have him go into battle knowing she spent the night with his buddy. But damn it, Carey, I'd hate worse to see him marry her after that."

"She didn't spend the night. She came home late. I heard her." Carey sighed and admitted her true feelings aloud for the first time. "I never really thought they were meant for each other. But I can't do anything about it." She frowned as she watched his spoon rock back and forth in his fingers. Tears came to her eyes again. "There are special problems for me."

Tom said nothing, just let her talk.

She took a deep breath, admitting what she figured by now he guessed. "You might as well know it. I've always been crazy about him." A touch of pink suffused her face. "He's just so cute and sweet. Innocent. Well, you know—"

Tom nodded.

She went on. "But I couldn't live with myself if I spoiled it for her. She'd think I did it on purpose. She is my sister."

He piled his dishes on her tray and started to rise. "I guess I'll sit on it for now. I may have to rethink things when he gets home. If she doesn't tell him, I will. But if I were Jack . . ." He smiled at her and pressed his big hand on hers.

She scrabbled for a tissue. It was a hopeless mess. Even if Jack and Ginny did break up. She'd never be able to take advantage of the situation.

Twenty-Five

Later the Same Day

Ginny stood leafing through the mail as Carey came in from school and her conversation with Tom. A lead weight dropped in Carey's stomach. Maybe she should leave, pretend she'd forgotten something. She could always go to the library.

Ginny didn't look at her, just handed her an envelope. "From Ted."

Carey frowned as she noticed the two envelopes Ginny had set aside. One was white. She'd seen enough to know that was from Steve. As for the other, it was blue. Jack. Her frown deepened. She didn't even want to think about him getting hurt.

Unaware of her sister's reaction, Ginny glowered at Jack's V-mail. Why couldn't he write a long one like Steve? A wave of self-pity engulfed her. It wasn't fair. And it wasn't fair either that he never got any leave. He'd been over there for three years. Other guys got leave. If he could have come home, maybe none of this would have happened. It just wasn't fair.

She straggled behind as she and Carey went upstairs together. She didn't want Carey studying her face, trying to figure out her problems. She finally got enough control of her emotions to ask, "How's school?"

Carey looked pained. "I feel like I'm in a sausage grinder."

218

With a brighter look, she said, "Speaking of sausages, how's Marjorie?"

Ginny chuckled in spite of her gloom. "Oh, that's not Marjorie. It's old Wells that looks like the sausage. Marjorie's our great tragedian. Hammy enough to feed a battalion. If they canned her, they'd have enough Spam for the army. I think she's finally given up on me. Anyway, I'm going on days next week and I don't think I'll have to put up with her anymore."

Carey teased, "They'll probably move her, too. Just to keep you on your toes."

"They probably will." Guilt pushed the laughter from Ginny's voice. Ever since that night, she'd not been able to live with herself. She didn't deserve to be happy after what happened. Maybe God would give her Marjorie as a punishment, to dog her the rest of her life. But it hadn't been her fault. The blue letter turned hot in Ginny's hand.

She went into her bedroom and closed the door. She'd read Steve's letter first. Maybe she'd feel better. He was always funny and sweet. Did he really love her like he said? Or was it like Shakespeare said, he "doth protest too much?" At least his letters were fun.

She tried to picture those quizzical blue eyes as he'd said goodbye. Had she really seen sadness mixed with that laugh he always had? He'd kissed her hard. More than a year ago. It seemed like a million. How much had he changed in that time?

For that matter, how much had she and Jack changed? He'd been gone three million years, it seemed. Did he still love her as much? He never raved about it like Steve. But maybe Jack was one of those guys who took everything for granted.

Laying aside her guilt for a moment, she considered the two of them. Her feelings for both confused her. She really wanted to marry Jack. If that were true, she must love him—yet Steve made her laugh.

And then that night with Red. She closed her eyes. She was so tired of struggling with that guilt. It hadn't been her fault and she wasn't ready to do anything about that now. Maybe I shouldn't ever. It really wasn't my fault.

Her conscience prodded. "Wasn't it?"

Well, even if it was, what about Jack? How many girls had he had? Would he tell her everything? She didn't think she wanted to know. People make mistakes. Maybe it's better for two people not to know too much.

She sat down on the bed and clutched the letters, staring at the wrinkled paper. Her eyes followed the tortuous paths of the crinkles, the creases twisting her mind with questions and doubts. How would I feel if he had an affair? Would a one-night stand be any different? Would he expect me to accept it and figure he was alone and far from home? Could I do that? She knew the threat was always there, but her own weakness had changed things. If I could forgive him, could he forgive me? But, with Red? His army buddy? Oh, how could I have been so stupid?

She closed her eyes tightly, forbidding the tears to rise. She shuffled the envelopes, afraid to open either. Steve's because he was too good to be true, Jack's, because, well . . .

She finally chose Steve's.

USS Starfish
June 2, 1944

My Darling Dearest Lovely Cruel Virginia,

Funny how even his opening lines had to outdo Jack's. Except that one he'd written when he got back to Hawaii from

Kwajalein, "My darling Ginny, What a beautiful name, Music to my ears. Ginny-Ginny-Ginny . . ." She moved to get that letter, but her guilt didn't want to let go. She couldn't face that yet. She picked up Steve's letter again.

I think I should have joined the army. Of course I wouldn't like slogging through the mud on those long hikes and as it is, I get shot at enough in the navy to last me a lifetime. But the trouble with this life is I'm either worked to death or bored to death. Today is one of the last kind.

I went on deck to read but that great Pacific sky, whose blueness defines the very color, made me even bluer. Bluer than the sky-blue sky, that is. It made me pine for you. (My muse is in a blue mood, too.) Blue skies and pine—pine trees. Nice image, what? All I see out here is the blue sea.

And speaking of blue (as I am), things are always as blue as the sky, but what is the sky as blue as? I don't know. Do you?

At least your eyes are not as, etc., etc. Your eyes are the color of the copper that flows from the flames of Vulcan's forge. Or perhaps the color of the flame that Prometheus stole from Zeus to give to mankind. It would be worth the torture of having one's entrails devoured for all eternity to have given your eyes such magnificence.

Ginny fell back on the bed, almost prostrate with laughter. He did go on. And on, and on. But it was wonderful.

She sat up and started the letter over, savoring the words while she laughed. It continued:

Give Marjorie my regards. I'll have to meet this gem when I get back. And I will get back to claim you, in spite of your protestations. Like Dante, I shall love you forever, my Beatrice.

By the way, does Marjorie have a really sexy voice? The kind that sends an invitation? If you reject me, I might fall for her instead of you.

Thank you for your beautiful picture.

Do you have any idea what a sight for these poor jaded eyes you are? You are lovely and I love you.

Problem is, since I hung your picture, I don't get any sleep any more. The guys keep coming into my cabin with stupid questions when what they really want is to sneak a peek at you. I had to throw a few punches to get them out. Now the captain takes his afternoon tea in front of your photo.

And I, poor fool that I am, lie every night and moon over it. "Oh, when, cruel damsel, will you be mine?" I sob into my pillow. But you will be mine. I have been assured you will.

I never told you, but before I departed for this floating bathtub, I went down to Summit and Cherry there in Toledo and had one of those storefront gypsies tell my fortune. She said, "Ah, you are zee lucky one. You will achieve all zat you dezire. I see a dazzling auburn-haired chick in your future." (Or something like that.)

So, you'll have to forget Jack and marry me, because it is fate. If you deny our fate, Zeus and all those guys will be very angry and I will forever be consigned to stay on this tub and be a cranky old sea dog. They might even make some stars out of me. But they have a dog star, don't they?

Well, my dearest, it seems the captain has just demanded my presence—probably has some new problem he wants me to solve—I'll be back and finish this later—

Bemused, Ginny turned the page. She'd never have guessed when she was with him at the USO that he would write such stuff. But she loved it. She almost believed him.

The rest of the letter held mainly funny stories about his shipmates. Only the very end said anything serious.

Here I am, back again. I had to run the ship. The rest of the guys just goof off all day.

We finally got a new officer to replace my pal, Jerry. I think I told you he got killed in the last business. I really miss him. He had two little boys, too.

Don't forget I love you.

Your Lonesome Lover,
Steve

P.S. The gypsies have spoken.
P.S.S. You know what happens if you cross a gypsy, don't you?

She traced the large, flamboyant "S" of his signature with her finger. Kilroy's big nose and bulging eyes peeked over the upper curve. The rest of his name was written in forceful, pointed strokes. Jack wrote his name in the small, hurried squiggles of a man who didn't like to write.

Carefully, she rose and put Steve's letter in the box, her hand lingering over the bundle for a moment. He was a nut, but a sweet nut.

Jack's thin blue letter lay on the bed. She picked it up then let it fall. She felt like a traitor. Tears threatened again, but she blinked them away. It wasn't her fault. She swallowed and lay back to read the letter. Three blacked-out spots marred the small page. The censors must be getting edgy again.

June 1, 1944

Dear Ginny,
They're really keeping us hopping
xxxxxxxxxxxxxxxxxxxxxxxxxxxxxxxxxxxxxxxxxxxxxxxx
xxxxxxxxxxxxxxxxxxxxxxxxxxxxxxxxxxxxxxxxxxxxxxxx
and I don't suppose we'll stay long. So, I wanted to write
while I had the chance.
Today is my birthday and I'm feeling blue. I didn't even
get cookies. I'm an old man of 26 and it seems like a hun-
dred years since I've seen you. Remember the ID bracelet
you gave me for my 23rd, just before I left for Belvoir? I still
wear it.

She lowered the page and sighed. If this war went on much
longer, she'd never get through all this. She hadn't even remembered his birthday. That other one when she'd given him
the bracelet, it had been such fun. They'd gone to Cedar
Point and he'd won her a teddy bear by shooting all the
ducks, and the Ferris wheel stopped while they were at the
top.

She threw the letter on the bed, sniffled and reached for a
tissue. When she'd had her cry, she picked up the letter again.

Goat and I and a couple of others are going downtown
later and get plastered. Well, at least sort of plastered.
Won't have much time to make a good job of it.
Actually, I guess I should be thankful I'm having an-
other birthday. When we were on that landing boat I
wouldn't have bet on it. I think we xxxxxxxxxxxxxxxxx
xxxxxxxxxxxxxxxxxxxxxxxxxxxxxxxxxxxxxxxxxxxxxxxx
xxxxxxxxxxxxxxxxxxxxxxxxso it may be a while before I can
write again.

Last night they xxxxxxxxxxxxxxxxxxxxxxxxxxxxxxxx
xxxxxxxxxxxxxxxxxxxxxxxxxxxxxxxxxxxxxxxxxxxxx
xxxxxxxxxxxxxxxxxxxxxxxxxxxxxxxxxxxxxxxxxxxxx
xxxxxxxxxxxxxxxxxxxxxxxxxxxxxxxxxxxxxxxxx

Annoyed at the loss of his words, she stared at the black lines that ran through the letter like railroad tracks. She wanted to know what he had been through. How he felt. She'd seen those clunky landing boats on the newsreels and pictured him huddled in the shell, terrified. At least she would have been. She'd never have been able to move when the time came. The black-outs in the letter told her he'd probably be on one again pretty quick. The news this morning had been full of New Guinea and the drive on Rome. They wouldn't send him to New Guinea, would they? She stared morosely at the blue page. How can I tell him about Red when maybe he's going into battle again?

The worst part of the whole mess was that she really didn't like Red. But even in her anger at her stupidity, her blood stirred. How could she not like him and still be aroused? She'd been a damn fool. Why'd she ever drink those martinis? He'd made her so nervous.

She remembered his touch, the excitement. He seemed larger than life. At first, the martinis helped her resist him, but she never should have had them. They were always lethal. Carey had been right, she never should have gone out with him in the first place. For a moment, she saw that impeccable uniform topped with the furry head of a wolf. He was an A-1 louse, and she was a fool.

She crumpled Jack's letter and tears rolled down her cheeks. She smoothed the page.

Have you seen Red? I am sure he'll contact you sooner or

later. Tell him the Sarge, Lt. Grimshaw, Goat, and I were all glad to get rid of him. I hope he teaches his greenhorns to shoot better than he does.

And tell him you belong to me. You are out of bounds for anyone but me.

She burst into sobs and tossed the letter across the room. What was she going to do? If only she hadn't gone.

Carey knocked at the door. "Ginny!" When Ginny didn't answer she opened it and stuck her head around the corner. Seeing the tears, she went over and put her arms around her sister. Almost afraid to ask, she summoned her courage, "What's the matter? Is it Jack? Is he okay?"

Ginny sniffled and nodded. "He's okay."

Carey closed her eyes and counted to three. Jack's okay! She pulled Ginny close and held her. Then she saw the crumpled letter on the floor and knew why her sister cried. "It's all right. We all make mistakes."

Ginny jumped back. "What do you mean, we all make mistakes?" What mistake did she mean? Carey couldn't possibly know. But what if she did? What if someone had seen them at the Hillcrest? But that was silly, even if they had, she and Red had a legitimate reason to be there.

She looked her sister over for any sign of an accusation but saw only sadness. She tried to think. She hadn't seen anyone there that she knew. She was sure of it. A shadow of alarm passed over her and slipped away. She was sure of it.

Carey reddened. She hadn't meant to say anything about what she knew. Strictly speaking, it wasn't even her business. It was between Ginny and Jack. But, then Tom—She didn't look at Ginny. "Tom was in the lobby that night. He saw you go upstairs."

The shadow took on the form of a man with crutches. Her

heart sank. She stuck out her chin. "Even if I did go upstairs, it wouldn't mean I—"

Carey looked at her thoughtfully. "No, it didn't. I'm still hoping that's true. You don't have to tell me."

Ginny started to cry again and felt blindly for the box of tissues. It was empty. She sniffled and looked imploringly at Carey. "Do you think Tom will tell him? He already told about Steve kissing me. There wasn't anything to that. He just did it. I couldn't help . . ." The thought of Tom writing to Jack about Red terrified her, but part of her almost wished he would. At least she wouldn't have to tell him, and then it would all be over one way or another. But Tom mustn't. "He can't say anything to Jack. I don't want him going into battle like that corporal—making up his mind not to come back."

Carey stalled. "Tom didn't tell him anything about Steve. He just said you were at the USO and implied that maybe Jack should be concerned."

"The nosy old thing. It's not his business."

"No, it's not. But Jack is his best friend."

Carey went to the linen closet and brought back a new box of tissues. "Here. I know he isn't going to say anything about the Hillcrest for now. He's decided you should have the chance to set things straight. And I think you should forget it for now. We've got plenty of time to worry about these things when they all get home." She closed her eyes again and added to herself, "Please, God, let him come home. In one piece, too."

She took Ginny's hand. "Come on, let's go down and hear the news. I want to see if they've taken Saipan yet." She didn't say aloud that she feared Jack was there. His letter seemed to expect that he would be in battle again soon.

While Carey tuned the radio, Ginny asked, "What did Ted have to say? How old's his letter?"

"He wrote it after D-Day. I talked to Toni and no one has gotten any bad news, so he must be okay. We don't know whether he was in that invasion or whether he's still flying over Germany. His letter says he's fine and busy, in more ways than one."

"What does that mean?"

She pulled a snapshot from her pocket and held it out.

Ginny took it and looked up in surprise. "Do you care?" In the picture, a smiling Ted stood with his arm around a tall, blond girl. She turned it over. "Jean Mees. London. April, 1944."

To Ginny's surprise, Carey's face glowed. "I'm delighted. It gets me off the hook. He said he's asked her to marry him."

"He told you that?"

"Let me read the line." She opened the folded page. "I've known for a long time that it would never work out for me with you. I just wanted to hope. You were my first love and I'll never forget you, especially for having that crush on me when you were a little brat. Great for the ego. It made me feel special. But now, I hope you will forgive me. I fell for Jean at first sight and I fell hard. She's a real trooper. Her family, like an awful lot of the English, has had an incredibly hard time. She lost one brother, a pilot, during the blitz, and another at El Alamein. Her folks are terrific and I know you'll love her. I've asked her to marry me. I hope you can be friends."

Ginny shook her head. "Men." She looked intently at Carey. "You sure you're okay?"

Carey smiled again. "I think it's swell and I'm just fine."

Twenty-Six

Restlessly Ginny glanced about the living room. Would this war ever end? Day after day, the news talked about Saipan. For more than three weeks battles had raged in the Mariana Islands, and only today, the ninth of July, the news reports said the last organized resistance had been overcome on Saipan. She hadn't heard from Jack since the letter he'd written on his birthday. She was sure he was fighting somewhere on one of those islands.

"Mom, I think we should do this room over." Ginny threw down the *Ladies' Home Journal* and got out the little Bissel carpet sweeper.

Her mom stared at the sweeper with a jaundiced eye.

"Well, the big vacuum's too much trouble."

"Ginny, it's eight o'clock at night. Why this sudden urge to clean?" She rose and hugged her daughter.

"We really need new draperies and at least some new pillows. I don't suppose you'd ever buy a new davenport."

Mrs. Fairfax smiled at Ginny the way she might smile at a child who wanted an ice cream cone in the middle of a snow storm. "Then what do we buy next week when you get antsy again?"

Ginny left the sweeper standing in the middle of the room

and plopped down on the sofa. Her mom was no help at all.

A twinkle glinted in her mom's eye. "Well, Virginia, I do need a new set of sheets for your bed. You can get them tomorrow on your lunch hour."

"Gee. Thanks, Mom." She stalked off toward the stairs.

"Virginia. The sweeper, please."

"Yes, Mom." She sighed as though it were entirely too much to ask that she move such a heavy object. But she put it away and went upstairs. If she couldn't get any cooperation, she might as well go up and listen to Bob Hope in her own room, where no one would pick on her.

She took the big box of letters down from the shelf of her closet and pulled out the latest from Jack. Tears threatened. She gritted her teeth. She refused to cry.

If she'd had any idea he'd be gone so long, she could have gone to college like Carey. She'd be graduating. But she'd figured he come home and they'd marry and have a family, and everything would be perfect.

Her hand went to the pile of Steve's envelopes. He hadn't been gone as long but his pile stood higher. The letters were fatter. Funny how the white sparkled at her while the little blue V-mails just managed to look sad.

She sat on the bed and stared at the box. *Dear God, isn't this war ever going to end?* She wondered how long the Japanese would hold out. They were such fanatics. Saipan had been no picnic.

She lay back and closed her eyes. Jack. Oh, Jack. Everything is such a mess. Maybe you're hurt. Maybe you're dead. But we would have heard, so you must still be alive. Are you going to hate me when you get home?

But it didn't seem like he'd be home for years and years. And if the war didn't end soon, she'd be old and ugly and he'd come back and find some young, pretty girl instead. Steve, too, if he ever got off that old tub. She hadn't heard from him either. She'd turn out to be an old maid. She started to hum, "Goodbye Dear, I'll Be Back in a Year." Some year. Would they ever buy that cottage outside of town?

Yesterday when they got out of work, she and Sylvia had splurged for waffles at the Tick Tock. She thought waffles shouldn't be just for breakfast. Jack used to take her for them late at night after the movies.

After she and Sylvia ate, they'd driven out to Perrysburg on her last bit of gas. A "For Sale" sign had taunted her from the middle of a green lawn where a white-frame house with green shutters sat among maples and pines. All of the houses sat back at least forty feet from the road, prim and snug under the protective shade of old, fat trees. Just what she wanted. Would she ever have it?

She looked up at her own ceiling, hoping that God was listening. *Bring him home. Bring him home. Make him forgive me.*

She rolled onto her stomach and started to cry.

The telephone rang in the downstairs hall but she hadn't the energy to get up and answer it. Let Carey get it. It's never for me anymore. Well, Eileen did say that she's going to have a baby. At least someone's happy.

She punched her pillow.

Carey's voice interrupted her moping. "Ginny. It's for you."

Ginny stood and straightened her dress, then shrugged. As if anyone could see over the phone!

Carey stood with her hand over the mouthpiece. She had a strange look on her face.

Ginny caught her breath. *Dear God, no.*

Carey gave a slight shake of her head then held out the phone. "It's Barb, for heaven's sake!"

Ginny flushed. Barb? What could she want? Did she

231

know? How could she know? Red certainly would never tell
her of all people. Ashamed and dreading what she might hear,
she took the phone. When she spoke, her words tumbled out
guilt-laden to her ears, high and off-key. "Barb! Good to hear
from you. It's been ages. How are you?"

A voice so quiet it was difficult to hear said, "Hi, Ginny."

For a long moment, Ginny heard nothing except what
might be a soft sniffling. She grew uneasy. "Barb? Are you
there? Is something the matter?" She thought she heard hic-
cups, or maybe a sob? Finally, Barb managed, "I need an address for Jack."

Ginny gasped. She wouldn't. Barb would never write Jack
about Red. She gave a strangled "Why?"

"Oh, Ginny—" Another strained pause, then, in a broken
voice, she blurted out, "Ginny, Red . . . Red was killed last
week. His rifle blew up. Jack would want to know. I should
have called you before, but I just couldn't."

Ginny winced as though she'd been hit in the stomach.
"Oh, Barb. That's awful. I'm so sorry." She waited, but heard
only more crying. "That's terrible. What happened? He was
still at Camp Perry, wasn't he?"

Barb blew her nose. "He was practicing. He said he should
be able to shoot better than the guys he had to teach." She
sighed. "He always used to laugh about the army putting him
there, of all places. His rifle jammed and exploded."

"Is there anything I can do? I know it's got to be hard, but
would it help to get away? You could come up here."

"I can't. I can't talk about it. I loved him so much." She
cried in huge, gulping sobs. At last she said, "I know Red was
a wolf. But Ginny, he just couldn't seem to help it. I used to
get hurt watching the women with him. He only had to look at
one and they'd fall at his feet. But I know he loved me in his
own way and if it hadn't been for the war, I think we'd be

married." She choked on the words. "I kept hoping he'd grow up, but he never had time."

Anger stirred in the pit of Ginny's stomach. Barb deserved better, but she could hardly say it. "What can I do?"

Ginny heard a deep, resigned sigh, then Barb said, "Nothing." The pause that followed seemed to last forever. Finally, she said, "Maybe I would like to come up and see you. I know we haven't known each other for years and stuff, but it's like we're old friends."

"I think that's a great idea. I'd love to see you." *Actually I wouldn't,* Ginny thought. *How can I face her?*

"But I guess it won't work. I promised his mom I'd come over this Sunday, and then I have to go on a tour. At least I'm supposed to, but I don't want to. You know I joined a USO dance troupe, don't you?"

Ginny started to say, "No . . ." then stopped. She'd started to say, "No, Red never told me." She bit her tongue. Did Barb even know she'd seen Red?

"Ginny?"

Ginny looked at the phone and realized she'd been silent. She spoke quickly. "No, I didn't know, but you're a wonderful dancer, Barb. Best I've ever seen, as a matter of fact."

"I don't know if I can do it, but Mom thinks I should. She thinks I ought to turn professional, and that this tour could be real important."

Relieved that she wouldn't have to face her, Ginny urged, "Oh, Barb, I think it's a great idea. It'll do you good."

Barb's voice brightened a little. "I was invited to go along with a group on a Bob Hope tour. But that won't be for six months, at least."

"You're the best."

Barb sniffed. "I don't know if I can do it without Red. I'm going to miss him so much."

"He was good, but you were the real star."

She didn't answer. Ginny hoped she hadn't said the wrong thing, but it was the truth.

After a moment, Barb managed to say, "Well, this is getting expensive. Do you have Jack's address?"

"APO 27, San Francisco, was the last one."

"Okay. Thanks, Ginny. Send me an invitation to your wedding when Jack gets back."

"Barb, I'm so sorry. Keep in touch will you? And if there's anything I can do—"

Barb's voice broke. "B-bye, Gin-ny."

Ginny sat there, her hand still on the phone after she hung up. Red, dead! A part of her felt vindicated, but then she remembered the man in Virginia with the red hair that almost waved at you from across the room. She saw him dancing with Barb the night they'd won the contest, the self-congratulating grin of his. And she saw Barb's face, too, when he ogled the waitress.

Her stomach tightened into a knot and the guilt flooded back. She had been part of the girl's pain. To make it worse, in spite of the anger and shame she felt, Ginny understood how Barb could have been so crazy about him. If she hadn't been drawn by his magnetism, that whole mess at the Hillcrest would never have happened. But he must have put Barb through hell. It was hard to understand the kind of love that remained through anything. She couldn't love someone who fooled around on her.

Someone who had fooled around. The implications of that thought sent liquid fire throughout her body. She jerked her hand back as if the phone were hot.

Would Red be the kind that "confessed"? Never. Not Red. Brag maybe, but not confess. His conscience never seemed to bother him, so he wouldn't have felt the need to unload his guilt on Barb.

She looked up at her sister who had stood by protectively, listening. "Red's dead. His rifle blew up."

Carey nodded and put her hand on Ginny's shoulder. Her fury for Red allowed him no sympathy. "I'm sorry for Barb. She's better off without him, though. What happened?"

Ginny told her Barb's side of the conversation.

Carey shrugged. It was easy for her not to like him after the way he'd tried to flirt with her at the Goodman dance. But she was even angrier than Ginny about what had happened in the hotel room. Ginny's anger was confused by feelings of guilt, and she struggled with the additional burden of shame. And Jack. And Barb.

Carey said calmly, "I hoped maybe someone, a jealous boyfriend or something, had got mad and shot him. I'm old-fashioned enough to think you reap what you sow."

Ginny reddened. "Oh."

Carey hugged her. "I didn't mean you. You've got to forgive yourself. You put yourself in a bad situation and he took advantage."

"Do you think Jack will forgive me?"

"He has nothing but foolishness to forgive."

"I thought you didn't approve of me."

Carey shook her head. "Who am I to approve or not? I just care about you both too much to want to see either one get hurt. I love you. We're sisters, aren't we?" She hugged Ginny.

"To the bitter end." Ginny hugged her back.

Twenty-Seven

June 1945

Jack shook his head as he watched Goat devour his C-rations, then dug into his own pack. Just another lunch in another foxhole, this one on Okinawa. "Did you ever think you'd see the day when you could down this stuff and be glad you had it?"

"I could eat these damn boots 'bout now."

"Yeah. Think I'd just as soon have boots as rice. When I get home, I'm never going to eat it again. Won't allow the stuff in the house." Jack leaned back against the sand and closed his eyes. A beatific smile spread across his face. "Potatoes and gravy. Chocolate cake. What I wouldn't give for a big red juicy tomato and a tall glass of cold milk."

"Me, I want some of Mom's chicken and noodles over a big pile of mashed potatoes!"

"Damn, I want to go home. I figured when Germany quit, the Japs'd give up." Jack looked over the ocean surrounding the island. Ships of all sizes dotted the horizon. Earlier in the month, the Japs had pulled a series of kamikaze attacks, but the skies and sea were quieter now, except for the U.S. planes that still crawled across the June sky like bedbugs on a blue sheet. The dock bustled with transports. "Do you realize we've been in this stinking army three years and eleven months? I used to dream of being a beach bum. Now I can't wait to get this damn sand out of my shoes. Hope this is the last damn beach we have to take."

"Do you suppose we'll get some warm bodies from the German front?"

"I dunno. I guess they'll have lots of mopping up to do. Might get some fire power out of it, though."

Goat looked at the dark spots on the beach to the south. The sarge said the Japs had pulled out of the Suri Line and were now fighting on the Oruku Peninsula. The marines were beginning their mop-up. The sound of guns was muted but ever present. "I sure hope we don't have to hit Japan. Though in some ways, I'd like to get a crack at those little bastards on their own ground. Give 'em a taste of what they've done to everyone else."

"That'd be sheer hell, though. That first time at Kwajalein . . ." Jack shook his head. Nothing he said could convey the terror of that first invasion. With Goat, he knew he didn't need to finish. He ticked off on his fingers, "Saipan, Tinian, and now Okinawa. Every time, I figured I'd never survive it. I'm still surprised to be here."

"Guess I ought to be thankful for these stupid dog biscuits." Goat curled his lip at the dry cracker in his hand. "And then again, maybe I ain't."

Between mouthfuls, Jack mused, "Speaking of surviving. Just goes to show. We figured Red had it made. Going home and all. Then we get that letter from Barb."

Goat shook his head. "It ain't funny, but it is. What'd ya call it? Poetic justice? The worst shot in the army gets whammied by his own rifle. Didn't the stupid bastard ever clean the damn thing?"

"I always say, when your number's up . . ."

"Well, poor bastard. But I guess he made a lot of women

happy in his day." Goat grinned. "Remember Hawaii?"

"He didn't make Barb happy." Jack found the subject depressing. He'd hate to think someone would make Ginny that miserable. He tossed the subject out with the wrapper of his crackers. The paper fell at a pair of boots planted on the edge of his foxhole. It was almost with relief that he looked up and recognized the boots of his sergeant.

"Andrews, we're going to clean out those Jap caves the marines took." He jerked his thumb at the three men behind him. "Take a detail up there." He nodded at Goat. "You, too, Carter."

Jack took off his helmet and wiped his brow. "What've they got in there, Sarge?" The marines were thorough. Chances were good there wasn't much alive. The problem would be mines or traps, he expected.

"Everything. I don't think anything's moving, but the Japs know their island's next. They've been holed up good here, waiting for us. So watch it. You never know when there's a crazy or even boobies. Be careful."

"Okay." Jack reached into his pocket for a cigarette and touched a piece of paper. Ginny's letter.

On the way to the caves, he thought about the letter. And her. Funny letter. She sounded sad and it was pretty short. It was incredible to him that it had been almost four years since he'd seen her. A long time. Did she really still love him? He reached in and touched the paper, trying to feel her presence, wishing it was her skin he touched instead of just a letter.

Funny how something as fragile as paper could be the only solid part of a relationship. It had become a link between himself and what he remembered as reality. This world of heat and jungle, of bugs and unseen enemies was a shadow world he hoped would one day just disappear. That paper was his passport back. His link with home.

Every time he went on another invasion, the thought of her became the most important thing in his life. Well, her and his rifle. But sometimes, when everything was quiet and he had time to stare at the stars, he wondered why it was so hard for him to visualize her, to hear her voice, her laugh. He touched his pocket again.

Suddenly he stopped and stood still. How could his life depend on a memory?

Goat almost ran into him, then froze and whispered, "What's the matter?"

Jack shook his head and moved forward. "Just had the oddest thought, that's all. Tell you later." He didn't like that thought. He knew he could depend on his rifle because he controlled it. He could depend on his buddies here in hell, but that was different. They depended on him, too. He wasn't crazy about needing some other person that much. When he clung to Ginny, he was clinging to a shadow. More and more, she felt less real to him, especially when he got short letters like this one. He took a deep breath. Later. He'd think about it later.

He held up his hand for quiet as his patrol neared the caves. The five of them moved silently through the brush and halted about a hundred feet from the entrance. The black mouth resembled an oversized domino once screened by vegetation. The marines had pretty well cleared that. Jack watched, but nothing moved.

From behind his shoulder, Goat spoke quietly. "How about a grenade?"

Jack nodded. Couldn't be too careful.

Goat pulled the pin and tossed the grenade at the domino.

Jack hardly noticed the noise, he was so used to it. Dust and debris flew into the air, clods and bits of stone showered the ground in sharp, flat-toned barks. Then all was quiet again. Nothing moved.

Jack nodded and the men darted forward, zigzagging in their leapfrog to the entrance. He slid around the wall and disappeared into the blackness, rifle ready. The stench of rotting flesh slapped him in the face like the whack of the water when he dove into the river at home. Inside the cave, the putrid odor was worse than the smell of the dead bodies on the beach. The foul air surrounded and swallowed him, forcing an involuntary "Ugh."

No sound answered him.

He motioned to the others and one of the men slipped in the opposite side of the cave entrance and was absorbed by the darkness. Jack learned the man's position from the stifled grunt that rose from him. He hoped they all weren't going to toss their cookies.

Goat slunk in front of him and flattened himself against the wall.

Still nothing.

The fourth man crept in on the opposite side and the fifth took Jack's place as he led the way inward. His foot hit something and he pitched forward, landing on a lump. He stretched out a hand and touched cloth and something that felt like a log. He drew back his hand and rolled away. It stunk. He shuddered.

He turned on his flashlight, surveyed the cave, then focused on what had tripped him up—the leg of a Jap soldier. The other men's lights joined his.

The front of the cave was maybe thirty feet across. The damp, rough lava wall was reinforced with concrete in places. It circled, then diminished and disappeared around a bend. Four dead men lay sprawled across the far end. The walls were stacked with broken crates and boxes.

He trained his light on the bend. Nothing. Not a sound.

Except for themselves, not a movement.

They inched forward, rifles ready, but Jack was sure from the odor he wouldn't find anyone alive. At least he hoped not.

As they rounded the wall, the tunnel opened into another space, smaller than the first. But then, maybe it only looked smaller because it was jam-packed, piled with empty crates, empty shell cases, and opened tins of food. All the evidence of life in a rabbit hole. Five more bodies sprawled on the floor, flopped against the crates.

One soldier lay in front of him, neatly stretched across the entrance as if to bar their way. Jack lifted the man's shirt gingerly with his bayonet, holding his breath, not from the smell this time but for fear the body was booby trapped. No wires. The trousers lay flat against the softened, lifeless form. He poked at one side. Only rotting flesh.

"Here. Someone give me a hand." He reached for the Jap's wrist, grasped with both hands and pulled. The arm came away in his hands. He stared at it for a moment. "Awwwgh!" he gagged and dropped the arm.

They all stared for a moment, then began to shake with a mad, convulsive laughter. Jack closed his eyes and clenched his hands, then looked for a place to wipe them. He shuddered at the sensation of that arm, still clinging to his hands like the ghostly pain of an amputated limb. He'd never get over the feeling of that thing in his hands. And he'd never forget the sound of that laughter, its mixture of fear and relief, exploding like a grenade, growing larger and louder as it rebounded from the cold, dark walls.

Twenty-Eight

September 1945

Jack and Goat leaned over the crowded railing to watch the San Pedro harbor pier loom into view. Jack raised his fist and brandished it at the sky. "We made it, Goat! By damn, we made it! San Pedro, California. U.S.A. I am going to kiss the ground. Yes, I am."

Goat clapped his hands, picked up Jack's duffle bag, and swung it hard toward the rail. Jack dove for it and held on for dear life.

Goat laughed. "You won't be needing that anymore, old buddy. You're home." He let go of the bag.

"Yeah. Home." He swallowed hard. Home. Ginny. Mom and Dad. Littlebit. "Yeah."

Not even an hour ago, as the first faint outlines of the coast appeared, then turned into a real, live homeland, the whole ship had resounded with a roar loud enough to scare the fish for a mile around. Now these men, who, like Jack, had been gone the whole four years of the war, were quiet.

Jack sneaked a look at Goat to see if he had tears in his eyes, too, then looked up to the heavens. *Thank you, God.* He felt like an old man who had carried a burden for years and now, finally relieved of it, he was left weak and trembling.

He watched the ship dock. He was home. Home. Hell was

behind him. The loneliness, the fear. He looked at Goat again. But yes, his friends were behind him, too. He wanted to reach out and hug him, but he didn't. He wanted to say, "I love you, pal." But he didn't. Instead, he wiped his eyes.

Goat sniffled and rubbed his fist across his nose. "Great moment, ain't it?"

Jack smiled and punched him. He pulled out his little brown book.

Goat laughed. "What timeless line do you have for us this time, Mr. Pyle?" He watched Jack write for a moment. "Too bad Ernie was killed over there. I'd have liked to read what he'd have to say about coming home."

Jack hadn't shown Goat the book since Saipan. Some of the things he'd written about Okinawa he'd torn out. There was more than he wanted to remember. Now he showed him the last pages, starting with the day Hirohito decided he'd had enough.

Japan asked for peace today, Aug. 10, 1945. Friday, Okinawa time. A great barrage of gunfire went up tonight in celebration. A great day for all of us, if it's true. Most of us here have seen the whole war through. We were at Pearl Harbor when the first blow was struck and on Okinawa when the last blow was struck, Okinawa being the last major invasion until we walk into Japan.

Goat turned the page:

We pulled out of Okinawa harbor at 8:15 Tuesday morning, August 21, 1945, in convoy. Arrived at Pearl Harbor, 7:00 a.m., Wednesday, September 7th.

Jack, watching him read the dates, shook his head. Once

again, he was struck by the oddity of the numbers. Beginning with the eleventh, his draft date, they were full of sevens, like a huge craps game. He had come home a winner of sorts, home in one piece. July 11, October 17, and December 7, 1941. August 14, August 21st, and September 7, 1945. On that July 11, 1941, he'd been inducted for a year's service. Once again, he told himself, it had been a hell of a year.

Goat looked at his watch, five after ten. He read aloud Jack's last entry. "We arrived in San Pedro harbor at 10:00 a.m., Wednesday, September 12, 1945." He laughed as he handed it back. "It's a good thing you don't write history books."

Jack leaned over the railing and watched the churning of the water alongside the ship. He hunched his shoulders. "That says it all, doesn't it?"

The ship shuddered and vibrated under his feet as it came to a full stop. Four years of pent-up passion suddenly shook him just as hard as the ship had. His chest was clamped by a hot straight-jacket, the burning stiffness moving up to constrict the muscles in his throat. He couldn't speak or release his grip on the rail. He stared at the harbor and tried to swallow, but his mouth was drier than C-ration crackers. Then the crush of bodies pressing against him and the noise and chaos penetrated. He picked up his duffle bag, and he and Goat joined their buddies surging eagerly toward the gangplank.

Jack paused at the bottom and took a deep breath. Slowly, resisting the shoves from behind, he put out his foot and with an emotion too profound for even a tear, put his foot again on his native land.

Home.

Jack and Goat, discharge papers in hand, bags at their feet, faced each other at the train station. The platform was a madhouse, but for them, they were the only two.

Goat shoved Jack on the shoulder as the conductor shouted the all-aboard. He was headed back to New York. He gave Jack an odd look, then said, "Oh, hell." He grabbed him in a bear hug. "You son-of-a-bitch, I love you, and I ain't gonna forget you."

Jack, still reluctant to hold a man so close, dropped his defenses and hugged him back. They'd lived a friendship that nothing could ever equal. He swallowed hard and managed a gruff, "Me, neither." He sure as hell wasn't going to cry.

But they looked at each other with blurred vision.

Goat smiled weakly and finally said, "I wish Red was here." He blinked and picked up his bag. "I'll write, buddy. You, too."

Jack nodded, then grinning, offered Goat a mock salute. His own train wouldn't be along for half an hour. "When you get your own cab, I get to ride free. On my honeymoon."

"Give Ginny a big kiss from me and tell Carey thanks for all those cookies." He laughed and shook his head. "The only thing I'm gonna miss about the army is those cookies." He mounted the steps of his train and waved. "You got it, pal, don't forget. Free rides when you come to New York. Artists have to live in New York."

Goat's train pulled out. Jack waved a last time, picked up his bag, and settled on a bench to wait for the train to take him back to Toledo. Back to Ginny.

Twenty-Nine

September 1945

"Stop!" Jack's voice trembled. He rolled down the window of the cab.

The cabby pulled up to the corner, then turned his wrinkled face to peer at Jack in question.

Jack inhaled and unclenched his fists. This was harder than he'd thought. For four years he'd dreamed of coming home. He wiped his sweaty palms on his trousers. He felt as if he were back in the jungle, only this time, the panic was of his own creation.

Everything looked about the same as it had when he'd left. Left for a year. Well. The trees still spread their shade on the lawns and roofs, the houses still stood in their not-very-neat little row. They looked a little more worn, perhaps, but weren't we all a little older and wearier?

What would his mom look like? Fear settled into the pit of his stomach, then a glow began to spread through him as he pictured her face when she saw him again. He smiled. "Let's go."

The cab slowly rolled down the block. "Say when."

The empty lot where he used to play ball lay beneath a shaggy growth of weeds. On the next lot, old Grumpy Galoshes pushed his lawn mower up and down his small front yard. The neighborhood kids hadn't known Grumpy well. Poor guy was a bit of a loner and just old. But he always wore big, thick boots, winter and summer, so the kids made fun of him. Did the old man know what they called him? Jack grinned, wondering what Grumpy would do if some strange GI jumped out and hugged him.

Jack could hardly speak and the cab nearly passed the gray frame house. In a last minute panic, he nearly yelled it: "Here. Stop. That's it. The gray one."

He gazed at it, devouring the details, the swing on the porch, the slight bow of the third step. His dad must have just cut the grass. It was as smooth as a crew cut on a new recruit. Bordering the walk, clumps of yellow and gold autumn mums basked in the late afternoon sun, their colors tawny and earthy. The tones, serene and unaffected by unimportant events like global war, were balm to his soul, restful after the hot, brash vegetation of the tropics.

The gray paint on the house wasn't as fresh as he'd remembered, and here and there some cream color showed through where the gray had flaked. Maybe he could give it a coat for his dad. Paint had probably been hard to get. He hoped his dad wasn't sick or anything. But flakes and all, it had never looked more wonderful.

He saw no sign of Mom or Littlebit. At the end of the block, a man and a woman walked toward him, and a few yards down, a strange kid dug in the dirt. It was about four-thirty. His mom would be in the kitchen, his dad still at work. Littlebit. Would she look all grown up? Was she thirteen? Fourteen? He wondered if she'd gotten a figure yet. He'd missed the brat. He couldn't wait to tease her again.

The cabby had waited patiently for a sign from Jack. He'd even turned off the meter. Finally, the old man cleared his throat and slowly unfolded himself from behind the steering

247

wheel. He walked around the car and reached for the passenger door. Jack beat him to it but allowed him to lift the duffle bag from the seat. Jack's feet stuck to the sidewalk, unable to move. His heart flip-flopped. He was home.

He fished in his pocket for some money. "Keep the change."

The cabby grinned at him and shook his head. "Uh-uh. No tip. If I had my way, I wouldn't even charge." He held out his hand. "Glad you're home. We been waitin' for our boys."

Jack swallowed hard and smiled back, enjoying the gap-toothed grin of an old, wizened face. Something else he'd missed, well-worn faces, not just weary ones. "Thanks." He turned back to the house and forced his rubbery legs to take their first step. Then he strode quickly until he reached the wooden steps, where he slowed and tip-toed. The door stood open as usual and he reached for the screen, its handle snug and familiar in his hand.

He opened the screen noiselessly and tried to ease it shut. It closed with a snap. He'd forgotten how tight the springs were.

He smelled browning beef and onions, and what? Bay leaf and celery. His mouth watered. The odor brought back the old family dinners with their familiar smells. As he walked through the living room toward the kitchen, he detected the lemony scent of furniture polish. His mom was a great one for elbow grease.

Her voice came from the kitchen. "Lizbet? Hurry up and get changed. I could use a hand."

Jack grinned, set his bag down, and tiptoed into the room. "What's for dinner?"

Her back was to him. At the sound of his voice, she jumped and dropped a tin of muffin batter. She whirled and flung herself at him. "Jack! Omigosh! You're home." She started to cry. "You're finally, really home." Her tears turned to sobs. "I was so afraid for you."

He held her and hugged her, touching her hair, almost crying himself. "It's okay, Mom. I *am* home."

She pulled away and started to laugh and sniff.

He bent over and picked up the tin.

"Here. Let me get it," she scolded. "You aren't going to lift a finger for a month." She took a rag from the sink and wiped up the batter splashes. "Guess I'd better make another batch."

"Where's Littlebit? How's Dad?"

"She should be back any minute and your dad's just fine."

He walked to the refrigerator and poured himself a glass of milk, then opened the vegetable drawer and pulled out a huge, dark red tomato. A real Ohio tomato. He bent over the sink and bit into it, letting the juice drip down his chin and into the sink. "Mmmmmm."

"Have you talked to Ginny? Does she know you're home?"

He shook his head. "I wanted to surprise her, too." He looked at his watch. Not quite five-fifteen. "She's probably at work. I'll try about five-thirty."

He lifted the lid of the big kettle and inhaled, sniffing again and again. "When I lived here, I thought Waikiki would be heaven on earth, but this is the real paradise."

His mom stirred the stew. Grabbing a fork, she speared a large potato and half a carrot, then handed it to him. She frowned, "Sorry it's only stew, but at least there'll be enough."

He laughed, "Anything but rice—" He was cut off by a yelp from the living room.

"Jack! Jack!"

He poked his head around the doorway as Littlebit flew at him and flung her arms around his neck.

"Hey, take it easy, kid. I'm fragile. You've got a grip like a bear." He eased out of her hug and held her at arm's length.

"Look at you. Almost grown up." He twirled her around. "How many boyfriends do you have?" She was prettier than he imagined a tomboy could be. A couple more years and she'd be a real knockout. Blond, straight hair. He could see a resemblance to himself at that age. Maybe just a trace of childish plumpness, but her features and bones were delicate.

She made a face and pushed him. "The boys in my class are all jerks." Then she laughed and said, "Except for maybe one. And I am all grown up, big brother."

His mom interrupted. "Give me a hand, Lizbet. We need to eat and let Jack get to Ginny."

Jack thought he caught a dark look on Littlebit's face. Could his little sister be jealous?

He asked, "Okay, Mom. What do you want me to do?"

"You can put the silver out."

"I wasn't supposed to do anything for a month, remember?"

She hugged him hard. "Oh, Jack. I can't believe you're home!"

He'd just finished laying out the silverware when the screen door to the kitchen opened. "Dad!" Jack's heart twisted. The old man looked like an old man, but he brightened as he saw his son. Some of the youth returned to his face.

His dad put his arms around him and crushed him. Their tears mingled.

Misty-eyed, Mrs. Andrews cleared her throat. "It's five-thirty. If you want to call Ginny, I'll hold dinner."

Jack pulled back, then clamped his hand on his dad's shoulder and gave it a squeeze. He turned toward the phone in the living room.

LAwndale 2-3459. The dial spun out the numbers one by one. He listened breathlessly to the ringing.

"Hello?"

Jack's heart leaped with a thump, one loud enough, he was sure, for Ginny to hear on the phone. "Ginny!" Her name came out like a croak and he cleared his throat.

"Hello?" She sounded impatient.

He laughed. Evidently she hadn't changed much. He spoke up. "Ginny? It's me, Jack!"

"Jack?" He heard a quick intake of breath, then she squealed. "Jack? Oh God, it really is you. It is, isn't it? Really you? Oh, Jack." She started to cry. "Where are you? Where are you?"

He pictured her face framed by that auburn page boy. He hoped she still wore it that way. "Home, Ginny. I'm home."

"Oh, God, Jack. I've been so afraid, so afraid something might happen at the last minute." She laughed and cried at the same time. "You really made it."

Yes, he'd made it. His heart skipped a beat. "Are you going to be home tonight?"

She sniffled. "No, you dope. I have a date. Oh, Jack. Of course I'll be here." She started to cry again. "Oh, Jack, I love you."

"Seven-thirty. I love you, too."

"Hurry."

Thirty

Deliriously happy, yet plagued with worries that it would never be the same with Jack, Ginny put the phone down.

She thumped down on the chair next to the hall table, the dial on the phone staring at her like a cyclops. Jack was finally home. Here. In Toledo. She wanted to scream from the roof, "Jack's home," but no one was around to hear. Instead, she jumped up, twirled and clapped her hands together. Carey would die when she heard. Where was Carey, anyway?

Her feet fairly danced up the stairs. What can I wear? I've got to wow him. Sliding clothes back and forth on the rod impatiently, she pulled out her new blue dress. There. He'd like that. The light wool was soft and feminine, and draped romantically across the front. Not too dressy, either. She turned to the mirror and pressed the dress against her waist.

Her face looked thin. Had she lost too much weight?

She yanked off her clothes and jumped into a steamy shower that turned her into butter. She found herself humming, and laughed aloud when she realized which song she hummed. Oh, well. She sang it loudly, defiantly, exorcizing a ghost. "Goodbye dear, I'll be back in a year, cause I'm in the army now . . . We'll buy that cottage just outside of town and

I'll never sing this again." She shouted to the world, "Yippee!"

When she stepped out of the shower, she gloated at the girl in the mirror and grabbed the fattest, newest towel she could find for a brisk rubdown.

"He's home, he's home." She sang again and slipped into the new satin slip saved for this very day.

"Don't think I've heard that one. What are you singing about?"

She hadn't heard her sister come in. She rushed at her and hugged her. "Oh, Carey! Jack's back. He's out!" Ginny hugged her. "He's home."

Carey blanched and shook with terror and excitement. Jack was back! Home and alive! But she couldn't face him, could she? How could she and let him walk away? But she had no choice, had she? She managed to say, "That's s-swell." Her face became a battleground. She lost and started to cry.

Ginny stepped back, surprised at first by the reaction, then deciding they were tears of relief. She'd been terrified, too, that something might happen at the last minute. After all this time, it was almost too good to be true. She put her arm around Carey's trembling shoulders. "He's okay, Sis. He's okay. He's out."

Carey hugged her again, smiled weakly and repeated, "Yeah, it's swell. Is he coming to pick you up?"

Ginny danced some quick, little steps. "Yes. Seven-thirty. You gonna be here?" She knew how much her sister would want to see Jack but she hated to share the moment.

Carey looked at the books in her arms and turned to leave. She said with a catch in her voice, "No, I've got to go to the library. Give him my love and tell him I'm glad he's finally back." She hurried off to cry in her own room. At least I won't have to bake any more of those darned cookies, she muttered to herself.

She didn't cry long. She had to get out of the house. Get away from Ginny's happiness. She walked downstairs and out the door.

Ginny was so happy she didn't notice the door slam or think about Carey's roller-coaster emotions. Her sister ceased to exist as she dressed for Jack.

Wonder if he's changed much? Will he look tired and worried? Very much older? It must have been awful for him.

She put the finishing touches on her hair and makeup, slipped on the blue dress, and surveyed her figure in the mirror. How does a guy act after he's been in the army for four years? Would he still be the same with her? Would he still take "no" for an answer? She wanted to be with him, but she didn't dare. If she ever got pregnant before . . . well, her mom would die. And she'd never be able to walk down the aisle in that white Skinner satin dress she'd been looking at in Lamson's department store. Carey'd be the maid of honor, and Sylvie and Eileen and . . .

She did another little jig. Jack was home. Four years. She remembered the call when he'd asked her to marry him. Then when he'd asked her again because he felt so silly about that call.

It had all been so long ago.

Could a guy who'd been in the army four years really not have had a bunch of girls? Part of her said it wasn't realistic to think he had never strayed. Yet part of her believed that guys could be true. She blushed, remembering Red. But it hadn't been her fault.

She gazed into the brown eyes reflected in the mirror through a gathering pool of tears. She dabbed at them carefully, trying not to smear her mascara. If she didn't ask him about other women, she wouldn't have to tell him about Red, Tom or no Tom. She hoped.

She put on the pearls he'd given her that first Christmas and frowned. Even after all this time, it still bothered her that his mother had picked them out. But they looked great.

She picked up her bag and went downstairs. What time was it? The clock said seven thirty-five. Women were the ones who were supposed to be late.

She sat crossing and uncrossing her legs on the little chair. She stared at the phone, casting a spell on that cyclops, forbidding it to ring. What if he'd changed his mind about her and was going to call and say he didn't love her anymore. But he'd said, "I love you."

She had said it first, though.

She rose, looked into the hall mirror, and made a face at herself. "Smile, girl, smile." She'd forgotten to ask how long he'd been home. Why hadn't he told her he was coming? She'd dreamed of him stepping down from the train, searching anxiously through the crowd for her. Then, there she'd be, in his arms, smothered with kisses. Now, maybe he wasn't even going to show up.

She sat again, her panic increasing, telling herself she was being irrational. Of course he loved her. Maybe on his way over, he'd heard a fire truck and gone chasing after it like he used to. She giggled giddily.

A car door slammed. She jumped at the sound and ran to pull back the curtain that covered the window in the front door. Oh, God, he's here. She started to tremble. *Don't be so silly*. She opened the door before he knocked. He stood there grinning from ear to ear, tanned and lean, his hair almost white from the tropical sun, his eyes bluer than she'd remembered. She suddenly felt shy and awkward and couldn't move.

He took her in his arms. "Ginny!" He smothered her face with kisses.

Between kisses she murmured, "Oh, God. Jack." She forgot to be intimidated by time and distance. Jack. At last. She was in his arms at last. The world beyond his touch vanished in a blur.

The kisses slowed for a moment and Ginny looked up. The door stood open and Mrs. McGillicuddy was watching from across the street, smiling.

Ginny grinned back, waved and kicked the door shut, taking him by the hand into the living room.

"Your mom and dad home?"

She'd forgotten how blue those eyes really were. Like an October sky. She gazed back, hungrily. He was gorgeous. She reached up and mussed the deep waves in his hair. "They went to play cards."

She felt him drape his arm about her, pulling her close, pressing his lips against hers, exploring again the softness, the fullness. He pressed his hands into her back.

The flood of passion in her response overwhelmed and frightened her. Things could get out of control quickly. She pulled back a little. "Let's take a breather. This is pretty fast."

Jack held onto her. "We're engaged, remember?"

"Mmm." She held out her left hand. "That's not what this says."

He nuzzled her neck, nibbling at her ear. "Want to go fix that tomorrow?"

She caught her breath, then pulled back and looked him in the eye. "Really?"

"Really."

Jack slid his hands down the hair that framed her face and

looked into her eyes. He let his gaze devour every inch, every pore of her face.

An inexplicable sadness suddenly overwhelmed him. He loved this girl, yet her face was almost that of a stranger. He hadn't looked upon it for four years and he had known it for such a short time before he went away. Did he really know the woman behind this face at all? Who was she really? For that matter, who was he? Not the same soldier who had danced with her in Virginia.

They had written letters, but paper and ink were too stifling to reveal much and he wanted to know the real Ginny, not some fantasy. They would almost have to start over. He started to kiss her again.

She returned the kiss for a long moment, then reached for a tissue and wiped the lipstick on his face. "Better go upstairs and wash that off. You're covered from the chin up."

When he came back, her face was bare of lipstick. She led him to the kitchen and opened the refrigerator. "Have you eaten? There's not much there." She laughed. "Carey hasn't baked any cookies for a while. Have you eaten?"

"Ah. Carey. Where is she? She okay?"

"She's at the college library. Said to tell you she's glad you're back safe." She opened the fruit drawer. "See anything you like?"

"Mmm. Mom had dinner. But I've got a yen for milk." He helped himself to a glass and drank it down like a starved child. "I don't think I'll ever get enough again."

"I haven't eaten, but I'm not really hungry." She brushed against him as she put the empty glass in the sink.

"Ginny, you're beautiful. It's been so long—" He took her in his arms. "Food can wait." He kissed her hungrily, then lay his cheek against hers.

"Do you love me still?" She sounded wistful.

He laughed again and hugged her. "Of course I love you, you silly goose."

"Where do you think we ought to go on our honeymoon?"

"Not Hawaii." He gave her that lopsided grin of his, the one that came when he thought he was being clever. "Depends." Mischief glinted in his eyes. "Are you still a virgin?"

That stupid joke of Red's! She blanched and drew back sharply. The world instantly crashed down at her feet. Why had Jack said that now? But, of course he didn't mean it. It was that joke.

He drew her to him and kissed her tenderly, but her bottled-up guilt overwhelmed her. Tears began to flow and turned into an avalanche.

He pulled back to look at her. "Poor Ginny. It's been tough, hasn't it?" He brushed the tears away delicately. "You don't doubt my love, do you?"

She turned away. "No, I . . . I just . . ." She couldn't say any more.

He took her shoulders and turned her back, staring at her with a puzzled expression. "Ginny?"

Ginny thought, he has no idea what he said. I should ignore it. He couldn't have been serious about his question.

She'd never made up her mind whether to tell him about Red, but what if Tom did? It would sound a lot worse because Tom didn't know the whole story. Maybe she should tell him now and get it over with. She was so tired of feeling guilty, so tired of trying to brush it away when it nagged her no matter what she told herself. "I . . ."

His expression told her he was getting impatient. She turned away quickly. "I need a drink. Want one?"

He frowned and shook his head.

She got a bottle from the cupboard and poured a shot of bourbon. She tossed it down, and it burned all the way. She made a face, shuddered, and poured another, gulping it before she changed her mind. She needed it. She was terrified of what he might say.

He eyed the bourbon with a raised brow. "Okay, Ginny, I give up. What's the matter?"

She lifted her chin and looked at him defiantly. She might as well get it over with. He had to understand. And she couldn't let Tom tell him first. Anyway, how many girls had he been with? In desperation and growing anger fed by alcohol, she glared at him. "Are you a virgin, Jack?"

"With that tone of voice, that's a hell of a question."

"Well, you asked me."

He stared at her, his tan face darkened. "Is that what this is about?"

She swallowed, afraid again. She lowered her eyes, unable to look at him. "Jack . . ."

"Yeah?" His voice was angry now.

"You know that when Red came home, he stopped here . . ."

He stared at her. He almost yelled. "You and Red?"

She opened her mouth but no words came. She reached out for him. After an awful moment she managed, "Jack, it wasn't . . ."

He didn't wait for her to finish. He glared at her, then turned and walked out the door, slamming it hard behind him.

Stunned by the swiftness of his reaction, she ran after him. In her panic she struggled with the doorknob, finally yanking the door open. As he stepped off the porch, she reached him and pulled at his arm. "Jack, it wasn't like that. Please, listen."

He jerked his arm away and kept on walking, his head high, his feet hitting the pavement so hard Ginny thought the concrete might crack.

His only word, hurled in pain, wrapped in fury, flew back at her. "Red."

She held out her hand. "Jack. Listen. It wasn't like that. Please, stop." Wasn't he even going to listen? It hadn't been her fault. She shouldn't be blamed. "It wasn't my fault. He got me drunk. I didn't know." But the car door had slammed and the engine snarled.

Jack gunned the engine. The car roared away.

"How many women did you have?" she yelled after him. She ran inside, slammed the door, and threw herself onto the couch and sobbed. She'd make him listen later. She had to.

Thirty-One

The Same Night

Carey claimed a table for herself at the university library, glad that she didn't have to make conversation.

She planted her elbow and leaned her forehead against her hand, shielding her face as she got out her microbiology text. She stared at it vacantly. Why be upset? Why cry? Jack was safe. He was home.

But he hadn't come back to her. He never would. He was Ginny's. She couldn't stand to see them together. Not tonight, anyway.

The words in the book in front of her didn't make sense. Determined to work her problems away, she read the page again but finally put it down and reached for her English lit, Joyce's *Ulysses*. His nocturnal wanderings around Dublin didn't interest her, either. Her own internal storm was enough.

She closed her eyes and tried to black out the world. So Jack was home. She'd known he'd come home someday. To Ginny. She'd known he'd be one of the first out with all the points he'd racked up. But the turmoil of her feelings when she realized he would really be here, with Ginny this very night, that she would have to face them sooner or later, had been a surprise.

261

How could the crush of a sixteen-year-old turn into this? What was so special about Jack that she should care after all these years, knowing he wasn't hers? Or was it because he wasn't hers that it had lasted so long? She thought about all his letters. Never too intimate, just warm and friendly. But they had been revealing. He'd shown her an introspective side she couldn't have guessed at.

Ted's great love for her hadn't lasted four years. There he was, over in England with his new bride. For the first time, she was angry with him. Not that she loved or wanted him—she felt betrayed that it had been so easy for him to forget her and get on with his life. Yet, that was what she'd tried to push him into doing.

Irritated at herself, she elbowed her books and *Ulysses* fell to the floor. She flinched and looked furtively around. Several pairs of amused eyes met hers and glanced away again.

She frowned down at the book spread on the floor and decided it was a symbolically appropriate place for Joyce and his hero. A place on the floor along with his Dublin alleys and bordellos. She was tempted to leave him there, but chose to be responsible and picked up her books, stuffing them into her bag. The cafeteria wouldn't be open but the restaurant down the street would be.

There was coffee but it was awful, probably left over from lunch. To banish the burnt taste, she ordered a hot fudge sundae with extra fudge, whipped cream, nuts, and defiantly, an extra maraschino cherry. The combination reminded her of the chocolate-covered cherries that were a Christmas tradition with her family. The memory of those candies consoled her a little with its reminder of family love and stability. The important fact was that Ginny and Jack would be together and Ginny would be happy.

"Hi. Want some company? Or do you need the whole table

for that concoction in front of you?"

"Tom! Every time I see you, I'm eating." She grinned sheepishly and poked her spoon at the mound of whipped cream. Embarrassed, she scooped up one of the maraschinos and offered it to him.

Tom laughed. "No, I'm done. I was over there when you came in. Guess you didn't see me."

"No. I wasn't paying attention."

"I noticed. Anything wrong?"

Suddenly, the fudge was no longer appealing as she remembered the cause of her misery and this binge. She pushed the sundae away. "Jack's home."

Tom smiled broadly at the news, but as he watched her face, he grew concerned. "That should make you happy. Shouldn't it?"

Her heroic decision that only Ginny's happiness mattered didn't seem as grand at the moment. She looked down at the napkin in her lap, confused and ashamed of her feelings. "Yes, it's just dandy. He's with Ginny right now and I'm having a green fit." Tears came to her eyes. "I just didn't know I would hurt like this.

"With him clear out in the Pacific, I was safe enough. All I had to worry about was him getting home alive. And here I am, jealous as a kid, watching my big sister with the prize." She sniffed and reached for a napkin.

He patted her arm. "Hang in there, honey. Those two just aren't going to last."

Carey frowned sharply as jealousy, hope, and loyalty clashed in a full-scale war within her. "Tom, they're getting married. They love each other and I haven't any right to feel the way I do."

"Carey, be honest with yourself. I doubt if Ginny has ever had a serious thought in her head. Of course she thinks she wants to marry him. But what she really wants is to marry Robert Taylor and live happily ever after. Jack just happens to fit that image."

Carey glared at him. How dare he say such things about her sister? She pulled the sundae toward her, dug her spoon into the melting mound and choked down three bites. A lump in her throat forced her to stop. "How do you know? What do you know about them, anyway?"

"That's two questions. One, as far as Ginny's concerned, we used to double date, remember? She's a nice girl, but she's young for her age. You're more mature than she is."

She squirmed inwardly. She was being pushed into a corner and his criticism made her angry. Ginny was her sister and good enough for any man. Even Jack. "You mean he's too good for her? She deserves a nice guy."

She knew her charge wasn't true, but she skipped past it. There was truth in Tom's analysis. Ginny was a total romantic, and Carey suspected Ginny hadn't any idea what love, and the sacrifices that love required, were all about. But the cold, hard fact was that her sister had Jack and she couldn't leave the door open for herself to enter their world. She couldn't even dare to dream.

Tom answered the rest of her question. "Point two. As far as knowing Jack, we go way back. He's one of the world's real innocents, a good guy who thinks everyone else ought to be just as good."

Carey pushed her sundae away again and dabbed with a napkin at the path of melted ice cream left by its slide. "C'mon, Tom. He's been in the army four years. He must have changed. At least a little."

Tom shook his head. "Not that way. When we were growing up, he had this girl. They were sitting on the swing and she kissed him, then unzipped her dress—"

264

Carey chuckled. "Yes, Ginny told me about that. Mary someone."

Tom looked surprised but let it pass. "The point is that Jack is just very moral." He laughed. "He'd like to be a little wild, I think, or at least he thinks it would be fun to try, but his nature won't let him. He's just a good guy."

"What are you trying to say?"

"The point is that he doesn't understand when anyone else isn't what he thinks they are or should be."

"If he loves her, he'll understand. It really wasn't her fault. You only saw her go upstairs." She told Tom about the martinis, and how Red had promised Ginny coffee and a nap.

He listened impatiently and when she was done, sat back and waved his hand in annoyance. "Well. She should have known better."

Carey suddenly realized that Tom didn't want to believe the story. In a way, it was flattering. He actually wanted *her* to end up with Jack, but the idea was futile. It wasn't going to happen.

Tom leaned forward and ran his finger around his coffee cup. "I guess that does put a different light on things." He frowned as he said it, then sighed wearily. "Ordinarily, I don't go around telling stories, and I don't like people who do. But this romance between Jack and Ginny has never seemed right to me. And you have to understand, it's hard to sit by quietly and watch your best friend make the mistake of his life. Especially when you know his family doesn't believe in divorce. It's not as if he could just walk away if things don't work out. It could ruin his life."

"But we can't play God, Tom."

He stirred his coffee vigorously. It splashed and he used Carey's ice cream soaked napkin to move the mess around. "I guess you're right. Especially since she was more stupid than sinning. They'll just have to work it out for themselves."

She reached out and touched his arm. "Thanks." She was tired of this conversation. Tired of struggling. It was time to change the subject. "How's Kathy?"

He beamed like a kid. "I'm going to ask her to marry me."

"That's swell, Tom! I can't wait! When do you think you'll commit this hari-kari?"

"I'm going to ask her Saturday. Have a big evening planned. I'll ask her after dinner. I've got reservations at Charlie Marks. I picked this up today." He reached into his pocket and withdrew a tiny box that revealed a one-carat diamond solitaire.

Carey gasped and tried it on, waving her fingers, admiring the pure white sparkle. She was pleased for Kathy but just a little jealous. Reluctantly, she slipped it off and gave it back. "It's beautiful."

Her voice trembled as she tried to gather her defenses. Now that she wasn't defending Ginny, her vulnerability smothered her again. "You'd better reserve the church, then. With all the guys home, it'll be one busy place." Everyone but her. Oh, hell. She was going to be a doctor. She didn't need some guy cluttering up her life just now.

Tom put the ring away and replaced his beatific expression with a sympathetic look as he stood. "Listen, I've got to go. Will you be okay?"

She swallowed hard and nodded, then dug her spoon into the sundae. She'd eat the damned thing if it killed her.

He hugged her. "If you want to talk anytime, you know how to find me. I hope things work out for you. I guess I shouldn't even think it, but I can't help it, Carey. You and Jack were made for each other."

Carey stirred her cold coffee and didn't look at him. Jack and Ginny were going to marry. Even if they did split up, and even if he did look at her twice, wouldn't it be weird for him to marry his ex-fiancée's little sister? No. It would never work. She had to get on with her life.

He picked up her bill. "I just don't think he'll ever be able to live with Red's actions. I wonder if you realize how judgmental *good* people can be?"

Thirty-Two

Later

Ginny flipped the sofa pillow she'd been sobbing into. It was wet and everyone would be home soon. She ran upstairs, tore off the stupid blue dress she'd worn just for him, and threw it on the floor. If only Red hadn't been such a rat, this whole thing wouldn't have happened. If only Tom hadn't seen her. If. Oh, Lord. What good were all those *ifs?* Her whole life was ruined, Jack would never forgive her. She'd be an old maid. Just because of Red.

A little voice tried to tell her she shouldn't have gone with Red in the first place, but that wasn't fair. He was Jack's friend. She'd trusted him and all she'd wanted was to hear about Jack. Again the voice prompted, *and dance?* No. Yes. Not with Red. It wasn't fair. But shame flooded over her again as the memory of her attraction to Red came back to taunt her.

She kicked off her shoe and it smacked the wall. Tears of frustration and guilt ran down her cheeks unchecked.

Jack had been so angry. She'd never seen him like that. He hadn't even let her finish. Maybe she should call him and try to talk to him.

She took a tentative step toward the stairs and the telephone. Would he be home yet? Would he have gone home?

Maybe she'd better wait. What would she say if he wasn't there? He was supposed to be with her. She couldn't face trying to explain anything to his mother and that snippy little sister of his right now. They'd probably be glad if she and Jack did break up.

Oh, Lord. What am I going to do? I've got to talk to him. He has to listen.

Downstairs, a key turned in the front door. Oh, no. Not now.

"Ginny?"

She stood still and brusquely rubbed the tears from her face. Carey mustn't see she'd been crying. Go away, Carey. *Make her go away,* she prayed. What'll I do? I can't talk about Jack now. Carey was always so disapproving about everything when it concerned Jack. She busied herself pulling on some slacks and a blouse.

Ginny finally gave up the battle to stem her tears and let them roll freely down her cheeks. She loved Carey, but when it came to Jack! A sharp pang of jealousy made her wince. What would happen if she and Jack broke up? What would Carey do? She'd never move in on him, would she? What if she did? Ginny shook her head, afraid to even think about it.

Footsteps sounded on the stairs. Ginny picked up her discarded dress and stepped into the closet. Maybe she'd think no one was here.

"Ginny? Are you home?"

She waited without moving until the steps had gone down the hall, but she couldn't stay in the closet all night, and it was too late to close the bedroom door. She gave up and threw herself on the bed, pounding the pillow, too angry to cry any more. Damn Jack. He could have at least listened. It wasn't her fault.

Carey came back down the hall and stopped in surprise at

the scene on the bed. "Ginny! What's the matter? Where's Jack? Didn't he come?"

Ginny kept her head buried in the pillow. In a voice muffled by the stuffings, she muttered, "I don't know where he is now, and I don't care. Probably out chasing some damn fire engine." She raised her head and hit her fists on the pillow again. The tears flooded back.

"Didn't he show up?" Carey demanded.

"He showed up all right. I hate him."

Carey leaned over and draped her arm over her shoulders. "Of course you don't hate him. It'll be okay, honey."

Ginny sat up and let Carey fold her in her arms. Between sobs, Ginny told her what happened. "He was here and everything was . . ." She threw the damp, misshapen pillow across the room. The stuffed elephant Jack had won for her at a church dinner tumbled from its seat of honor on a chair. "I wasn't going to tell him, but he asked me if I was a—" A new rainstorm broke and she finally managed to wail, "—a virgin."

Carey looked at her, stunned. He couldn't have. He wouldn't. "You mean he actually came out and asked you that? The nerve!"

Ginny shook her head and sniffled, "He was kidding. I knew it. Red made some smart remark about the Virgin Islands that time we were in Virginia, and it's been sort of a standing joke." The memory of Virginia quieted her for a moment. They were so in love then. This had to turn out all right.

She swallowed hard and hiccupped. "But I got upset and he knew something was wrong and I thought about Tom, and he kept asking what was wrong, and then I told him." She wailed. "I knew if Tom told him first, it would sound awful."

Carey got the box of tissues. "Here. It seems like I've been doing this for the past four years."

Ginny nodded and tried to blow her nose, while trying not to laugh and hiccup, too.

"Hold your breath," Carey ordered, but had to laugh herself. "You look like a squirrel with a mouthful of nuts."

Ginny let the air go and smiled weakly for a moment, then started to howl again, "He wouldn't even listen. He just stomped out. What am I going to do?"

"You'll call him tomorrow when he's had a chance to think."

"Maybe you could talk to him." Even as she said it, she knew it was a silly thing to say.

Carey shook her head. "I'm just the cookie kid. I can't stick my nose in, but maybe I could get Tom to talk some sense into him."

Ginny gasped, horrified. "Not Tom. He hates me."

Carey took her sister's hand and shook her head. "He doesn't hate you. It's okay. I ran into him at the coffee shop by the university and we had a long talk. I told him how Red took advantage of you after getting you drunk and he's backed off."

"Great. I just blew my whole life away because he's an old tattletale, and I figured he'd squeal, and now you tell me he's backed off." She started to cry again. "It's not fair. My life is ruined."

"I wasn't even sure you'd tell him at all. I never figured you'd tell him the first time you were together."

"I didn't mean to. It just sort of came out. And Tom with his big mouth wasn't any help." She threw herself back on the bed and covered her face with her hands. "Tom must think I'm a real jerk."

Carey tried to console her. "No, he doesn't, honey. He just thinks . . . well, putting yourself in a spot like that with

Red wasn't smart. But it wasn't deliberate. That ought to count for something." Remembering Tom's words, *I wonder if you know how judgmental good people can be,* she had a sinking feeling the odds were not good.

And as far as Tom went, she wondered if she had spoken too hastily. He still didn't approve much of Ginny. She sighed inwardly. Oh, Lord. It's bad enough that I have to be stuck on the guy, I have to play God and try to fix things up for her.

She truly loved Ginny and wanted her to be happy with Jack, but she ached for herself as much as for her sister. She drew a deep breath and straightened her shoulders. She had to put her feelings for Jack behind her once and for all. He'd never been part of her future and never would be more than a brother-in-law. She would concentrate on more important things, like being a doctor.

Jack walked into The Office Bar and looked around, vaguely remembering the location but not the room. At least it looked like a nice, quiet neighborhood place to relax and forget his troubles, maybe even get drunk. That was one of the promises he'd made to himself over there. He'd been back in the states four days now. Time to fulfill that promise.

He picked up a beer at the bar and looked around for Tom. He waved from the corner booth. Just like old times. Many was the time they'd had that extra beer and many was the time Tom had pulled him away from an argument when things got too warm. He thought again about the night with the squeaking crutches and grinned at his friend.

Tom grinned back and stirred as though he might want to hug him, but Jack gave his friend's shoulder a shove. All of that army macho had left him too embarrassed to be soft around men, even his oldest and best friend. "Okay, you old

SOB. How you been? I won't even ask if you've been behaving yourself."

Tom laughed. "I could ask you the same thing."

"Don't change the subject."

"Times have changed. Kathy keeps me on the straight and narrow."

"Yeah, and old drunks don't hope to be college presidents. How's it going?"

"That, too. How do you like the bar? Ron bought it last year. Used to be the Windmill, remember?"

Jack looked around, realizing why it had struck a familiar yet blank note when he walked in. "Oh yeah, the fishnets are gone. Good name for an alibi."

"Speaking of offices, have you talked to yours? You get your old job back, don't you?"

"Legally, they have to take me back. They probably could find a way around it if they wanted to, but they didn't. I can start right away. Except I'm going to take a few weeks off." He scrutinized the other men in the bar, wondering if any were veterans. Not too many of the right age group around yet. GIs were being demobbed in quick succession, starting with the guys with long service time and points. He wondered how many actually had more points than he did after four years, all overseas.

Jack searched his friend's face and decided Tom didn't look much older. He wondered how he looked to Tom, if the war showed on his face.

Tired of living with war on his mind, he asked, "How's work going? You head of the college yet?"

"Not yet," Tom chuckled smugly. "Tomorrow, maybe. Anyway, it's great. How's Ginny?"

The muscles in Jack's jaw tightened. He studied the foam on his beer with great interest. "I used to dream about this beer on draft. That and big, red, ripe tomatoes."

Tom asked again, "How's Ginny?"

Jack ignored him and took a long drink.

Tom huffed and frowned at him. "You haven't answered me. What's the matter?"

Jack drained the glass. "Why should anything be the matter?"

Tom watched the charade with the beer. Ginny couldn't have told Jack about Red already, could she? If her error had prompted his remark, then he'd been right about Jack's self-righteous streak. He couldn't handle it. Or didn't want to. Tom felt guilty about his ambivalence, but he admitted that Jack and Ginny deserved a chance to get to know each other again. "Okay. Nothing's the matter, but how's Ginny?"

"Who's Ginny?" Jack picked up the glass, walked to the bar, and sat down, pushing his mug toward the bartender.

Tom followed and shoved his beer forward, too. Against his better judgment, he said, "I know it's not my business, but I happen to know the story. Did you listen to her at all?"

Jack ignored him until they got back to their booth. Finally, he said, "What's to listen to? She was with Red. Of all the men in the world, it had to be Red."

"But it wasn't like that. Look, I've never been happy about you and Ginny. I don't think that's a surprise to you. But I hate to have you end this relationship with the wrong idea."

Jack glared at him. "Didn't you hear me, Tom? Red! It was Red. I could forgive anything else."

"I don't think you could. You've been good yourself so every one else has to be." Tom gave a long sigh. "Not that it's bad to be good, but sometimes, when you know you've done the right thing, you just don't have any sympathy for anyone who hasn't." He was growing annoyed. "Didn't you have girls over there?"

"What's that got to do with it?" He pictured Emily with tears in her eyes as they'd said goodbye that last time, the night before his outfit left for Kwajalein. She'd written a couple of times when he was on Saipan, but that had petered out. Still, they had come very close to making love. With a mixture of guilt and pride, he grudgingly admitted, "Actually, I wanted to but I didn't. I kept thinking of Ginny."

Tom nodded and wanted to say *See, I told you so. There's no one as difficult as a good man.* Instead, he tried to explain. "He got her drunk. She didn't know until it was too late." He told Jack the story he'd learned from Carey. "It wouldn't have been much different if he'd grabbed her in an alley."

"Shit." A lump bounced down Jack's gullet to his chest. For a moment, he didn't know whether to laugh or cry or yell. He should have known it wasn't as simple as he'd thought. He should have let Ginny talk. But it didn't make any difference. The damage was done. A wooden man sat in Jack's stead.

He looked at Tom and shook his head. "That's too bad, but it doesn't make much difference." He stared into space and exhaled slowly, as if relieved of a big weight. "At least she didn't do it on purpose."

Tom waited, hoping he'd come to his senses.

"You know, I had this dream all the time I was over there about this wonderful girl. Even then, it was kind of scary when I couldn't see her face or hear her voice anymore. I used to worry about it. It had been so long.

"And since I've been back . . ." He paused awkwardly. "Since, well, you know, I've given it a lot of thought. Do you realize I hardly even know her? It's like the whole relationship was just a fantasy. We'd only gone together a month when I got the draft notice. I didn't mean to get engaged, but everyone was. It seemed the thing to do. Three months before the big hero goes off to the army. Three months to be filled with deathless love that will rise above the threats of separation, war, and death."

His face turned red and he squinted. He wasn't about to cry over this now. "It was all sort of a Charles Boyer movie. What was it? Something about the dawn coming up. Well, we had three months to act out the great tragedy, play like we were in love. And then I went off to camp.

"Do you know how we got engaged?" He gave a bitter laugh. "Red started it, actually. Old Red was quite a lady's man. His girl, Barb, was coming down for the weekend, so wouldn't I invite Ginny? She said she couldn't." He gave an ironic laugh and went on bitterly, "Her reputation and all that. So, suddenly I found myself engaged and she came to Virginia."

"But you did love her."

Jack let his breath out slowly in a deep sigh and shook his head. "I don't know. I'm not sure I really did. I needed to think I did."

He closed his eyes, remembering. "At first, the idea of having a girl at home was fun. Someone to come back to when my year was up, a not-too-distant future to look forward to. I'd come home and we'd go together for a while and everything would be fine.

"Then, when the war started, she became even more important. She was someone who would make it worth my while to live through that hell."

His eyes were shadowed by pain. "You know, it's funny. I thought being back would be like paradise. But then, I thought Hawaii would be paradise. So, here I am back home, and I'm suddenly swamped with problems and decisions. I've done more figuring just since I got back than I have in my whole life. Maybe I should re-enlist. In the army, all I had to do was say, 'Yes, sir,' and hope I didn't get a bullet in my head."

Tom nodded. Amusement flickered on his face for a moment. "I know what you mean. Sometimes I wish I was back in school, where all I had to do was have a good time and do some studying."

Jack stared at himself in the mirror over the bar. He saw a nice-looking blond young man, maybe a little tired and thin. Did his eyes show the emptiness he felt? The lighting in the bar was too dim to tell. "You know, when Ginny said it was Red, I lost it. Now I don't feel anything. It isn't even a matter of forgiving her."

"I told you—"

"I know. But to forgive someone, I have to feel something. It's like she closed a door and there isn't a door knob, not even a door any more."

He clenched his glass, his knuckles white. He wanted to throw it. "But it had to be Red. That's the worst of it. He and Goat and I had some great times, and we went through hell together. I'll never forgive him, even if he's dead." There were tears in his eyes now. "Never."

Tom shook his head and sighed. "Too bad. I thought maybe I could talk you and Ginny into making it a double wedding with Kathy and me."

Thirty-Three

"Ginny, telephone," Carey called from the hallway. Her heart flopped as her sister trotted downstairs. She looked so thin. The past months had been awful. How could Jack treat her like this? He was supposed to love her. Didn't that count for anything? Even Tom had been unable to soften Jack's refusal to have anything to do with her. All Jack could say was, "Red," and change the subject.

Ginny picked up the phone, not caring if it was Glenn Miller. "Hello."

"Ginny?"

"Yes." Her answer was somewhere in the clouds. She didn't recognize the caller.

"It's Steve. I haven't been gone that long, have I?"

Steve, she thought. Wow. Was he home already?

After a moment of silence he repeated, "Ginny? It's Steve."

Belatedly, she managed to put a little enthusiasm in her voice. "Hi, Steve. I'm sorry. I haven't been feeling well." That was certainly true. "Where are you? Are you home?"

"I have a leave. I don't have as many points as some of the other guys. From the sound of your voice, I may have to stay in the navy for good. Remember, I'll turn into an old sea dog, unless you relent and marry me."

She winced at the word "marry." She'd probably never get married now, never walk down the aisle in a white dress. Probably be an old maid. But Steve's teasing brought back happy memories when life was fun. She never could resist his humor. "Steve, you're a darling. It's so good to hear your voice."

"That's the nicest thing you've ever said to me. When can I see you? You can't be married already 'cause you're still at home, so I still have time to win you from old what's-his-name."

She sat down hard on the little chair. No, she sure wasn't married. But in spite of herself, she enjoyed his banter. "You have no idea how glad I am to hear from you."

"That's swell. I'm here in chilly old Detroit and I can be there tomorrow. Do you have a date?"

Her gloom, not far away, returned. "No, I don't." She hadn't the courage to tell him about Jack. He might ask the wrong questions.

"Good. Get yourself all dolled up, my girl, 'cause I've been waiting three years to get you in my arms, even if it's only to dance."

Part of her melted at his words, only to freeze again at the thought of Jack. But it was hard to stay depressed with Steve around. She couldn't suppress a smile. "What time?"

"What time?" he complained happily. "I deposit my heart at your feet and that's all you can say? What time?" He laughed. "Six-thirty. We can have supper."

"Sounds wonderful."

He crooned, "Goodnight sweetheart, until we meet to-morrow," and hung up.

Ginny sat smiling dreamily at the receiver in her hand. He had a nice voice.

Carey tiptoed into the hall. "Sorry, I didn't mean to listen, but I couldn't help hearing. Going to see him?"

"Tomorrow night."

"Swell. Where're you going?"

"He said something about dancing." She hopped up the first two stairs but turned and looked at her sister. "Do you think it's awful of me to be glad to see him?"

Carey reached up and patted her sister's hand. "I'm glad you're going. Jack's been a jerk and it's almost six months. I think it's just dandy you're going out."

"Ginny!" Steve grabbed her by the waist and twirled her around. When he put her down he tried to kiss her, but she was laughing too hard. He missed his aim and brushed her ear with his lips.

"You're crazy. You know that, don't you?" she gasped.

"Yeah. That's what I've been telling you for three years. Crazy about you." He took her hand and stood back a little to admire her. "You look delicious." He brushed her cheek gently with the back of his hand. "A bit pale, and a bit thin, I think." Then he grinned. "You must have been pining for me."

"Natch. During the whole war, I never had another thought." She looked down at her dress. Was it a bit roomier than usual? She hoped she didn't look skinny.

He sighed loudly at her "Natch," and pretended to swoon at her remark. Then he took her in his arms and kissed her until she blushed. When he stopped, she put her hands to her face. Her cheeks felt warm.

He said, "Do you remember the first time I kissed you? Old what's-his-name was staring at us?"

"You mean Tom." After all that had happened with Jack, the image of Tom's disapproving face seemed almost funny now.

"Tom, Dick, or Harry. Who cares?" He kissed her again and held her locked in his arms. "I made reservations at the El Dorado Room. Okay?"

"Great. Let me get my coat." She pulled back gently, her gaze fixed on his face. He looked better than she'd remembered, even though he would never be as handsome as Jack. She swallowed hard at the thought. She took her coat from the closet, then hung it back up and exchanged it for a lighter one.

He rattled his keys. "You might want the heavy one. It was snowing in Alaska when I left."

"When were you in Alaska?"

"Oh, just Detroit. Believe it or not there was snow on the ground. It felt like Alaska."

She switched coats again. "Funny we often have a snowstorm early April. Aren't you ever serious about anything?"

He held her coat then took her in his arms. "Yes. About you."

In spite of the sweet things he said, Ginny shook her head. They were nice to hear, but she couldn't escape her blues. She pulled back a little out of his reach. "We'd better go or we'll be late."

In the car, he turned to study her. "You haven't mentioned Jack."

At the sound of his name she flinched, then straightened her shoulders and raised her chin. She said curtly, "That's over."

"Want to talk about it?"

"No."

"Does that mean you're available?"

"I hate men. They're rats."

Steve tilted his head and turned a quizzical look on her. His eyes teased her gently. "All men?"

She shrugged. "Almost. You don't count. You're a friend."

He gave her a quick hug and started the car. "Okay, friend. I suppose I should be hurt, but I'll settle for that for the moment. Let's go eat."

He dropped her off at the door of the Commodore Hotel and drove ahead to have the car parked.

She waited in the lobby. Just standing in a hotel again, any hotel, brought back her shame and pain. She squirmed inwardly and eagerly turned to Steve for comfort as he entered.

There's no use crying over spilled milk, she told herself. Taking a deep breath, she concentrated on the details of the ornate El Dorado Room as they entered. A lot of men were still in uniform, some in civvies, but they all seemed to be with pretty girls. She felt jealous and lonely as they good naturedly jostled and greeted each other, all crowded around the horseshoe-shaped mahogany bar. Less than half the tables, clothed in white linen, were occupied, and it was too early for dancers.

Still, it was nice to be out and doing something. "This is nice." Their table was against the wall, affording a view of most of the room.

Steve shrugged and nodded. "It is, but I wish we were on the wharf in Frisco."

"I've never been to San Francisco. Never been anywhere, for that matter." She gave an exaggerated sigh. "If I'm going to be an old maid, I'd like to travel and have some fun."

He took her hand, holding it tightly, but that amusement was still in his eyes. "Never an old maid."

She withdrew her hand. "You always laugh at me."

"Only because you delight me so."

Before she could answer, the waiter appeared with shiny maroon menus and handed them a wine and cocktail list.

282

"Would you like something to drink while you decide?"

Ginny bit her lip. She hadn't had a drop of alcohol since that night with Red. Of course, she hadn't gone out anywhere, either. She didn't want to make the same mistake again, but surely Steve was safe enough.

She looked from the cocktails to the wines. In all the movies, they always ordered sherry as though it wasn't really a serious drink. Maybe that would do. She looked at Steve, uncertain. "Sherry?" There he went again, mocking her. For a moment, she was tempted to kick him under the table.

"All right, make that two. Harvey's *amontillado* for the lady, and do you have a *fino Macharnudo?*"

The waiter raised an eyebrow but assented.

Ginny noticed the look and when he'd gone, she asked, "What was that all about?"

"I don't think he's used to men ordering sherry. I wouldn't, except I thought I'd keep you company. And then it's a rather good wine, too. I think it might be too dry for you, but you'll like the amontillado."

Her curiosity was aroused. He seemed to know a lot about everything. She realized that for all the time she had known him, she knew very little about him. She didn't even know what he did before he enlisted in the navy. He was an officer, so he must have gone to college somewhere. It was strange that she'd never asked. But then, Jack had been her dreamboat, and it had been enough to have Steve for a friend.

She studied Steve's face. It was a pleasant face—one that would be easy to look at over morning coffee. Compared to Jack, she'd always thought Steve was very ordinary. But now, she became aware of the strength in his face. And there was a serenity she had never noticed before, never thought to look for. She'd been too busy laughing at his clowning.

The arrival of her sherry interrupted her examination. Not

quite trusting herself, she reached for the glass, but let her hand rest on the table.

Steve half-grinned and nodded encouragingly. "You'll like it. Has a nice, nutty flavor."

The taste wasn't exactly what she'd been worrying about, but she took a small sip and made a face. "It's strong."

He grinned. "Like love, the second time around is always better."

She shook her head and said, "You're hopeless," then took another sip. It was better. Good, in fact. She started to say, "You're . . ."

He beat her to it. "You're right." Then he repeated again, whispering, "You're right. I am hopeless." For the first time, he looked sad as he leaned over and kissed her gently, not even bothering to look around to see who might be watching. "I've been hopelessly in love with you since the first night we met."

Suddenly all those funny letters were no longer so amusing. She felt like crying. How could he have loved her that much? How could she have been so blind? She gazed into his eyes and saw the warmth, the fire that had been banked there, hoping for a breath of encouragement to flare it up.

Reluctantly, she pulled her gaze from him and looked furtively around the restaurant, expecting it to be all but deserted. To her surprise, almost all the tables were occupied. She decided she didn't care if everyone did see. She kissed him.

He gave her that lop-sided smile loaded with mischief. Sort of like Van Johnson's. She'd never noticed how white and even his teeth were. He really wasn't all that ordinary, was he? What was the rest of this man really like?

She said, "You never said what you did in real life."

"As opposed to the fantasy life of risking my neck in a tin can, you mean?"

She tried hard to frown at him. "You know what I mean."

"I went to Notre Dame. My degree is in literature. I plan to get my doctorate, the pursuit of which was so rudely interrupted by the war. Then I plan to teach at a university, hopefully Notre Dame. My specialty is mystical poetry—Dante, St. John of the Cross, Thompson, etc., etc., etc."

"Oh."

Again, the mischief showed. "I can see you're really impressed."

Ginny shook her head. She remembered that he'd mentioned Dante before, but it hadn't meant anything. She thought he'd used it like people talk about Romeo and Juliet.

"I don't think I've known any men interested in poetry."

"You just haven't been in the right circles." He reached over and touched her cheek. "Do you have any idea why I love you?"

Her dream of Jack and the vine-covered cottage in Perrysburg began to fade. She shook her head. "I just figured you were kidding."

"Eileen once said you were shallow. She didn't know you, though. You're a dreamer. And I like dreamers." He took her hand in his and kissed it, kept kissing it while he said, "I told you once before, you have depths you know nothing about."

"Me?" She was touched, but didn't really understand.

"You don't believe me. I'll show you." He stopped kissing her and cupped both her hands in his. "What do you see when you look out into the night?"

She thought for a moment. She felt silly, but she closed her eyes and took a deep breath. "My favorite scene is the river at night. It's like a long satin ribbon, shimmering with stars and lights. Sometimes I imagine it's a long sash around my waist, trailing on forever. And when I'm up high in a building and look out, the street lamps over the river look like a diamond necklace."

She paused for a moment, embarrassed. She'd never said such things aloud before, but she couldn't resist the look in his eyes, urging her on. "When I was a kid, I used to watch the tree just outside my window, bowing in the wind, almost dancing, I thought. I used to look at the patterns the leaves made against the sky. Except after I saw *The Wizard of Oz*, my favorite branch turned into the Wicked Witch of the East."

She laughed, then, embarrassed at revealing her secret life, she looked shyly at him.

He sat there smiling at her.

Wriggling, she said, "What do you see?"

"I see night as a great womb, nurturing love." He quoted:

> "I have been here before,
> but when or how I cannot tell:
> I know the grass beyond the door,
> The sweet keen smell,
> The sighing sound, the lights around the shore.
>
> You have been mine before,
> How long ago I may not know:
> But just, when at that swallow's soar
> Your neck turned so,
> Some veil did fall—I knew it all of yore.

"Gabriel Allegheri Dante," he finished. The three words stated a fact, a name, but his voice said, "I adore you."

She looked into his eyes and swallowed hard. This guy would never chase fire engines.

Off in the corner, a small combo began to play and a young

286

woman stepped up to the microphone, crooning, "Kiss me once, and kiss me twice . . ."

Steve took Ginny's hand. "As the song says, it *has* been a long, long time." He led her onto the tiny dance floor.

Her hand felt small and secure in his.

He held her close and murmured, "I've been waiting for this forever." He sang softly, his breath warm against her ear as he finished the song.

She rested her cheek against his and let the music and words envelop her. Where had this guy been all her life?

Thirty-Four

Jack scraped the last drop of hot fudge from his dish. Tom watched in amusement. "The dishwasher won't have to wash that when you get through with it."

Jack looked sheepish and continued scraping. "I've been home six months but I can't get enough of this. I used to lie in my foxhole and picture this. I got so sick of rice. One night, Goat and I were on patrol and we found a crate of fruit cocktail washed up on the beach. It was cold from being in the water." He closed his eyes, enjoying the memory. "It was wonderful."

Tom nodded and said, "I can imagine." He changed the subject. "Have you talked to Ginny?"

"No."

"Don't you intend to?"

Jack closed his eyes, slamming the shutters on the past. "It's over."

Tom wasn't ready to let it go. "She really didn't do anything that awful, you know. She just wasn't smart."

Jack stared into his empty dish and sighed. "I know. It isn't that. I hate Red for what he did, but not Ginny. It's like I said, I just don't love her. There's nothing I can do about it."

"How does Ginny feel about all this?"

288

Jack sighed, irritated. He couldn't help how Ginny felt. Although, he doubted that it would matter to her for very long. He didn't think her emotions ran very deep. "I haven't talked to her."

"Don't you think you should?"

Jack tapped his spoon and looked over at the small crowd near the door of the Purple Cow, waiting for tables. The little restaurant was mostly a sandwich shop, with ice cream and desserts, but it was a popular stop before and after the theater. On the wall, a cow chewed her cud, ignorant of her purple hide, unaware that the accompanying nursery rhyme proclaimed it was better to see than be her. If he were the purple cow, at least he could eat in peace. "Maybe we should leave."

"Okay. In a minute. I want some more coffee." As Tom turned to signal the waitress, his face broke into a big grin. "Wait a minute. I see someone. I'll be right back."

He rose and made his way to the door where Carey stood with her back to him. He tapped her on the shoulder.

She turned and her face lit. "Oh, hi, Tom. I was just leaving. Doesn't look like there's much room."

He motioned to his booth. "Look who's here. Come join us."

"I don't want to intrude. Just give Kathy my love."

"No. Look. Kathy's hair isn't that short, is it?" He turned her to face the booth.

Jack! Her heart did cartwheels. This was the first time she'd seen him since—since he'd left. Since she was a kid with a crush on him. She tried to breath deeply, but her pulse raced. She hated the idea that she, like Ginny, was in love with that wavy hair and the smile that showed perfect white teeth, but she felt helpless to resist. He was more gorgeous than ever.

He was looking in their direction, but his face was unrevealing. Even from across the room she could see his eyes, eyes the color of a clear winter sky. His golden South Seas tan had faded and his hair wasn't as white as Ginny had said, but he was still gorgeous. Her fingers itched with the desire to run through those deep waves. She clutched at her handbag to keep her hands still.

"Come on." Tom tugged her toward the booth.

Her face was fiery hot and she was sure it was beet red as she approached the table. Jack nodded coolly and smiled. Her heart sank, but even when he was just being polite, his smile dazzled her.

Tom poked him on the shoulder. "Don't you know who this is?"

Jack sat, confused. She did look familiar, but if he'd ever seen anyone as gorgeous as this, he'd have remembered for sure. "Uh. I guess—"

Carey blushed and Tom crowed triumphantly, "It's Carey!"

Jack's eyes opened wide. It was. He inhaled slowly, wondering how this gorgeous creature could be that kid sister who sent him fudge and all those letters.

Great fudge. Great letters, he thought inanely. She was stunning. He stuttered, "Yu-your pictures sure didn't do you justice." His gaze was riveted by the dimple in her chin. It was the one thing about her that made her look like Ginny. The blond hair that used to be long and straight now waved gently over the collar of her beige chesterfield coat, its slim tailoring promising a tall, thin figure.

A hint of embarrassment showed in her green eyes as she said, "Hi, Jack."

He realized he was staring and finally had the presence of mind to stand and let her slide into the booth. Tongue-tied, he mumbled hastily, "Thanks for the cookies. I was always the most popular guy in the outfit when your boxes came."

Carey was as confused as Jack looked. She wondered if he had any idea how she felt about him. Probably not. Ginny never would have told him, and their letters had always been just the words of friends. What had Tom told him, if anything? Surely nothing.

Smiling, she brushed his thanks aside. "Anything for our boys. Your letters were fascinating. That story about the little Japanese boy made me cry. It must have been awful."

Jack looked down at his dish. "Well, it was. Some of it, anyway." He looked up and studied her face, touched by the warmth he saw there. Funny. He had never told Ginny some of the stories he'd told Carey in those letters. Maybe he'd been able to write to Carey like that because he hadn't thought of her as a girlfriend. Somehow, he'd been able to write what he couldn't have said to anyone else.

He cleared his throat, embarrassed by the silence.

Tom stood and took his check. "Listen, you two, I've got to go. Good to see you again, Carey. We'll get together for lunch."

Absently Carey looked up at him. "Uh-huh. Swell, Tom. Give my love to Kathy."

He looked smug as he left.

Jack rose and moved to the other side of the booth where he could look at her without being too obvious. Then he forgot to worry about it. He couldn't take his eyes off her face. He found himself blabbering and repeating himself. "You've changed since the last time I saw you."

"Yeah, well, that's what happens with little sisters."

The waitress came over and cleared the empty dishes, rattling them so loudly Jack thought she might break one or two. She glared at him and then back at the small crowd near the door. "Will that be all?"

"I'd like a hot fudge sundae, please, and coffee," Carey put in firmly as she tried to keep a straight face.

The waitress sighed, looked pointedly back at the crowd again, and left.

They broke into laughter and found it hard to stop. She wiped the corners of her eyes. It wasn't really all that funny, but she was nervous. What about Ginny? Did he love her at all? Carey's conscience told her she ought to be angry with him for the way he'd treated her sister. Yet her heart wasn't listening. As she gazed at him, its rapid pounding drowned out every other sound in the room, roaring in her ears like a formation of planes taking off.

He broke the silence. "How's Ginny?"

She stiffened. "Do you care?" She cared about her sister, but did he? How could he sit there and ask so indifferently, as though Ginny were some mutual acquaintance?

With a fork, he drew lines on a paper napkin in front of him, then looked into her eyes. Her green eyes, like his favorite marble, a green emmy, he had when he was a kid. "I care about Ginny, Carey, but I'm not in love with her." Those eyes were beautiful. "I'm not sure I ever really was—we never really were."

His words made her angry. "You can't care much. You won't even talk to her. And what do you know about how Ginny feels?"

He told her about his battle to understand himself, his anger with Ginny, with Red, and the final realization that their romance had never been more than the immature dreams of two young people caught up in a war. "If we'd had more time together, we might have known a long time ago it wasn't real love."

She knew he was right. Ginny the dreamer, with her vision

of Robert Taylor in the rose-covered cottage and happy ever after.

Ginny had told her about the date with Steve. About *him*, Steve. Even though Carey knew that what Jack said was true, she was hurt by his calm indifference. "How do you know how Ginny felt?"

"Well, the USO bit, for a start. Only I wanted to believe we were in love. I needed to believe it."

"She was lonely and bored. Didn't you have a girl?" She blushed, realizing that she had no right to ask that, but she had to get rid of the ghost of Ginny or else get away from him.

He looked at her thoughtfully, then, believing he owed her an answer, told her about Emily, but ended, "We never . . . we only kissed." They were both silent, embarrassed. "Ginny and I . . ." he stopped again but knew he had to set the record straight. Finally, "We didn't."

Carey's cheeks grew hot. She wanted to slide under the table. They were talking about her sister. Yet a giant weight lifted from her heart and went flying out into the night.

The constraints finally lifted, they talked. She told him about Steve dating Ginny now. "He's the one Tom saw at the USO, but there was never anything between them. Back then, you were too much competition for him. But it turns out he's an English professor and spouts poetry to her. Very romantic. He's probably just what she needs."

"As opposed to me. She said I was totally unromantic." He laughed. "She was always on at me about those v-mail things. " He laughed. "They were kind of small."

His eyes glinted in amusement, then he became serious again. He reached out and took Carey's hand. "I'm glad about Steve. I hope she'll be happy."

His touch sent shock waves running up Carey's arm. The din of the restaurant became the ringing of cathedral bells.

She started when the waitress slapped down the bill and complained, "Are you finished?"

They looked at each other and broke into laughter again. Jack rose, picked up the check, and told the waitress, "We've just begun."

In the car on the way home, Jack heard himself humming. He stopped abruptly, embarrassed. He never could carry a tune. He watched Carey from the corner of his eye. She looked straight ahead. Her profile, calm and serene in the dim light from the street lamps, suggested a depth to Carey that he'd never sensed in Ginny.

He wondered what it would be like to marry a doctor. Maybe it would be good. She'd be independent. Not expecting him to amuse her all the time, and he did have his art. Does a doctor have time to iron shirts? Well, he could iron but maybe they'd have a maid.

He thought about Goat's words, "When you get to be a famous New York artist, you can ride free in my cab." Or something like that. Would she want to be a doctor in New York City?

He pulled the car to a stop in front of her house and shifted in his seat to face her. Funny that his story with Ginny should end like this, with her kid sister here beside him. Yet every fiber in his being shouted at him, *this is no kid.* Carey was, is, the kind of woman a man dreams about but seldom finds. He reached out, touched a lock of her hair that gleamed from the shadows, and spoke tenderly, "It's been great."

Sitting there in the dark, beside him in the car, she trembled. How could she be so warm when it was so cold outside? She cleared her throat. "Glad I caught that bus." Glad she'd been restless and hadn't been able to study. Glad she'd wandered into the Purple Cow.

"Me, too." He reached over and pulled her to him, his lips

finding hers. He kissed her gently, tentatively, then hungrily. The warmth spread to his ears. After a moment, he pulled back and got that silly look of his. "I think I hear a fire engine."

She put her hands to his cheeks and drew him back to her. "Oh, no, you don't, you old dalmatian. Those were bells you heard." Their lips met again and the bells chimed so hard her heart thrummed. The world spun dizzily like a ride at the amusement park. Outside the car, houses and trees and streets vanished in the night.

Jack pulled back but held her face in his hands. "You're right. Those aren't sirens, they're bells."